The Memory of Home

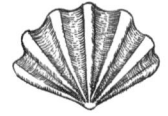

Other Books by
JUNE HALL MCCASH

Eleanor's Daughter: A Novel of Marie de Champagne
First Place in 2019 International Chaucer Award

The Truth Keepers: A Novel

Marguerite's Landing

The Boys of Shiloh

The Thread Box: A Collection of Poems

A Titanic Love Story: Ida and Isidor Straus

Plum Orchard
Winner of the 2013 Georgia Author of the Year Award for Best Novel

Almost to Eden
Winner of the 2011 Georgia Author of the Year Award for First Novel

*The Jekyll Island Club:
Southern Haven for America's Millionaires*
(co-author William Barton McCash)

*Jekyll Island's Early Years:
From Prehistory through Reconstruction*

The Jekyll Island Cottage Colony

The Jekyll Island Club Hotel
(co-author Brenden Martin)

The Cultural Patronage of Medieval Women
(edited by June Hall McCash)

The Life of Saint Audrey: A Text of Marie de France
(co-edited and co-trans., with Judith Clark Barban)

Love's Fools: Aucassin, Troilus, Calisto and the Parody of the Courtly Lover

The Memory of Home

June Hall McCash

TWIN
OAKS
PRESS

Copyright © 2023 June Hall McCash

All rights reserved

This book may not be reproduced or transmitted, in whole or in part, through any means electronic or mechanical including photocopying or electronic transmission without prior written permission from the author, except short excerpts considered normal for review.

The Memory of Home is a work of fiction. Names, characters, places, and incidents are either the product of the author's imagination or are used fictitiously. Any resemblance to actual persons living or dead is entirely coincidental.

ISBN-978-1-937937-31-7

First Edition 2023

Printed in The United States of America

Twin Oaks Press
www.twinoakspress.com

Cover photo by the author

Design: Art Growden

*In loving memory of Bart
with whom I began this journey.*

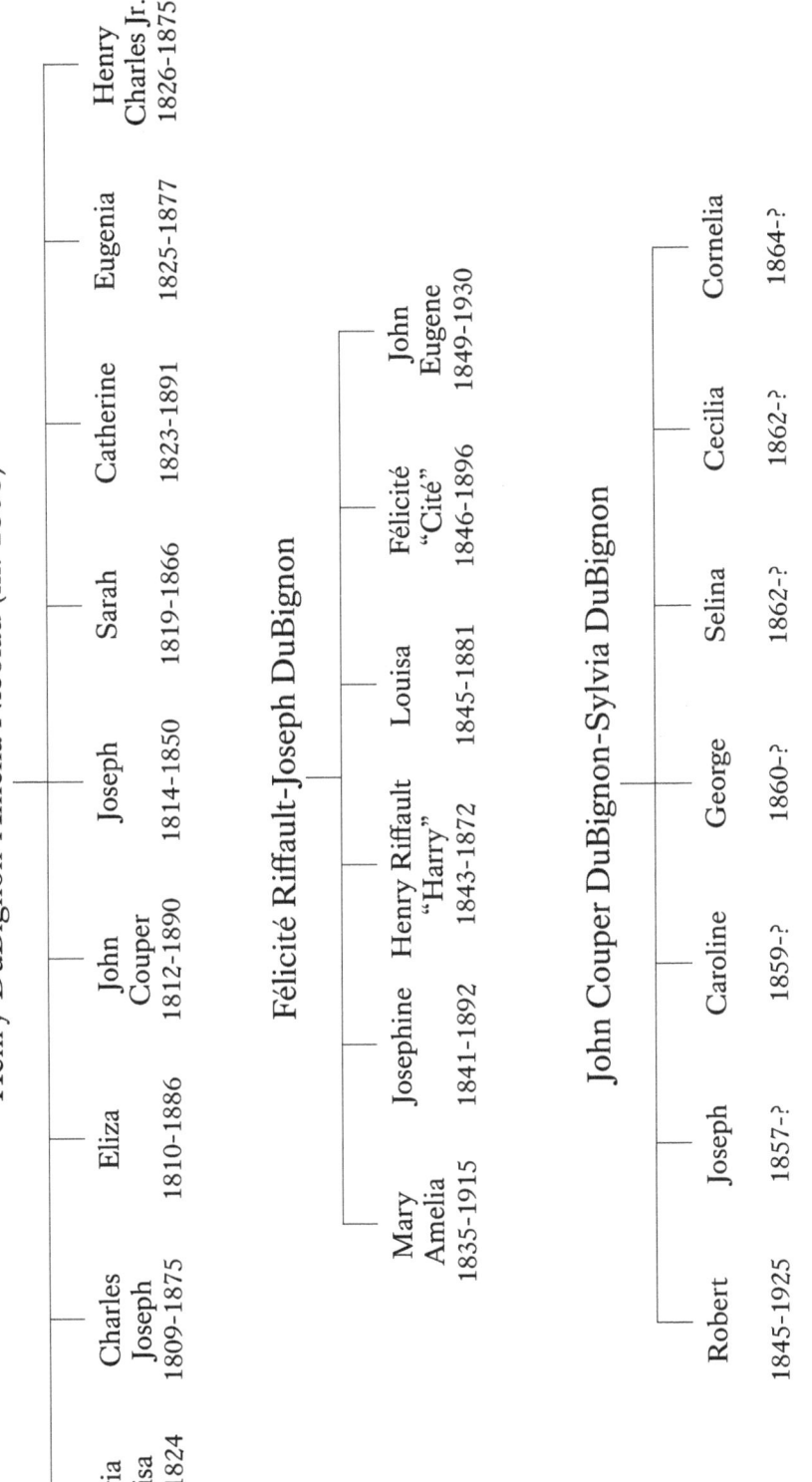

CHAPTER 1

Jekyl Island, Georgia, March 1853

Henry DuBignon Jr. leaned against the front-porch railing, half-heartedly watching his sister Eliza work furiously on her knitting. It was late afternoon, but the sun had not quite reached the horizon, and there was still ample light for her to see what she was doing. She frowned at her knitting needles, which clicked as she worked.

"What're you makin'?" he asked, not really caring.

"A shawl," she answered.

"Why bother? Winter's over."

"I can use it on cool evenings, and winter will come back."

Their brother John Couper DuBignon, nearby, ignored them both, slumping in a wooden chair, tilted back, his feet perched on the porch railing and his interlaced fingers resting on his belly, as he gazed out over the tranquil marsh glowing in the setting sun. The three of them often gathered like this on the front porch of their family home to enjoy the sunset and catch up on events of the day. Daylight was growing longer, and the sky's pre-twilight displays, reflected in the wide expanse of saltwater and spartina grass that lay between the island and the mainland, were often glorious, as they were this afternoon. The reddish clouds on the western horizon suggested the possibility of rain in the night.

"You look upset," Henry said to the frowning Eliza. "Somethin' wrong?"

"You know perfectly well. Why do you even ask?" she replied.

He let out a long sigh. "I hope you're not going to bring that up again."

"How can you not care?"

"I do care. Of course I do, but I try not to think about it every waking moment. At least he's out of our lives."

"But our family's reputation is ruined," she said.

"It's done, and there's nothing we can do about it except carry on. Maybe in time people will forget. Maybe we can restore our good name and make things like they used to be."

"Not likely," Eliza muttered.

Their widowed father had humiliated the family with his recent marriage, not to his mistress of ten years, Sarah Aust, who had given birth to his three illegitimate children while their mother was still alive. That would have been bad enough, but at least they had all expected that. Instead, already in his sixties, their father had gone and married his mistress's twenty-year-old pregnant daughter, Mary Aust, rocking the DuBignon family to its core. When they refused to accept his "bride," who was younger than all his legitimate children, he had quit the island and moved inland to a place called Ellis Point, leaving his two unmarried sons, Henry and John, in charge, but totally inexperienced to run a plantation.

If he was going to act the fool in such a way, he could at least have given us more preparation, Henry thought, *but he never trusted us to do anything right.* Henry, who was youngest of all the siblings, was as angry at his father as Eliza was, but he was determined somehow to redeem the family name and wealth. He would prove to his father that he and John could restore what he had thrown away. He was determined to bring back the former glory he imagined the plantation had during earlier times, when his father was still an upright member of the community, a respected planter, a wealthy man, even a bank president everyone admired. But the old man had sacrificed it all to take up with that woman, a widow with two daughters—Sarah Aust.

Their mother had managed to forgive him the first time the English woman bore him a son, but only after he promised her that it was over and would never happen again. Then, when the second bastard was born, their mother, angry, hurt, and outraged, had left her husband for good to live with her son Joseph and his wife, Félicité. Nothing was ever the same after that. The household, once filled with laughter and dignity, was now dark and lacked the spark of life that Henry recalled from his childhood. All grace and gaiety in the home had vanished.

He had heard his older brothers and sisters talk about all the good times they had once enjoyed at balls and barbecues among the plantation gentry. But he had been too young to attend and had only the vaguest memories of afternoon boat races and family picnics. He longed for that imagined splendor of the old cotton plantation that had been settled six decades ago by his grandfather—a French émigré of noble blood.

Now, the plantation had fallen on hard times, thanks to his father's antics, along with the loss of some of the slaves and the falling price of cotton. But Henry was resolved to return it to its former glory, if only to spite his father. He wanted it to be worthy of his family's aristocratic origins, but he knew that much of the burden would fall on him. His brother John, even though he was older, took little interest in business matters. He could help supervise plantation activities like planting and picking, but Henry knew that he was the one who would have to make the trips to Savannah, negotiate with cotton agents, whom the planters called *factors*, and handle any other business matters. It was he who would have to go into Brunswick or Darien to buy the various goods needed on the island—things they could not produce on site, like coffee and sugar.

It would be hard to restore the social and business connections his father had once had, but he would seize every opportunity to do so, whatever it took. He would accept any invitations that came his way, dine and drink with fellow planters and wealthy friends at the Oglethorpe House in Brunswick, dance with the best-connected ladies at the balls in Brunswick or on St. Simons—anything he had to do to increase their wealth and raise the darkened spirits of the house, especially Eliza's.

He thought about his sister and her gloomy outlook. She had just turned forty-three and was the oldest of those still at home, and she had despaired of ever finding a husband and having a family. But her situation was not unusual. In many families, it was an unspoken expectation that the oldest daughter would remain a spinster to take care of her parents in their old age. *I suppose our father's new wife will be his caretaker now,* he thought.

There was no doubt that all his other sisters would wed. One of them, Sarah, had married a man named Thomas Bourke fourteen years ago. The youngest, Eugenia, at twenty-four, was planning a wedding only a month away to a young Carrollton lawyer. And it was a certainty that their only other sister Catherine would soon marry as well, for she was the prettiest of them all and possessed by nature the even temper and sweet-natured demeanor men liked in a wife. She had many admirers, but her heart was set on Robert Hazlehurst Jr., who was training to be a doctor and didn't want to marry until he felt he could support a family in a secure and refined manner. Catherine was waiting patiently, never doubting his intentions. Soon, he, Eliza, and John Couper would be the only ones left at the family home. The only other white people on the island were Félicité, the widow of their brother Joseph, and her six children. Their older brother, Charles, the firstborn, had long ago left Jekyl, marrying into a well-to-do family near Milledgeville and now running his father-in-law's Woodville Plantation there.

Henry didn't think it was so much Eliza's age and apparent fate as the family's "maiden lady" that bothered her. He knew she had long since resigned herself to that. Instead, it was the most recent disgrace their father had brought to the family. She never seemed to forget, not even for an hour, the shame and anger she felt when he married Mary Aust, who was pregnant with his child and more than forty years younger than he. At least now, thank God, the couple had left the island and moved to Ellis Point on the other side of Brunswick. *Good riddance!*

Henry's older brother, John Couper DuBignon, gazed out over the varying colors that danced in the marsh waters and reflected the changing hues of the sunset. He too was thinking of their father and how quickly he could turn his back on his children. He had learned its sting even as a young boy, and it had altered his life. The incident at the swing had changed everything. He had committed a single, youthful indiscretion and his father had been furious with him. He had lectured John in a loud voice, almost yelling about his "inappropriate behavior" and his "shameful actions" toward their cousin Fannie Nicolau. *Hypocrite*, John thought.

He had been barely in his teens, just a year older than Fannie, and they had played together since they were children, laughing, teasing, and tickling, romping together like puppies. They were fond of one another, and his family had thought they might even marry someday. Then, when they reached adolescence, all that had changed. All of a sudden one day, Fannie was upset and would have nothing more to do with him. Both her father and his were angry and chastised him unmercifully, though he had no idea what he had done that was so wrong.

Only his sister Eliza had stood by him. He remembered how, when she was younger, she always tried to be the peacemaker, hating to see friction in the family. She had written to Fannie trying to persuade her to forgive John for his "indiscretion," even though she herself didn't know what it was, and to let their relationship be like it was before. She alone had made that effort. He remembered quite clearly Fannie's reply—that she would always see him as a "fond cousin" and that she wanted to "let the matter rest forever in oblivion." Nevertheless. It was the end of their carefree friendship, and he missed her.

He and Fannie had enjoyed so many days of fun together. He could talk with her about almost everything, and he had teased her that very morning by putting a frog in her lap to watch her scream and jump about to shake it off. Later, they had both laughed about it. *But the incident at the swing changed everything,* he thought once more. It was something he would never forget. It had happened on a warm summer afternoon, as John was pushing Cousin Fannie in the swing that hung from a massive oak tree on her father's Marengo Plantation.

She called out, "That's too high, Johnny. Slow me down."

He reached out to catch hold of Fannie's waist and slow the swing, but he aimed too high, missed her waist, and found himself clutching both her budding breasts in his hands. He was startled. Then, with a playful smile, to tease her, he rubbed his thumbs across the little nipples that had sprung up. Fannie gasped, jumped out of the swing, and burst into tears as she ran toward her father's house. John was bewildered. What had he done? He'd always teased Fannie. What was so different this time?

"Fannie, what's wrong? Don't be mad," John called to her retreating back, but she did not answer. Later, his uncle confronted him.

"How dare you touch my daughter like that." His face was red with fury.

"I'm sorry," John said, "I didn't mean—"

"You filthy boy. I would never have expected such a thing from you. You stay away from Fannie from now on."

And then it was his father's turn.

"Haven't we taught you anything? How could you do something like that? You've shamed the entire family." John hung his head and wanted to die. Fannie had been his friend, and now she wouldn't want to see him anymore. He hadn't really paid much attention to her changing body nor realized that things had suddenly become restricted between them. His father had refused to tell his mother or his sisters what had happened. "You'd be too shocked by it," he had told his wife.

John swore it had been an accident, grabbing her like that, but he learned that day that he should have let go at once and apologized. Instead, he just stood there, dumbfounded by all the ruckus it caused. He hadn't understood at the time why it was so bad. He had seen men in the fields do the same thing to women and girls who worked alongside them. He had even seen his father stroke the breasts of a slave woman when he thought no one was looking. John thought it just a playful act. But, after everyone in the Nicolau family got so upset about the incident, Fannie wouldn't spend time alone with him anymore. It had caused a breach in the family and John knew he was to blame.

From that moment on, he lost all interest in plantation belles. He would pay no mind to the young women his age who minced about in their hoop skirts and hid their coy smiles behind lace fans. He avoided them altogether, fearing that he might do something else to offend them and upset his parents. No one had ever taught him any rules about things like that. They just got angry if he did something wrong. How was he supposed to know?

The only girls he'd dared touch after that were slave girls. They never made a big fuss about little indiscretions. They didn't dare. He'd learned that from his father. He found them just as attractive, but less pretentious and more available, and he wanted nothing more to do with those uppity white girls who were no fun any longer. He felt safe here on the island. Now, all these years later, he had his own woman—Sylvia—a pretty caramel-colored slave who had borne him a son when she was only fifteen. He'd been drawn to her combination of swarthy beauty and innocence when she was still a young girl. At first, she had seemed frightened and unwilling, and his attentions had made her cry, but over time she had given up and grown accustomed to him. He no longer wanted a life without her. She was all he needed. Now that his mother was dead and his father was gone, he felt free to acknowledge his affections more openly. The island was the only place that provided him refuge and privacy from the prying eyes and judgments of the world. It was his home and his sanctuary.

He was happy to let his younger brother, Henry, the only one named for their father, represent the plantation's interests to the outside world. John wanted no part of that life. No one bothered to invite him to social events anymore, for they knew he would not come. Only once, at their father's insistence, had he made any effort to enter that scene. After his brother Joseph, a state legislator, had died in 1850, their father insisted that John put himself forward as a candidate to replace him, just as Joseph had replaced their elder brother Charles. Everyone in Brunswick had been pleased with the service of both Charles and Joseph, and they had assumed John Couper DuBignon would be like his brothers. They soon learned that he wasn't. He'd tried for a short while to obey his father and do his duty in the state capital of Milledgeville, but it was not his place. He knew it almost at once. It required social skills he did not possess, ambitions he did not want to develop, and an interest in political and economic issues he did not have. He had left in the middle of the legislative session to come home, again infuriating his father. Once he returned from Milledgeville, he had never left the island again.

The resplendent yolk of sun sank rapidly once it started its descent, poising for only an instant on the horizon before sliding beneath the rim of the earth. The sunny afternoon was over. It was time to go in and light the lamps. Eliza rose, picked up her knitting basket and went inside. Henry followed her. Only John Couper chose to linger on the porch, enjoying the peace of the island and the last glimmer of the vanished sun and watching the fireflies emerging from their winter sleep, as they began to sparkle in the grass.

CHAPTER 2

DuBignon Cemetery, Jekyl Island, March 1853

Standing at the foot of her mother's grave at the north end of the island, Félicité, the widow of Joseph DuBignon, gazed with tenderness at her children gathered around. Her two youngest daughters huddled close to their mother's side, while the two oldest stood to the side of the tombstone, each holding a hand of their four-year-old baby brother, Johnny, who shuffled restlessly between them. Her thirdborn and only other son, Henry Riffault, whom everyone called Harry, was alone at the grave's head, standing as tall and straight as his ten years would allow. As the oldest boy, he considered himself head of the family now. It was one of the few things that could still make his mother smile.

"I miss *Grand'mère*," her daughter Josephine said in her plaintive twelve-year-old voice.

"So do I, my darling," Félicité echoed. "More than you can imagine." She had lost her beloved husband, Joseph, to pneumonia just three years earlier. He had been only thirty-six, and they had counted on a long life together. Then, only a week after his death, his mother, who had come to live with them after her husband's infidelity, succumbed to the same illness that took her son's life. Now, less than two years later, Félicité had lost her own mother as well. The three graves lay side by side in the small DuBignon cemetery on the north end of the island.

"May I say the prayer today, Mother?" Harry asked, his voice still that of a child.

"Of course you may," she answered.

"Dear God," he began, "please give our father and our grandmothers peace in your kingdom. And tell them we miss them. May they be happy in Heaven and bless us here on Jekyl Island." He added "Amen," then opened his eyes and looked to his mother for approval.

She smiled and nodded at him. "That was a very nice prayer, Harry." She was proud of all her children, especially her oldest son, who took his responsibilities as man of the house quite seriously.

"Can we go home now?" asked Johnny, whose real name was John Eugene, though his mother never called him that unless he had done something naughty.

"Blow them all a kiss, and we're off," she said.

Once they had all made the necessary gestures toward the three graves, Johnny broke loose from his sisters' grip and started racing down the road. "You can't catch me," he yelled back to his siblings.

They all laughed as Harry was by his side in a flash. "Who says so?" he taunted his little brother playfully.

After her husband's death, Félicité, now a bereft widow with six children to feed, the oldest only thirteen, had moved her family from the coastal town of Brunswick back to Jekyl Island and into the house she and Joseph had built when they first married. She had a fierce love for the island, for it was where they had begun their married life together and where they had been happiest and most carefree. She felt closer to him here than anywhere else on earth.

She wanted her children to know the island as she did and to share wonderful memories of their own there. When anyone asked her about her decision, she told them that she did it partly to save money since she didn't know what her economic situation would be once her husband's estate was settled. The other reason she gave was that she would have the support of Joseph's unmarried brothers and sisters who still lived in the family home there. As an only child, she had no siblings of her own to turn to. She knew there would not be much opportunity for social life on the island, but she didn't care, for she found no joy in gala gatherings without her husband.

As it turned out, she had no real financial worries. Although Joseph had been young and only at the beginning of his promising legal and legislative life as justice of the inferior court, and then as county delegate to the state legislature, he had invested wisely. He had been a well-respected man, and it was not surprising that he was elected to replace his older brother Charles in the assembly after he had moved away to Milledgeville. Joseph was liked and trusted by all who knew him, especially those who had served with him in the Glynn Hussars or the Brunswick Guards. Félicité remembered how handsome and distinguished he had looked in his uniform, how much she'd loved him and loved him still. She was grateful for the time they'd had together, though its brevity made it all the harder.

Félicité was also the sole heir, as an only child, to the estate her deceased father had left her mother so many years ago. It was not vast, but she found herself comfortable and well enough off to remain independent and to deprive her children of nothing they needed. *Thank God*, she thought, *I'd hate to be one of those destitute widows with many children to feed and no way to support them.*

The family frequently visited the small cemetery on the north end of Jekyl on sunny Sunday afternoons. It was a peaceful spot beside a small creek that ran along the edge of the salt marsh. Most important of all, it was a place where she could feel close to Joseph, whose tomb was flanked by the graves of both their mothers. She had loved them all. Her mother had been a solid rock during her daughter's long period of grieving, never giving *herself* the time she too needed to grieve for Joseph and Amelia, who had been her best friend. Her health had finally given way under the strain.

Félicité did not look forward to the long walk back. The sun was hot, and the road was dusty from a lack of rain. Resurrection ferns, clinging to the branches of the live oak trees along the way, were dry and brown, but she knew that all it would take was a good rain to bring life to them again and turn them a rich springlike green. *If only it were like that for human beings,* she thought.

"I'm tired, Mommy," Johnny whined as they trudged down Plantation Road. He usually seemed to have boundless energy. But not today.

"I'll carry you, little brother," Harry said, stooping to let Johnny climb on his shoulders. Félicité smiled again at the efforts of her oldest son. He was much too young to bear such a burden, but she knew he wanted to help. They were all good children. The two youngest girls could be a little clingy at times, but she always welcomed their hugs. She thanked God for all of them, for they left her little time to indulge in such weakness as loneliness.

She watched the children as they distracted themselves along the road, stopping to pick wildflowers or chase a lizard or a squirrel. It's good, she thought, that they can shake off the sadness and find joy in such simple things. She was glad that, for a time at least, she had brought them back to the island, where most of them had been born. Although it wasn't the same for her without Joseph, it had become instead a place of healing.

The children danced along the road, ignoring the desiccated ferns and the withered cotton plants in the dry fields that drew her attention. It was uncanny how the island always seemed to reflect her feelings.

Things were uncertain now that Joseph's father had remarried and moved away. She wondered how the plantation would fare under the supervision of her two unmarried brothers-in-law. No doubt it would be a struggle for them to learn in such a short time all they needed to know. And neither of them owned a single acre of the land. The island still belonged to their disgraced father, *God forgive him*, even though he no longer lived there. John Couper and Henry Jr. had found themselves suddenly in charge, with little experience in their new responsibilities. The outlook was uncertain.

As hard as it would be to leave the island and move back to the mainland, it was something she had begun to consider in recent weeks. While she hated the thought of leaving Jekyl, which would always feel like home to her, it was time to think of her growing children now. They had been here three years already, and her two oldest daughters would soon reach an age where they needed opportunities for more social life. She watched them as they walked along the roadway. They were both in the bloom of their youth, almost young women now. She needed to think of their future more than her own. Although she hadn't decided yet, the question was uppermost in her mind. But she knew that her two boys would hate the idea of leaving the island, for to them it was heaven, filled with adventures and freedom. She would have to weigh carefully the needs of all her children. It would be a difficult decision, but one she knew she would soon have to make.

CHAPTER 3

Jekyl Island, April 1853

Little by little, the DuBignon sons' and daughters' raw memory of the unsavory behavior of their wayward father began to fade, and his unmarried offspring began to speak of it less and less. Even Eliza managed to set aside her resentment long enough to help her sister Eugenia prepare for her upcoming wedding on April 12. She was to marry a young lawyer from Carrollton named Archibald Turk Burke, and both Eliza and Catherine were as excited as the bride. All morning they had fluttered about the bedroom, giggling like young girls, and making suggestions, as they helped Eugenia organize her trousseau. Her bed was scattered with neat piles of sheets, lingerie, the few pieces of jewelry she owned, and the clothes she planned to take with her. The two were beginning to grow a bit nostalgic at their sister's impending departure.

"What's Carrollton like?" Catherine asked in her gentle voice.

"I don't really know. Archie seems a little nervous about

taking me up country. All I know is it's all the way up in northwest Georgia—almost to Alabama. He's warned me that it doesn't have the kind of plantations we're accustomed to here and that a lot of people there still live in log cabins." She smoothed out a wrinkle in a sheet with her hand.

"And what did you say?" Catherine asked.

"I told him I'd be willing to live in a teepee in the middle of nowhere as long as he was there."

"A good answer, sister." Catherine nodded her approval with a smile. "You'll be a fine wife."

"Hmph. Well," their older sister Eliza said with a scowl, "I wouldn't give up my comfortable life and go so far away for any man. I don't think you should let him drag you down."

Eugenia and Catherine exchanged amused glances. They knew that their older sister was more soft-hearted than she appeared, but she often chose to display a gruff exterior to hide her emotions.

"I'm sure he won't, Eliza. It's just a beginning," Eugenia assured her. "We have to start somewhere, and they need a lawyer in Carrollton. It's a new town, I know, but it will grow."

As the sisters chatted, Henry and John sat on the front porch, trying to cheer themselves with a glass of whisky. They could hear their sisters through the open window, laughing gaily as they helped Eugenia organize her trousseau.

"Women have it so easy," Henry muttered as they listened.

John gave him a wry smile but said nothing. He didn't begrudge their cheerfulness. In fact, it was rather good to hear his sisters chatter on without a care for a change. He took another sip of his drink and relaxed as he listened to their conversation. Henry, who was on his third glass of whiskey, was more like their sister Eliza, rarely forgetting his problems, in his case the pressure of dealing with the management of the plantation. The most serious issue the brothers had to cope with was their loss of so many workers. Their father had taken some of them with him when he moved off the island and promised six others to Archibald Burke as their sister's dowry.

Henry leaned forward and commented in a soft voice, so as not to be heard inside, "You know, Archie doesn't even plan to take those six slaves to Carrollton, but rather hire them out to coastal rice growers to boost his income."

"I know," John said. "And most of them don't want to go."

"What do they even know about rice growing?"

"They don't want to leave their families, I guess," John said. "That's what slave life is like. They can't control anything that happens to them. They have ties here, yet they're being ripped away to some future unknown world." He knew his Sylvia felt that way. Her father had been torn away like that from his family and sold to another planter. Her people had not come here of their own accord, but for some of the younger generations it was the only home they knew.

He let his mind drift to their limited time together. Even now, she and their son still lived with her mother in the slave quarters, while he lived in the big house with his brother and sisters. He hoped he could change that someday and find a way for them to live together.

Their liaison had been his choice, not hers, but he thought that, over time, she had come to care for him. At least he hoped so. But whatever *her* feelings, he cared for her in ways he didn't know how to express. He had come to find his meaning in her deep dark eyes, her full soft lips, and in holding her in his arms whenever they could be together. She had become a part of his life that he never wanted to do without. He knew they could never marry like Eugenia and Archie. There was a law against it. There was no place they could live where they would be accepted as a couple, except here on the island. Thus, here they would stay. He considered her and his son his family now, and he planned to keep it that way.

"I just wish Papa hadn't taken so many of our prime hands," Henry complained. "We needed them, and replacing them would be expensive, even prohibitive right now."

They had learned in the past year that there was more to running a plantation than they had realized when their father was in charge. They were already aware that growing cotton never resulted in a steady income. Everything depended on the crop. If the season produced a good crop, as this one promised to do, the income could be more than sufficient. But they also knew that unforeseen factors could always affect the yield—weevils, storms, runaways, so many possibilities. Nothing was ever certain. But they knew no other life.

John was fourteen years older than Henry, but even given their age difference, they had shared the same boyhood experiences, discovering, each in his turn, the secrets of the island—on its beaches and in its woodlands. They had hunted the deer, boar, and wild turkeys in the forests, tried to imitate the songs of the mockingbirds, and spied on the roseate spoonbills nesting on the banks of an inland pond. They had caught the ocean's fish and crabs and run through wrecks of seabirds on the beach, scattering them in a wild flutter of wings. On warm afternoons they had swum with their brothers in the river that separated the island from the marshes and where dolphins sometimes swam close enough to touch. They had both roamed the shore, looking for eggs laid just above the tide line each summer by giant sea turtles, and they had watched the eventual hatchlings scurry frantically toward the sea.

Even as grown men, when their father was in charge, they had sometimes ridden their horses from end to end of Jekyl, trying to catch the wild ponies or galloping through shallow waters of the incoming tide just to make splashes. Sometimes they would look for Indian relics, especially arrowheads left by long ago native hunters. On days like that, they still felt like boys again, free to roam the island as they wished. How all that had changed! Henry had grown more restless of late, now that so many new responsibilities had been placed on them, and he was sometimes drawn to the livelier life in the cities just to forget, though he claimed it was only to make important connections. John, on the other hand, was content on the island and, problems notwithstanding, he intended to live there forever.

Under their management, the previous season hadn't yielded as much as they expected. The profit was meager, but at least adequate to live another year without undue hardship. They could only hope that things would go better in the future.

For Eugenia's wedding they tried to forget their worries and just enjoy the family event. They were all there—the brothers and sisters, Félicité and her children, and a few neighbors who had decided for the occasion to ignore their father's scandal. It was the last happy time they would share for many months.

The following year, to their horror, yellow fever swept the area. The DuBignons were familiar with the disease, for it had taken the lives of two of their siblings. They had lost a brother and a sister some years ago to the awful disease, which folks in the area called "the black vomit." They remembered how the two had suffered from fever, chills, convulsions, and other symptoms too awful even to think about. The epidemic began in midsummer. By September, daily reports of yellow fever deaths in Savannah mounted to more than sixty or seventy a day. Darien, which was even closer, was also hard hit with hundreds of deaths. Wealthy people were leaving the towns in droves to escape the dread disease, fleeing to their more isolated plantations or country homes where they thought they would be safe.

"This couldn't happen at a worse time," Henry complained to his brother, for it was the time of year when it was imperative for him to go to Savannah to make arrangements with their cotton factor to have the season's bales of Jekyl's long-staple sea island cotton sold and shipped, as well as to place orders to replenish necessary plantation supplies for the coming year. The crop promised to be good this year, and it was almost picking time. And now this—the risk of infection.

"I can't put off a trip to Savannah much longer," Henry said as they surveyed the abundant crop. "Time is getting short for cotton negotiations, and we're well overdue in placing our orders for the coming season."

"I can go in your place, Henry," John offered. He was the older brother after all.

"I appreciate the offer, but you're no good at business matters, John." They both knew it was true. "No," Henry said firmly, "I'll go."

Jekyl Island, Friday, September 8, 1854

Only a few days later, in mid-afternoon, before the details of Henry's trip could be settled, John noticed storm clouds gathering over the island.

"Looks like we're going to get some rain—right here at pickin' time too," he said as he and his brother sat astride their horses on the edge of the cotton field watching the workers. The fields were almost white with bolls of luxuriant cotton, just as the season had promised. Weary-looking slaves were bent over the stalks, monotonously picking with both hands to fill the long, heavy sacks they dragged behind them. Although the cotton stalks grew tall this year, it was back-breaking work, John knew, as he watched the workers bent over in the field. He had made certain that neither Sylvia nor their boy was a field worker. He had no objection to their working in the cotton house, but he never wanted them to work in the fields.

"Maybe it'll pass over," Henry said in a hopeful tone, frowning up at the sky.

"Maybe, but we always get *some* rain this time of year," John replied.

By late afternoon, the sky was growing dark, and a stiff breeze began to blow. The brothers returned to the barn and handed their horses over to Samson to be fed and brushed before the inevitable raindrops began to fall.

"This might be more than a rainstorm, Henry," John observed grimly, as the brothers walked from the barn toward the house.

"What do you mean?" Henry asked.

"Seems there's a lot of wind behind it. We'll have to wait and see."

The storm grew stronger throughout the night, and rain began to pour, beating on the rooftop of the big house. John lay awake much of the night, listening to the heavy thumps of rain and the howling gale.

The whole household was aroused suddenly in the early morning by a loud crash. John threw off his sheet and got up to look out the window. A heavy limb had fallen onto the roof of the front porch. Even in the dim light of early dawn, he could see the devastating effects of the storm. He woke Henry, and together they peered from an upstairs window toward the only cotton field visible from the house. It stood full of water. Many stalks were broken, and their wet bolls lay on the ground. Some of the plants had even been uprooted and washed from the furrows.

"My God," said Henry. "Do you think we can save any of it?"

"I'm not sure," John answered, stroking his beard thoughtfully. "Not much, if any. I'm afraid. We may have lost the entire crop. Even if we manage to save some of it, it will be graded far lower than we expected. And all this rain could cause boll rot. There's no question that it will affect our yield."

Henry could only stare in dismay. All that work wasted. And all the money he had expected to make from this marvelous crop vanished beyond a doubt. The storm could not have hit at a worse time.

The danger from the wind had subsided sufficiently by Saturday afternoon for John to put on his boots and wade out to the nearby field. He stood there for a few moments, surveying the damage. It was worse than he had feared. Frowning, he leaned over and brought a handful of the water to his lips. Salt. A tidal surge as well as a storm. The taste was unmistakable. It was diluted with rainwater to some extent, but it was bad enough to ruin the crop for the year, and a salty soil could affect next year's crop as well. The fact that most of the cotton was waterlogged and mud-soaked didn't help the situation.

"Damn," he muttered, dreading to give the news to Henry.

He remembered how his brother had first reacted when their father decided to leave the island plantation in their care. He could still picture Henry's big hopeful grin.

"We'll be lords of the manor now, John," Henry had said before he realized all the responsibilities and how many workers his father intended to take with him. "We'll have plenty of money to spend, and we can do whatever we want."

"Don't be too sure," John had replied in his laconic way. He'd lived through far more vicissitudes in plantation life than his younger brother and he was skeptical of Henry's optimism. Everything, he knew, depended on the crop and the possibility of unforeseen events. Their father's and grandfather's problems had even included British invasions and a government embargo. Nothing, he thought, was ever certain.

The storm proved to be the worst hurricane in fifty years, wiping out much of the crop up and down the coast. It would be a hard winter for them all. John was glad it hadn't happened their very first year as caretakers and added to their problem of inexperience and insufficient labor.

"At least we didn't lose any of our people in the storm," he told his brother, trying to cheer him up after they had surveyed the destruction. He was glad there was no loss of human life, while

Henry was concerned only with the fact that they had lost no more slaves.

Despite the yellow fever and the hurricane, Henry could delay his trip to Savannah no longer. It was essential to go now and see what he could buy with their restricted means or on credit to get them through the coming fall and winter. Even though they had little cotton to ship this year, they needed to place orders for winter supplies of shoes and clothes for the workers as well as items they couldn't produce on the island—like sugar and coffee. He was not eager to undertake the risk, but it had to be done.

It was already mid-September by the time he finally set out for Savannah on the daily packet boat. Because of the yellow fever, he planned to keep to himself for most of the trip, staying at the City Hotel, as he always did, and remain for only two days to place his orders as quickly as possible and report to their cotton factor the results of the storm at Jekyl. Since there had been such devastation all along the coast, he knew it would come as no surprise.

On Wednesday morning Henry went first to Factors Row, a line of four to five-story buildings between Bay and River Streets, where his cotton agent had his office. As he made his way up the cobblestone streets, he noticed how the whole area seemed less busy than usual. It was as though a pall had settled over the entire city. Henry climbed the stairs to the iron-railed walkway that joined the buildings together and made his way toward the factor's office. Like the streets outside, it was usually a busy and noisy place, with well-dressed men gathered around tables fingering cotton samples, making notations, and debating the quality and value of their crop. Today there were only two men in the office.

"Good morning, Mr. Snelling," Henry said as he entered and recognized the agent.

"Morning, Mr. DuBignon," said the man behind the sorting table "It's good to see you. What can I do for you?"

"Not much, I'm sorry to say."

"I gather Jekyl didn't fare well in the recent storm."

"I'm afraid not. We'll have little to ship this year, and I'm not completely sure what condition it will be in. We'll let you know as soon as we have it all baled."

"Sorry to hear that. But it's the story of most coastal plantations this year." He shook his head in sympathy. "By the way, have you met Mr. Lamar?" Snelling said, gesturing toward the distinguished-looking gentleman standing nearby.

"Charlie Lamar?" The two men shook hands as Henry introduced himself. "Henry DuBignon. You may not remember me, but we met as children at boating events, when our fathers belonged to the Aquatic Club of Georgia."

"Ah yes, those were good days, weren't they? I remember you and your brothers well," Lamar said. "Good to see you again."

The men exchanged a few more pleasantries, before Henry turned to leave. Lamar picked up his hat to walk out with him.

"I was wondering if you'd care to join me for a whiskey and a bit of lunch," he said once they were outside on Factor's Walk.

Henry hesitated. He would welcome the whiskey, but he knew that a crowded restaurant risked exposing him to yellow fever. Nonetheless, he was flattered to be invited for a meal by someone of Lamar's status. He was the son of a wealthy and powerful man named Gazaway Bugg Lamar. One of his claims to fame was reflected in his very name—Charles Augustus Lafayette Lamar. He boasted about being the godson of the Marquis de Lafayette, the hero of the American Revolution who had passed through Savannah in 1825 and attended Charles's christening during his triumphal return to the United States.

"I'd be much obliged," Henry answered, as the two of them descended the steps and headed for a nearby tavern.

Henry and Lamar had encountered one another through the years, both in pleasure outings at the boat races and through their connections in the cotton trade, but they had never been friends. Over a meal of meat pie and potatoes, accompanied by several whiskies, the two men bonded.

Henry completed his orders for the plantation's needs, mostly on credit, and returned to Jekyl with renewed optimism toward the future. His encounter with Lamar had made him even more determined to find a way to buy more workers to make up for the ones their father had cost them and to work them hard to make the plantation thrive.

"We can just plant fewer fields," John had once suggested.

"Nonsense. I want to see this plantation blossom like it did in the old days." Henry would hear of nothing else. "We must find a way to get more slaves."

John wrinkled his brow at his words, but he said nothing.

CHAPTER 4

Jekyl Island, March 1856

Félicité and her two oldest daughters were settled comfortably before the fire in the parlor enjoying a cup of tea. It was late afternoon, a time of day they all treasured when their duties were done, the younger children were playing outside, and the three of them could converse like adults, which both the girls were rapidly becoming. Their mother sat quietly, sipping her tea and peering thoughtfully into the flames as the girls chatted. Finally, with a sudden motion, she set her teacup firmly on the table beside the settee and turned toward her daughters. It was obvious she had something important to say.

"I've been thinking, my dears. As you know, your aunt Catherine is getting married in the fall and will be moving to Brunswick in November, and I suspect Eliza will soon follow her," Félicité said "Then only your two uncles will be left here."

"I wish we could leave too," said Mary Amelia, the older of the two girls. "I never get to see my friends out here."

"Me either," her sister Josephine echoed, with a pout, tossing her long dark hair across her shoulder.

"I'm almost seventeen now," Mary Amelia said. "A lot of my friends are thinking about getting married, and I've never even had a suitor." She looked as though she were about to cry.

Her mother was not surprised by their reaction. It had become increasingly obvious that the two of them were no longer little girls, content to play with their brothers and sisters. Instead, they were eager to be part of the fancy balls and parties the younger set enjoyed. Now they could attend such events only rarely and in cases where they could stay overnight, for Félicité would never allow them to be rowed back to the island at night. It was far too dangerous. And Mary Amelia was right. She was old enough at least to begin thinking of marriage. Josephine, at fifteen, would not be far behind. Félicité understood, for she too sometimes felt lonely for her old friends.

"Well then, you're going to be happy with my news," she said with a smile, "I've already begun construction on our new house on Union Street in Brunswick. If all goes well, we should be moving in by late summer.

"Really?" Josephine squealed with excitement, set down her cup with a careless rattle, and leapt up to give her mother a hug. Mary Amelia's face glowed with joy.

"Really!" their mother said, laughing and pleased by her daughters' enthusiasm.

"How wonderful!" said Mary Amelia. "Why didn't you tell us before now?"

"I wanted it to be a surprise," Félicité said, delighted by their reaction. It had taken her a long time to make up her mind, and she had wanted to give her boys as much time on the island as possible, but she could put it off no longer. The older girls' futures were at stake.

She dreaded telling her sons, for she knew they would not welcome the news. They were perfectly happy living on Jekyl. What boy wouldn't be, with all its beaches and wild woods to explore and two doting uncles who were teaching them to ride and hunt? She had heard both boys proclaim loudly, like their uncle John, that they wanted to stay here forever. But they too needed to learn to interact with others their own age and behave properly in a more complicated world, their mother had decided.

She waited until the next day to tell her sons of her decision. Although she had expected their disappointment, she was surprised by the intensity of their reactions. They both looked at her in disbelief, and Johnny began to sob. Harry ran from the house, fighting off his own tears.

"What about Lucy?" Johnny asked, once his sobs had become only teary hiccups. He and his brother had found the fawn alone in the woods. She seemed too young to be on her own.

"Maybe somebody shot her mother," Harry had said, approaching the fawn with care. She did not move as he touched her. "She seems lonely."

"Can we take her home?" his little brother asked.

"Yes, and we can feed her," his brother said, "but we can't pen her up. She needs to be free." They put a rope around her neck, led her home, fed her copiously on acorns, corn, and crabapples, and named her Lucy. Then they let her go, but she came back each evening for a nuzzle and her daily meal. Now she was a yearling, but she still came alone and seemed to belong to none of the small herds that emerged from the shadowy woods each evening looking for food. She let them pet her and rubbed against them like a faithful horse.

"Lucy will be fine," his mother answered. "She's old enough now to fend for herself."

"But she'll be all alone."

"She'll find a mate and they'll have a family," she assured him, hoping it was true, for the boys had come to love the little doe and think of her as their own.

"But who will feed her?" the child asked.

"There are plenty of acorns and nuts in the woods, and all sorts of plants for her to eat. She'll be all right." She took John Eugene in her arms to console him, but Harry was gone for the rest of the day. He didn't reappear until suppertime, and Félicité was worried. When he returned, his face was dark. He ate without speaking and went straight to the room he shared with John Eugene.

They were both young, and she knew they would get over it, but she could appreciate why they were so upset. *It's hard,* she thought, *but it's the right thing to do. One day they will understand.* When they were older, they too would want to live in a place where there were friends their own age and pretty girls to court. She couldn't deprive her daughters of their opportunity. Life, she had long realized, was never easy, and one often had to make choices that could hurt, but she had to do what she thought best, no matter how difficult it was. Still, she lay awake most of the night, knowing that she was the source of her sons' misery.

Before she had made her decision about the house, Félicité had wanted to be sure that her financial situation was sufficient to build a comfortable dwelling back in the town. In fact, she found herself rather well off, all things considered, given her inheritance and savings. Even though back on the mainland, she knew she would miss Jekyl's quiet beauty and all those things that reminded her of those happy years with Joseph, she also knew that the days would be easier for them all and that her children's futures depended upon it. It would certainly be more convenient for their education and Sunday worship, not to mention social activities.

She would miss her brothers and sisters-in-law, but she didn't need their support so much anymore, now that Mary Amelia and Josephine were of an age to be a great help in almost any situation. And she didn't want to be left on the island with only Joseph's two unmarried brothers to count on. They were good-hearted, she thought, but John and Henry had little life experience and didn't know much about children. Now that Catherine was getting married, she wondered how long Eliza would stay on the island.

Félicité had surveyed the several lots Joseph had once bought as investments in Old Town Brunswick. After considering them all, she had chosen one on Union Street as the site for her new house. The location was ideal, just north of where Union Street crossed Gloucester, the main road in the little town. The house would be just two doors down from the family of Urbanus Dart, who, like Joseph, had served in the state legislature and who was a family friend. It was a welcoming and convenient neighborhood for her and her children. The empty lot that stood between the DuBignon house and the Darts' was still for sale, and she would encourage Eliza to acquire it if she should decide to move to Brunswick and build a house of her own. That way they could be neighbors. As she pondered the possibilities, she felt a sense of excitement stirring inside—something she hadn't felt for a very long time.

By late July, the house in Brunswick was complete. Félicité and John were supervising the loading of the barge that would move her household goods back to the mainland. The children bustled about, making sure all their favorite belongings were appropriately packed and on board, even the boys, who had become reconciled to their mainland fate.

"Put that heavy armoire on the side opposite the piano. We need to keep things balanced as much as possible," John called out as the two black men, grunting and sweating with their load in the summer sun, carried the chifforobe down the dock. It was the last of the heaviest pieces, and it would be easier now to place the smaller items among them. "We're sure sorry to see you go, Félicité," John said as he watched the men load. "Things won't be the same around here without you."

"I'll miss you too, all of you, but I won't be far away. Perhaps you should come with us."

"Never," he answered firmly. "I'll live on Jekyl Island until the day I die. It's in my blood."

CHAPTER 5

Jekyl Island, 1856

Although the DuBignons were sad to see Félicité and the children go, their spirits were lifted when later that year, on November 20, their sister Catherine finally married her beloved Dr. Robert Hazlehurst. She was already thirty-three years old, but she had waited patiently for her suitor to feel secure enough in his profession to take a wife.

"You make a beautiful bride," Eliza assured Catherine just before the wedding, though a part of her was sad to see it finally take place. The last of her sisters was leaving the island. She would be the only white woman left on Jekyl now. She wore a mask of joy during the wedding, but for weeks afterward, as Eliza and her brothers prepared for Christmas, she settled into a quiet melancholy, trying to ignore Henry's delight in having one less mouth to feed.

She waited until after the new year to announce casually to her brothers, "I'm thinking of moving into Brunswick in the spring."

She didn't feel the same profound attachment to the island that John and Henry did. Although she enjoyed the sunsets and occasional quiet walks or carriage rides, it was far less appealing to her now that all her sisters were gone. Life would no doubt be more interesting in Brunswick, and she could leave the men to their own pastimes and habits—many of which she found distasteful—tracking their muddy or sandy boots onto a newly cleaned floor without the least apology, chewing those disgusting wads of tobacco, or smoking their smelly pipes.

"Who'll look after us?" Henry asked, using his most plaintive voice, the voice he'd used as a little boy.

"Oh, for goodness sake," she said. "You're grown men. You can look after yourselves."

"Where will you live?" Henry asked, assuming that he and John would be expected to cover her costs from the plantation income.

"Catherine has invited me to stay with her for a while. Then perhaps I'll build a house of my own."

Once Eliza too had left the island, Henry and John missed her for a few weeks, but by early fall they'd both realized how much freer they were now to indulge in what they considered manly behavior. John could pursue more openly his relationship with his beloved Sylvia, which he'd tried to keep a secret from Eliza, though he suspected she knew. She must have noticed the little boy with the gray eyes and honey-colored skin, who bore an uncanny resemblance to her own brother. She must have wondered at least, but she had never said anything.

Henry, on the other hand, had no such secrets. Nevertheless, her departure allowed him not only to save money, but to come and go more freely whenever he saw fit. He could spend unaccounted-for time in Savannah or Darien, without having to explain his absences to his sister. It allowed him to seek more freely opportunities to benefit the island. Although he enjoyed the peace and quiet of Jekyl, he continued to discover the city entertainments and livelier activities he had been missing.

He went more often to Savannah, where he sometime met with Charlie Lamar and his friends. Their encounters took place in taverns for the most part, and conversations usually focused on the issues of the day. He listened to his companions complain that Yankees were "too damned critical" of slavery in the South when it was "none of their business." The men, with their glasses of ale before them, were worked up over those abolitionists, who had been on the rise and more outspoken ever since the publication a few years earlier of that book called *Uncle Tom's Cabin*. Henry, who still felt new to the group and didn't really know much about the issue, mostly kept quiet and listened. Slavery was something he took for granted. But it seemed that many plantation owners were steamed up about the North's call for abolition. One of the most outspoken of the men was Charlie Lamar himself.

"You didn't hear that kind of talk when Yankees had slaves of their own," Lamar said, "but now that they've got all those factories and don't need them anymore, they criticize the South. Well, by damn, we still need them."

"They're just a bunch of hypocrites," another voice added.

Henry nodded, along with the others. "We need to be able to make our own decisions here—not be dictated to by some northerners who don't know pea turkey about the South," Lamar added.

Most of the men in the group were highly opinionated and not shy about speaking out, and they all seemed to agree with what Lamar was saying. He was only two years older than Henry, but he seemed to hold sway over the group with his strong personality and imperious self-assurance. It didn't hurt that his well-to-do father had recently moved to New York, leaving his son in charge of his vast enterprises in Savannah. As a result, Lamar had his finger in many Savannah pies. His wealth, along with his quick temper and blunt nature, had made him a veritable legend in the city.

No matter what calamities might occur, Lamar seemed impervious to them, always coming out on top. Or so it appeared to Henry. When he was fourteen, Charlie Lamar had lost his mother and five siblings in the nighttime explosion and sinking of his father's new steamer, the *Pulaski*, as they traveled on its maiden voyage from Savannah to New York. He had been the only Lamar child to survive the disaster. More recently, he had suffered massive financial losses when a fire roared through his uninsured warehouse and cotton press, destroying about 5,000 bales of cotton. He'd even lost a highly-valued race horse that had been stabled in the area during the conflagration. Overall the losses were rumored to total hundreds of thousands of dollars. Most men would have been completely ruined by such a disaster, but Lamar was resilient, determined, and already hatching a plot to recover. He brought up one possibility during one of those tavern conversations when Henry was present.

"I just don't want the U.S. government interfering in my business," he grumbled. "Who the hell are they to say we can't import any more slaves from Africa?"

It wasn't a new law, but one that had been passed by the U.S.

Congress in 1808, before most of the men involved in these tavern debates had been born. The state of Georgia had outlawed it even ten years earlier, but it was the federal government that enforced it. It was not illegal to buy and sell slaves, just to bring them from Africa.

"What difference does it make?" Lamar argued. "They all came originally from Africa, and, I tell you, we're doing God's will to bring them here, taking them out of that heathen land and bringing them to Georgia where they can hear the gospel and be brought into a blessed state. We're paving their way to Heaven." Men nodded all around the table.

"I tell you it's a good thing we do when we import slaves. It's fortunate for them and does them more good than it does us," Lamar went on.

Henry listened silently to Lamar's ranting. He rarely voiced it himself, but he agreed that they couldn't raise their cotton without slave labor. The conversation only reminded him that he still needed more of them on Jekyl Island. He and his brother could not afford to buy most slaves. But those brought directly from Africa never cost as much as those born in America. They were harder to train. They didn't speak the language and were often sullen and irascible at being so recently enslaved. They were a people accustomed to their freedom, but he knew they could be broken.

Lamar continued his speech. "We bring 'em here and civilize 'em—as far as they can be civilized, given that they're not fully human. Even the U. S. Constitution recognizes that they're worth only three-fifths of a white man."

As he listened, Henry was glad it was himself and not his brother John who had come to Savannah on business. He knew that John viewed his woman Sylvia and their boy as fully human as himself, and that statement would have raised John's hackles. Ever since that relationship had started, at least since the boy was born, John's ideas about race and slavery seemed to have changed. Henry, on the other hand, wasn't much interested in the question of their humanity, but he did care about the need for cheap labor.

Even though Henry agreed, Charlie annoyed him. *He thinks he knows everything*, Henry thought. Lamar could be arrogant and overbearing, but Henry put up with it primarily because the Lamar connections could perhaps be useful. Only occasionally did he lose his patience entirely.

One of those occasions occurred in January 1858. Lamar had invited Henry along with many others to a festive dinner after the closing of the races at the new Ten Broeck Race Course in Savannah, one of Lamar's newest possessions. He had bought the old Oglethorpe track the preceding January, refurbished it, and changed its name to Ten Broeck Race Course. Now, in his usual flamboyant style, he was entertaining friends there, treating them to a lavish dinner following the day's last race.

It rankled Henry that Charlie Lamar never seemed to suffer financial woes. Even given his recent setbacks and the current financial panic that was gripping the whole country, causing some banks to close and many businessmen to despair, Lamar spent as he pleased. Although Henry resented Lamar's arrogance, he accepted the invitation, hoping it would lift his gloomy spirits at his own financial setbacks. He had still not been able to buy the slaves he needed, while Lamar could buy whatever he wanted.

It was January 9, the closing day of the second annual meet

at Ten Broeck, but instead of lifting his spirits, everything about the day seemed designed to contribute to his foul mood. A general mist pervaded the atmosphere, and several of the races had been canceled. Some of the horses had fallen ill, one had been seriously injured, and another had died before the race began, but the most important race of the day would still go on.

It was a four-mile heat for a stake of $3,600 between three entries: a four-year-old sorrel mare named Lizzie Macdonald, by far the favorite, and her two competitors, Moidoire and Dallas. Most people were playing it safe, and odds were running in favor of Lizzie McDonald. But when the skittish mare hesitated at the starting gate, hearts fell. Dallas took the lead, and the screaming of the crowd intensified. Lizzie trailed for the first mile, but as she ran, she seemed to gain confidence. By the end of the second mile, she had taken a commanding lead, which she held onto for the rest of the first heat. The second heat followed a similar pattern, though this time it was Moidoire who was out in front. In the end, much to the relief of the gamblers, most of whom had bet on the favorite, the mare prevailed and took the stake. Nobody had made a lot of money, but even a small amount was welcome.

Those in the Ladies Stand, where men and women mingled after the race, appeared to be in high spirits and determined to enjoy themselves. Liquor had flowed freely among the men throughout the race. Now they were ambling down the steps toward the makeshift dining room below where Lamar was holding his dinner to celebrate the end of the racing season. Henry DuBignon was among them.

Lamar, standing on the top step, raised his glass, and shouted toward his friends. "A toast to Lizzie McDonald, a great little filly."

"She's not a filly. She's a mare" Henry shouted in a loud, scornful voice, slurring his words, but jubilant to call out Charlie's inconsequential error in public.

"You're right, Henry," Lamar riposted in a mocking tone, not liking to be contradicted. "If she was human, she'd be too old for your father. He likes the fillies, I'm told." Those close enough to hear his words erupted in laughter. Everyone knew the story of Henry's father who in his dotage had married his mistress's young daughter, and it seemed they would never forget. Henry was enraged by Charlie's taunt, but the other men, who had been drinking as much as he had, found it hilarious.

"How old is that new wife anyway?" someone yelled. "We hear she's still a filly!"

"Don't know about *her*, but I hear *he's* still a stud," another loud voice echoed from the crowd.

"You shut your mouth, Charlie Lamar, or I'll shut it for you," Henry growled. His eyes narrowed as he reached into his pocket and began to push his way toward Lamar with a knife in his hand. The throng of men suddenly grew quiet, despite their inebriated gaiety.

One of the younger men clapped him on the shoulder. "Let it go, Henry. They're just joking!" He patted the shoulder in a conciliatory gesture. "Come on now, let's go outside and cool off."

Henry jerked free from his grasp but halted in his menacing approach toward Lamar and let the man lead him away, cursing as he went. Those in the stands breathed a sigh of relief and filed on into the dining area. Once outside in the chill air, Henry's head cleared a bit, but his anger didn't cool. He stood there, alone for a few moments.

Finally he muttered to himself, "Damn you, Charlie Lamar. You think because your daddy's so rich, you can say or do anything you damn well please. Well, you don't make fun of my father, fool that he is." He took a deep breath, drew out his knife again, and stumbled back inside. As he threw open the door of the dining room, Lamar was standing at the head of one of the long tables, talking to a dapper-looking gentleman wearing a green vest beneath his black jacket and a darker green cravat to match.

Bystanders could see Henry beginning once more to make his way toward Lamar, the knife open in his right hand.

An old gentleman, already seated, stood up to block Henry's path. "Come on now, Henry," he said, "the men are just havin' a little fun. They didn't mean anything. It's nothin' to get so het up about. We don't need any trouble here."

Henry shoved him aside and snatched up an almost empty champagne bottle, took the last swig straight from the bottle, and held it up by the neck to threaten the man.

"Get out of my way, old man, or I'll do something you may regret."

"Hold on, Henry," Lamar said, his anger rising. "That man is my Uncle Phinizy. If you hit him with that bottle, rest assured, I'm gonna kill you." By now, Charlie had drawn his pistol from his waistband and was pointing it at Henry.

"I'm not kidding, Henry. Put it down. Now."

Henry, angry and drunk, gave a snarling laugh, drew back the bottle and struck the old man on the left side of the face. Lamar's Uncle Phinizy staggered back and fell to the floor, his cheek bleeding. Then Henry, still out of control, hurled the bottle toward Charlie Lamar, barely missing his head. It smashed into the wall behind him. Almost simultaneously Lamar fired. The ball slammed into Henry's face just below the right eye.

"Goddamn it, you sonofabitch, you shot me," Henry yelled, dropping his knife. His hand flew to his eye as though he could hold back the blood gushing from his wound.

By this time, the room was in pandemonium, with men scrambling to avoid the weapons. Lamar lowered his revolver, the latest model Colt Walker, and tucked it back in his belt. "I warned you," he said, moving to help his uncle who was scrambling to get up off the floor.

"Somebody go for a doctor," a bystander yelled, and several men rushed forward with their handkerchiefs trying to staunch Henry's blood.

"I have a carriage outside. I'll take him uptown to find a doctor," a man unknown to Henry offered, and off they went. Lamar stayed behind to see to his uncle.

The doctor probed Henry's wound to see if he could retract the lead ball lodged high in his cheekbone just below the eye.

"Mr. DuBignon, I'm afraid I'll do more damage if I try to dig it out. Let's give it until tomorrow to see if it'll work its way a bit more to the surface. I'll try to stop the bleeding and give you some laudanum to help you get through the night."

Henry, still angry, checked in to the City Hotel to pass the night.

It was late afternoon, almost dark, when there was a knock on the door of Henry's room. He was lying down, hung over and groggy from the alcohol and the laudanum the doctor had given him. He managed to stumble to the door.

There stood Charlie Lamar.

"Henry," he said, as he stepped into the room. "I'm sorry about what happened. I guess we were both a little drunk."

"Not too drunk to shoot straight," Henry said bitterly, his hand pointing to his bandaged eye.

"I was aiming for your arm," Lamar confessed. Anyhow, I want to make it up to you."

"How can you do that?" Henry's laugh was bitter. "I'm blind in that eye now, probably for good."

"I know. I heard, and I'm really sorry. I'll take care of your medical bills, of course. But I want to make it up to you. I have a proposition that will be beneficial to you and your brother on the plantation."

"I'm not interested in any proposition from you, you sonofabitch."

"Just listen to what I have to say. You might change your mind."

Henry said nothing. If he weren't so groggy, he would have thrown Lamar out of his room. As things stood, he knew he didn't have the strength.

"Then get it over with and get out."

"Now Henry," Charlie said in a placating voice. "As you know, we're all going through a bit of a financial pinch right now, and from what I hear, you and your brother could probably use a little money and some new slaves to bring in your crop this fall."

"We can't afford them. We'll just have to make do."

"Not necessarily. I have a plan to bring in some new, shall we say, 'worker apprentices' from Africa. They don't cost as much as those on the domestic market, and I need your help."

"It's illegal, Charlie. You know damn well that importing slaves is against the law. As badly as we need them, I'm not sure I want to go that far." His head hurt, but his mind was clearing.

"We won't call them slaves. As I said, they'll be 'apprentices.' There's no law against bringin' in immigrant apprentices."

"You're not gonna fool anybody. I heard you've even been quarreling with Howell Cobb about the importation of slaves. Must be nice to have kinsmen so high up." Henry's voice was sarcastic. He knew that Cobb was President Buchanan's Secretary of the Treasury. "Isn't he your cousin or something?"

"Something. By marriage," Lamar said with indifference. "And it's true we've had words about it, he and I, and we'll never see eye-to-eye. I don't think the law is just, and I told him so. He's managed to stop some of my earlier efforts, but he won't know about it this time. What I'm proposing is a way around that law, in case we're stopped?"

"What are you talking about?"

"I'm going to find a pleasure yacht, outfit the hull as a slaver, leaving the exterior pristine, exactly the same."

"How will you ever be able to pass inspection at the ports of entry?"

"That's the beauty of my plan. The cruiser won't have to land at a port of entry if you're willing to cooperate. For a goodly sum, of course, I'd like to land it at Jekyl Island."

"Jekyl Island? We don't have a dock big enough for a boat like that."

"I thought we could anchor at the south end somewhere in St. Andrews Sound and unload the cargo in skiffs."

"Why Jekyl?"

"Well, it's a private island, an enviable one. There's no lawmen snooping about. Once the Africans are unloaded, preferably by night, we'll move the vessel up the Little Satilla River so nobody will associate it with Jekyl. Then we can get the darkies cleaned up and ready to move in small lots to sell them upcountry. Quietly of course. We won't advertise except by word of mouth and only to those we think might be interested and trustworthy."

"Why on God's earth should I help you? And it sounds risky."

"No risk, no gain. I'm willing to pay handsomely for the privilege."

"How much?" Henry asked.

"Would $10,000 suffice?"

The large amount surprised him, but he wanted to make Lamar pay even more. "Make it $15,000, and it's a deal."

"You drive a hard bargain, Henry."

"You'll get most of it back if the slaves are worth it. As you said, we could surely use more to work our land. Could we get first pick?"

"Why not?" said Lamar.

Suddenly things were looking brighter for Henry, despite his sightless, bandaged eye. Charlie held out his hand for a handshake to close the deal. Henry hesitated, but finally he took Lamar's outstretched hand, and they shook on the pact.

Unfortunately, the doctor in Savannah was unable to extract the ball from Henry's eye the next day, but he recommended a doctor named Carnochan he knew, a Georgian who practiced medicine in New York and had the skills to do the job and maybe even save his eyesight. He would write to the doctor immediately and make the arrangement.

Well, why not? Henry thought. *If Charlie Lamar is footing the bill, why not indeed?* He wrote to his brother John that he was taking a ship for New York City to see a doctor right away.

"I'll explain everything when I get back," he wrote. "And I think I've found a way for us to take care of our problems on the plantation."

The letter was enigmatic, leaving John with more questions than answers, but while his brother was away, he consoled himself by bringing Sylvia and their boy to live with him at the big house for a full week. He didn't care what the servants thought. Only Sylvia was uncomfortable with the arrangement.

"John, they say I'm the massa's gal, and they treat me different, and folks in de quarters ...well, they don't seem to wanna be friends with me no more."

"They better treat you and Robert real good, or they'll answer to me."

"Please don't make no trouble."

"Don't you worry," he said.

She didn't like being at the big house. She thought nothing good could come of it, but she had no choice. He wanted her there, in his soft bed with feather pillows. He liked the contrast of her smoky skin against the white sheets, her dark fleece-like hair, usually hidden under a bandana, splayed out on the pillow. It was like being married, even though the laws of Georgia forbade a legal marriage between the races. But John liked feeling married. He wanted her there, by his side and in his bed despite her discomfort. He thought again that they needed a house of their own—nothing fancy like this—just a small house somewhere in the woods, far away from prying eyes.

By the time the week was over, Sylvia was expecting another child, and John had made up his mind to build a new cabin in the pine thicket north of Wylly Road, where they could all live together, undisturbed, for as long as they liked.

CHAPTER 6

Jekyl Island, 1858

When Henry returned to Jekyl Island, the ball removed, but still blind in one eye, he told his brother John Couper all that had happened, including his agreement with Charlie Lamar.

"It will solve a lot of our problems, John. We'll either have more slaves or the money to buy them."

John did not try to hide his annoyance. "You should have talked it over with me first, Henry. I'm in charge here too," he said. "I don't want any trouble with the law."

"Would you have agreed?"

"I'd have to think about it." John said. "I don't much like the idea. Maybe for that amount of money it's worth considering, but you're going to get us in trouble. It's a good thing all the womenfolk are gone. This would really have upset Eliza and Félicité."

"If they were still here, we couldn't do it," Henry acknowledged.

"Or we surely couldn't have told them."

"They'd have found out."

"Well, it's good they're gone."

"How many people does he plan to bring in?" John asked.

"We didn't talk about that. As many as the cruiser will hold, I expect. A couple of hundred at least, I'd guess. Maybe more. Do you know a pilot who could steer the boat into St. Andrews Sound in the dark?"

"There's a fellow over on Cumberland named Clubb, James Clubb. He might be willing, and he's a good pilot. Knows the waters well. He won't steer you wrong. But I don't know if he would do it or not, considering it's illegal."

"Well, we can worry about that later, John. Let's don't talk to him about it yet. We don't want word to spread. I'm just hoping that this will help us get back on a sound financial footing. And he said we could have first pick of the Africans. We need them. The years have been rough, with so few workers."

John shook his head. "We're gettin' along all right, and I don't much like the idea. I just hope it's worth the chance we're taking."

"We'll just have to wait and see, won't we?"

Jekyl Island, mid-November, 1858

John and Henry were on edge as they waited impatiently for word from Charlie Lamar concerning when the shipload of "apprentices" would arrive. The brothers became increasingly nervous and irritable as the day grew closer. As planned, they had fired their overseer as soon as most of the cotton was in, telling him that Henry would take over his duties for the following season. Now all they could do was wait.

Finally, on November 20, a coded letter from Lamar arrived telling them to be prepared for "the expected visit" any time after November 25. Three days later, the two brothers published a notice in the *Savannah Daily Morning News*, warning "All Persons" against landing or trespassing in any way or for any reason on Jekyl Island. They set up a makeshift light to mark the island's southernmost point in case the ship arrived by night, and they posted a trusted slave to keep watch. Now all they had to do was wait. Their nerves were frazzled to the breaking point, and they snapped at each other at the slightest irritation.

On the evening of Sunday, November 28, the watchman, Samson, spotted a small skiff carrying three white men making its way toward Jekyl's south end through the dark waters of St. Andrews Sound from the direction of Cumberland Island. The black man waited and peered toward the dark waters as they approached. As they grew nearer, he thought he recognized one of them—the assistant lighthouse keeper from Cumberland—Horatio Harris.

"Mr. Harris, is dat you?" he called into the darkness.

"It sure is, Sam. We're here looking for Mr. Clubb. D'you know where we could find him?"

"Yessuh. Dat light been givin' some problems, so he come over to fix it. Now he gone up to de big house to get paid, I reckon."

"Well, we need him. Can you take us to him?"

"I'se supposed to be on watch here."

"I 'spect the men you're watching for are these two here," Harris said, gesturing toward his companions, who were getting out of the boat.

Samson had never seen them before, but they looked tired, scruffy and weather-beaten, as though they might have been at sea for a long while. He wasn't sure if they were the ones he was watching out for or not, but he agreed to lead them to the house. The walk took half an hour, and when they arrived, Clubb was already on the verge of departure. Harris introduced the two men from the skiff as Nick Brown, the red-bearded captain of a vessel called the *Wanderer*, and William Corrie, its owner, who might have been a handsome fellow had he not had the appearance of one who had not shaved or bathed in weeks. His hair, like that of Brown, was unkempt, windblown and stiffened by salt, and his skin, toughened and burned by the sun.

"We understood that you were to be our pilot to bring our ship into St. Andrews Sound and eventually up the Little Satilla a way," Corrie said. "I'm told there's a bar we need to cross."

Henry DuBignon had brought up the topic with his Cumberland guest earlier in the evening, but they hadn't yet settled on a price. Now Clubb eyed the men suspiciously.

"I understand the going price is fifty dollars," Corrie said.

"I'll do it for five hundred," said Clubb.

"What?" Corrie said, his voice angry. "That's ridiculous, my good man. I won't pay it."

"Then I won't do it," Clubb answered.

"Come on, James," Henry DuBignon said to the lightkeeper. "You know that's not a fair price."

"I won't do it for less," Club answered. "I know what you folks are up to, and I won't get involved for fifty dollars."

"Forget it then," said Corrie. "We'll do it on our own."

"You'll find yourself stuck on a sand bar in shallow water if you try," Henry warned. "Those are dangerous waters for a large ship."

"Well, I won't pay it. It's highway robbery." Corrie's jaw was set.

"Come on, you two," Henry urged. "Let's come to an agreement. It's got to be done, or the whole expedition will have been a waste."

"I won't do it for any less," Clubb said again. "It's the middle of the night, and I've heard rumors about a slaver called the *Wanderer*."

"Where did you hear any such thing?" Henry asked. He was shocked because no one had mentioned the name of the vessel.

"There's talk here and there."

Corrie balled up his fist. "Damn it," he said, turned toward the door, and started to walk out.

"Hold on, Corrie," Henry stepped forward. "John and I will pay it out of our share." He turned to Clubb and added "As long as you keep your mouth shut."

Clubb nodded.

"Now let's get it done before daylight," Henry said. The men shook hands in agreement and turned to leave.

John grabbed his brother by the shoulder,

"What d'you mean... 'John and I will pay it'? Don't you think you should have talked with me about that first?" He was the older brother, and he was getting tired of Henry's making decisions without discussing them with him. He knew his younger brother had a better head for business, but it was irritating nonetheless.

"John, we can't waste any more time or the authorities are going to get word of this before we can get the Africans sold—especially if there are already rumors out there. Let's not argue about it now. Time's wastin'." Without waiting for a response, Henry turned on his heel and followed the others.

It was almost dawn by the time the *Wanderer* was safely anchored in the Sound. It dropped anchor long enough to allow repeated small boatloads of shivering Africans to be rowed to Jekyl's shores. To speed up the process, the DuBignons contributed their own larger yawl to help bring them ashore.

As John got his first glimpse of them, he was aghast, not only at their weak and emaciated appearance, but at the stench they brought with them. Some of them were so weak they could hardly walk.

One of the women in a recently landed skiff was barely able to stand. She was holding in her arms what appeared to be a newborn baby, wrapped in rags to protect it from the November wind. When one of the sailors tried to take it from her, she clutched the infant even closer to her bosom.

"*Mba*," she said loudly, her eyes suddenly afire, as she held on with all the reserves of strength she had left.

"Let her keep it," John shouted to the sailor in his most commanding voice as he stepped forward to hand her out of the boat. "I'll help her."

Several of the new arrivals, all naked, were retching on the sand. Some had sores and new scars over their bodies. Others coughed and scratched. Their movements were stiff, and some could not walk without help. Clearly, they needed medical care.

"We should send for Robert to come. We've got to get a doctor here. They need medical care," John said to his brother once he had settled the woman and the baby in a suitable spot. "I'll go fetch him."

Henry nodded. Even he could see that some of the Africans were sick. He feared they'd be worthless in that condition, and if they died, then all this would have been for naught.

"Go ahead," he said to his brother. "And hurry. Just be careful no one else knows why you've come—not even Catherine. And send some of our most trusted people from the quarters down here, even if you have to take them out of the fields. We're gonna need help to get them fed and cleaned up." John nodded, mounted his horse, and set off at a gallop.

He had not been gone an hour before some of the workers showed up in a work wagon, Polydore and Old Jack among them. *I'm glad John had the sense to send those two*, Henry thought. He knew that both of them had experienced the trip from Africa themselves and would know what the new captives had been through and what they needed.

He watched as Old Jack passed among them, speaking occasionally and making sounds of sympathy. The dark-skinned man seemed to understand the language of some of the captives, among them the woman with the baby. After a few murmured words, he reached for the child and this time she did not resist. He wrapped the small bundle in his arms and gazed tenderly at the child for a moment. Then, when the baby began to whimper, the old man leaned down and gently handed it back to her, watching with satisfaction as she put the infant to her breast with a grateful smile.

"Get some buckets of water to wash these people," Corrie barked. "They carry a foul odor."

Of course they do, Henry thought. They'd been at sea for many weeks without any kind of proper bath or toilet facilities and God know what else. He was tempted to point out that Corrie himself didn't smell much better but decided not to mention it. He didn't like taking orders from Corrie, but it was no time to get into an argument.

Polydore was standing at his elbow with another request. "Dey be hungry, Mas' Henry, but we ain't brought nothin' to feed 'em," Polydore volunteered. "We didn't know dey was comin'."

"My God, man," Corrie cursed. "Didn't you make any preparations at all?" he castigated Henry.

"Of course we did. We just didn't know when you'd get here. I'll take care of it," Henry responded.

He put Polydore in charge of organizing a few men to make a quick return to the plantation. "Take the wagon and load it up with soap, buckets, as many blankets as you can round up, and bring the cornmeal and rice reserves in the storage area behind the kitchen as well as some jugs of fresh water. And hurry."

"We ain't got no cookpot big enough to fix food for all dese folks," Polydore reminded his master.

"Is there something on the ship that would suffice as an ample cookpot?" Henry asked Captain Brown, who was in charge of transporting the captives from the ship.

The captain nodded and ordered the crew of the next skiff that arrived to bring back the large, iron cookpot they had used on the *Wanderer*.

The Africans kept arriving throughout the darkness of early morning, hundreds of them, in the small boats that made their way between the ship and the sandy shore. While they waited for the cookpot and the supplies, the other DuBignon slaves built up a great fire to try to keep the shivering captives warm. It would also serve for cooking when the men returned with the sacks of corn meal and rice the DuBignon brothers had stored. They would make up a large amount of what the slaves called a "hodgepodge" to feed the new arrivals. It was a tasteless, unsalted gruel, but the hungry newcomers ate it greedily.

It was mid-morning by the time all the captives had been unloaded, and the sun was high. James Clubb finished his guidance of the ship through the sound and sailed her up the Little Satilla to anchor in a cove far enough away that she couldn't be spotted from any seagoing crafts offshore. From there, Clubb was rowed back to Cumberland with the promise of payment as soon as the slaves were sold, and the crew set out to clean the ship and dispose of all the bondage equipment below deck.

It was early afternoon by the time John arrived back on the island with his brother-in-law, Robert Hazlehurst, armed with his medical bag.

"Good God!" said Robert when he saw the large number of people in such wretched conditions, all of whom he was expected to treat. By now, many of the captives were cleaner and in better shape than they had been the evening before. They had rested and been fed, and most of them had regained enough mobility to walk about, though their movements were stiff and they tired easily. Others, however, still lay on the ground in a miserable state. Robert knelt beside them first, opening his medical bag and taking out his new stethoscope. He spent hours examining the ones who seemed to be in the worst condition, as well as the new mother and her baby and the few sick children. Then he reported back to John and Henry.

"There's one man dead. The others are suffering mostly from skin diseases, diarrhea, and wounds—from beatings, I expect."

His voice was scornful. "Some of the women have infections from what appears to have been abuse, most likely at the hands of randy sailors. It would help if I could talk with them."

"Call Jack," Henry said to his brother. "He and Polydore seem to understand some of them. Maybe they can help."

Robert did what he could, working throughout the rest of the day and into the night cleaning wounds, lancing boils or carbuncles, applying poultices and calomel, dispensing sulfur, camphor, Dover's Powder, and anything he felt would help. After what seemed like endless hours of examining the neediest captives and providing whatever remedies he had at hand, he reported back to his brothers-in-law.

"I've done what I can for them. Most of them are young, in their teens, I'd say, some even younger, and that's in their favor. They're suffering primarily from malnutrition, a need for fresh air, and joint stiffness, but I think that, along with some decent food, the remedies I've given them, and a bit of rest and exercise should get them on the mend, most of them at least." His words were reassuring. "Now I'm tired, and I've got a practice I need to get back to before morning. I'll check back in a few days and see how they're doing."

"I hope we'll have most of them out of here by then," Henry said.

"Where are they going?" Robert asked.

"God only knows. Lamar is taking care of the sales. We're just the landing point."

"Well, if you plan to sell them for a decent price, you'd best get them in better shape than they are in now. And, by the way, I'll send you a bill. Maybe Lamar can pay it from his ill-gotten gains."

"Please don't tell Catherine and Eliza about all this," Henry cautioned.

"Don't worry. I won't shock the ladies. They'd no doubt be quite appalled at what their brothers are up to. But I won't tell them. And for future reference, if you ever get mixed up in anything like this again, leave me out of it. I won't tend to any more illegal shiploads of African captives. I don't want to be involved."

John nodded, and Henry extended his arm, offering to shake Robert's hand. The doctor hesitated for a moment, then, with a palpable lack of enthusiasm, took his brother-in-law's outstretched hand.

"Thank you, Robert. I appreciate what you've done." John said.

Robert nodded and said, "Can you get some folks to row me back to the mainland now?"

As soon as all the captives were tended and fed, the red-bearded Captain Brown managed to flag down and board a steamer that made a daily run between Brunswick and Savannah to let Lamar know of their arrival.

Another day passed before he and Lamar arrived back on Jekyl aboard a different steamer called the *Lamar*, aptly named for its builder, Charlie's father. Among the men to emerge from the vessel were Nelson Trowbridge, a well-known slave trader and a part of the expedition, and Captain Brown. One other man Henry recognized was John Tucker, a member of the Savannah City Council, who owned a large plantation on the Savannah River.

"What's he doing here," Henry asked.

"I'm hoping he's one of our buyers," Lamar assured them.

Finally, the last one to disembark, to the surprise of both John and Henry, was their brother-in-law Thomas Bourke, the husband of their sister Sarah, who stood looking about in a bemused manner.

"What are you doing here, Tom?" John asked.

"Lamar stopped in Brunswick and asked me to come. He said they needed someone trustworthy to guide them to the island."

"Well," John said. "I guess we don't have any secrets anymore. The whole family knows by now, I expect. I hope they didn't tell Sarah what it was for."

"They didn't even tell me. He just said I needed to come, that it would be of help to my brothers-in-law."

"Well, I guess you can see now what Henry got us involved in," John said. "I hope you won't tell Sarah."

"Your secret's safe with me, John."

As John talked with Tom, Henry was busy overseeing Lamar's selection of the slaves he planned to take to South Carolina.

"I'll take that one, that one, those three...," he was saying, as Corrie made a chalk mark on the back of each boy or girl, man or woman he chose.

"What are you doing," Henry asked.

"Selecting the healthier ones I'm taking to sell in South Carolina. I'm taking about a hundred of them. The sales are all prearranged."

"You told me we could have first choice," Henry said, his voice angry.

"Be reasonable, man," Lamar said. "I can't take people in their conditions." He pointed to some of the sicker ones. "I wouldn't get a good price for them. They'll heal, and you'll have a fine group, no doubt."

"But—" Henry sputtered.

"Good lord, man, you know we've got to get them sold as fast as possible. The rumors are already out. You'll still have hundreds to choose from. There were more than 400 'apprentices' in this shipload," Lamar said, in a dismissive tone. "Plenty to go around."

Corrie had informed John and Henry that they had left Africa with 487 captives. But they had arrived with only 409, including the newborn.

"What happened to the others?" John asked.

"A few died. We had to get rid of the sick ones to keep fevers from spreading. Then, we started to get short on food and water. We couldn't feed them all, but we kept the best ones alive."

"Good heavens, man. Did you just kill the others?" John was shocked at the man's indifference.

"Well, not exactly. Either they just died or we dumped them in the sea."

"Good God! You mean you just threw them overboard to drown or be eaten by sharks?"

"It was the only thing we could do to save the cargo," Corrie replied, his tone nonchalant.

What kind of men are we dealing with here? John wondered. He could never tell Sylvia what they had done. She would be horrified, he knew, for she was a tender-hearted woman who, despite all she had been subjected to in her life, still cried when she had to wring the neck of a chicken for dinner.

CHAPTER 7

Jekyl Island, 1858

John stood silent as he watched Lamar make his selections. He looked the captives over from head to foot, examining their teeth and groping their bodies here and there to feel the strength of their muscles or the firmness of their breasts. As he touched and poked, many of the Africans flinched, eyes flaring with fury or filling with tears of humiliation and fear. Lamar, indifferent to their reactions, gave only an occasional grunt, a nod of approval, or a frown of displeasure. John tightened his lips, imagining Lamar touching Sylvia or Robert that way, and he could feel his face redden and his hands tighten into fists with anger. But he said nothing.

He and Sylvia had another son now as well—Joseph—named for John's dead brother. When he had first seen the captive infant brought ashore in its mother's arms, he thought of his own son as a newborn. *So tiny and helpless*. He could only imagine the horrible conditions that must have surrounded the baby's birth.

"A good cargo overall." Lamar grinned with satisfaction. "Load the ones I chose onto the ship," he said to his men, "and let's get on our way." They drove the selected people like a herd toward the steamer, as the crew prepared to set out for the coast of South Carolina, where the captives were to be sold to prearranged coastal planters.

Just before he boarded the sidewheel steamer himself, Lamar took John and Henry aside. "If any strangers approach the island, make sure you hide the Africans," he said.

"We put an ad in the paper warning people not to land here," Henry said, "just like you asked us to."

"Be cautious. I don't think it's too big a danger, but watch out," Lamar told them. "Even if the law should gather evidence, no Southern court is going to convict men of our stature over such a trivial matter. As I've said before, a man of means and influence can do pretty much as he pleases here. Now guard them well," he said, as he climbed aboard, the last one to do so.

The crew cast off. Standing beside his brother on the dock, John could feel the engine's vibrations as the steamer began its journey up Jekyl Creek toward St. Simons Sound and into the open ocean. Sunlight reflected in the murky water that swirled in the wake, the vessel's hisses of steam growing fainter with the distance. Under Lamar's orders, its whistle remained silent. John was glad to see him go. Lamar had taken more than a hundred of the captives, the best of the lot. John knew Henry would be annoyed by that, but to him it was a relief, for there was no way they could have fed and cared for them all for very long.

Enough time passed before Lamar's next visit that most of the Africans, being young and resilient, had begun to regain their strength, if not their spirits. Old Sam and Polydore were assigned the task of remaining with them, to make sure that none tried to escape and to instruct them in what they needed to know to survive in this new world. The captives themselves had added a little meat to their diets, thanks to their skill at trapping small game and catching fish barehanded in the shallow waters.

Many of them seemed to take comfort in the fact that others of the newly enslaved had filed teeth and body tattoos not unlike their own. Although all the captives were not of the same tribe or spoke the same language, their ways were similar in many respects, and they were finding non-verbal means of communicating with each other. Sam and Polydore were also beginning to teach them the language the slaves spoke on the island, made up of words from various African tongues with English, Spanish, and a little French mixed in.

As John observed the captives' efforts, he could see that many of them were intelligent and resourceful—values that Lamar had not bothered to assess as he poked and prodded their bodies. During Lamar's absence and before he could send his minions back to pick up more Africans to sell, the DuBignon brothers selected those they wanted to keep at Jekyl. They decided that forty slaves, a mix of boys and men, women and girls, would make up a fair equivalent of the $15,000 that Lamar owed them. Taking the captives on hand as payment, instead of waiting for money that might never show up, seemed to them a safer bet. Among those that John insisted on keeping, over his brother's objection, was the woman with the newborn baby.

Most of the new captives had learned to fear the white men back in Africa or on the *Wanderer*. They had noted that they almost always carried guns and sometimes a whip at their sides. So far, the only use of a gun they had seen on the island had been to shoot a rattlesnake in the brush. Whips were another matter. They learned particularly to fear white strangers. Polydore and Jack had made sure they understood that it was necessary to hide if white strangers approached. Most of them were quick to learn, but as much as possible they clung to their African ways, consoling themselves with ritual dances around a fire and chanting, the sounds filled with sorrow that went unnoticed by their white captors.

Henry and John checked on the captives every day, knowing that Lamar or his men, eager to have them all sold as soon as possible, would return soon for those who were left, fearing that the rumors about the *Wanderer* were growing on the mainland. They were wary of federal authorities who tried to enforce the law prohibiting the importation of slaves, but they also knew there was nothing the law could do without concrete evidence. Their most important goal was to keep the "evidence" out of their sight and grasp.

"Lamar's sure that everything will be all right," Henry assured his brother.

"We can only hope he's right," John said.

It was already mid-December, and thus far, no one else had come to the island. He didn't know what was happening on the mainland, but there were no major problems at Jekyl.

Then, late one morning as Henry was riding toward the Africans' encampment to check on the captives, he encountered a lone white man on foot trudging rapidly along the path toward the big house. He stopped his horse and eyed the man with suspicion.

"Who the hell are you?" he asked in an angry tone. "You're trespassing on private property? What are you doing here?"

"I'm Edward Gordon, a federal deputy," the man said. He flashed his badge and then pulled out a folded document. "I'm on my way to deliver this warrant to John DuBignon. Would that be you by any chance?"

"No, I'm his brother, and John DuBignon is not on the island. Now you get on back to where you came from, and don't trespass on this property again. How'd you get here anyhow?"

"My boat is tied up at on the river side," he gestured back toward Jekyl Creek.

"Well, get on your boat and get out of here. Now," Henry said in a loud voice, his hand resting on the stock of his rifle. "You're not welcome here."

The man made no protest and started back toward the creek. Henry watched for a moment, then turned his horse around and began to gallop toward the big house without waiting for a response. He needed to warn John to hide. He would be safer somewhere besides the family home should the lawmen return.

After his breathless ride, Henry leapt off his horse and rushed into the house, where he found John in his bedroom changing his boots.

"You've got to get out of here. There's a federal deputy on the island, and he's got a warrant for you."

"What? A warrant? On what charge?"

"I didn't stop to ask. I just told him you weren't on the island. Now go and hide somewhere until he's gone. I'll ride back and make sure he left."

"Thanks for the warning. I'll pay a visit to Sylvia and my boys, I think." He gave Henry a conspiratorial smile, jerked on his last leather boot, and ran out to the barn where Samson quickly saddled his mare. Then, John mounted and rode rapidly toward the cabin he had built for them in the woods.

Henry waited until he was out of sight before he remounted his own horse and headed south again toward the place he had encountered the deputy. It was not far from the captives' camp, and he wanted to make sure the lawman had left the island.

He was more than halfway there when he found Polydore running toward the big house. Polydore began to wave his arms and started to yell, "Mas' Henry, Mas' Henry!"

"What's the matter, boy? Did you see that deputy?"

Polydore glanced back toward the camp and began to talk in an excited tone.

"We couldn't help it, Mas' Henry." he said. "Dey took one of dem boys away,"

"Hey, slow down and tell me what happened. You said 'they.' Were there more than one?"

"Yessuh, dey was another man."

"Did you recognize him?"

"Naw suh. It wadn't our fault, Massa. Dem African folk did everything we told 'em. When dey saw the white mens comin', dey run into de woods and hide. But one of dem men found a boy under a bush, and dey done took him."

"Dammit to hell," Henry muttered. Well, the deed was done,

and there wasn't much he could do about it now, except scan the riverbanks to make sure they were gone. He gazed up the river and toward the marsh. At a great distance he could see three figures in a small skiff, already paddling down one of the tidal creeks toward Brunswick. There was nothing to do now but wait.

The deputy didn't return, but in the following days, John and Henry scoured the newspapers, reading every story they could find in the *Savannah Republican* and the *Savannah News* about the "wild African boy" captured at Jekyl Island and brought to Savannah, and then about his surreptitious rescue from prison by a group of unknown men. Lamar's henchmen, no doubt, they thought. Now the boy had disappeared again, and the brothers relaxed a bit. But within days they found articles containing reports of more "savages" believed to have been part of the *Wanderer* cargo, who had been apprehended as "evidence" by the authorities. The U.S. attorney's office had also seized the vessel itself along with her logs and record books.

Legal authorities in Savannah began rapidly to study all the evidence, which led to a hearing that was to begin on December 18. Among other things, the court would consider the testimonies of those they believed to be eyewitnesses to some part of the landing and its aftermath. Among them, they called the DuBignons' brother-in-law Dr. Hazlehurst, Clubb, Harris, and a man named Luke Christie, who had been the pilot of the *Lamar*. Finally, when they learned that, as a result of the hearing, the case was to go to trial, the two brothers really began to worry. Was it possible they could go to jail for their part in the matter?

If tensions weren't high enough already, one afternoon in mid-January, their father Henry Sr. returned to the island. It was not the first time he had come back since his marriage to Mary Aust, but such visits were rare. He was not in a good mood. He climbed out of his boat, a scowl already on his face, and ordered the six black men manning the oars to wait. Steadying himself with his silver-headed cane, he began to trudge down the sandy road toward his old homestead.

When he arrived at the big house, his mood had not improved and his feet hurt. There, sprawled on the room's two sofas and enjoying a warm fire in the parlor of what was once his home, he found his two sons. Their eyes widened in surprise when he walked in, looking every bit his seventy-one years and obviously not happy to see them.

"Papa!" John said at once and stood up to greet him with a tentative smile.

His father did not return the smile. Instead, he began to rage at once. "I leave you two in charge and look at the mess you've made of things. You'll ruin the family name and the reputation of Jekyl Island."

Henry Jr., still seated, scoffed, "I think you've already taken care of that, Father. I don't think we can make it much worse."

"How've you been, Papa?" John asked quickly, trying to calm the anger that crossed his father's face at the remark.

The old man sat down on the sofa John had vacated, to rest from his walk. "Just fine," he said. "Until now."

As he sat, Henry Jr. rose, went to the sideboard, and, despite the early hour, poured them all a glass of whiskey.

"I think we might all need this," he said, handing his father a glass. "How's your new family? I hear Mary's pregnant again—for the fourth time, is it? Three daughters already. You don't waste any time, do you?" He made no effort to hide his sarcasm.

His father sat silent for a moment, sipping the amber liquid and staring sourly at his youngest son and namesake. "I didn't come here to discuss my daughters," he said. "I just want to understand what you two are up to and why. I left the island in your charge, thinking you had the sense to take care of it, and what do you do? Make a devil's bargain with that scoundrel Charlie Lamar—the same man who shot you in the eye hardly more than a year ago." He peered at his son. "I see you didn't lose it entirely."

"I made a trip to New York to let Dr. Carnochan remove the ball. He's from Savannah, as you may know, and I felt I could trust him more than those Yankee doctors. I didn't lose the eye itself, just the sight of it," Henry said with a bitter laugh

"Well, maybe that explains why you're so shortsighted now. What on earth could you have been thinking of?" his father retorted.

"Papa," John interrupted their angry exchange, his tone placating. "We've had a lot of financial problems of late, and we needed the money."

"Yeah," Henry said, "we needed to get more slaves to make up for all those you took with you or gave away in dowries." He swirled his whiskey around in the glass and took a large swig.

Before his father could respond, John said, "Henry didn't mean to get us into anything this serious."

"Well, you're up to your necks in it now," his father said. "I heard your names were bandied about at that hearing in Savannah.

And I can assure you, there's a lot of talk in Brunswick as well. It's going to go to trial, you know."

Henry nodded. "Lamar assures us that he'll take care of everything."

"We'll see about that," his father said dubiously. Then his tone changed a bit. "I wish I had some means of keeping you out of jail, but I don't. As you know, whatever influence I once had around here is gone, thanks to all those narrow-minded people up and down the coast. But keep in mind that it's still my island you're representing. I never broke a federal law and I do not want one broken in my name. Why can't you two be more like your brother Charles?"

"We didn't marry and fall into a money pot like him," Henry retorted.

"Well, it's your own faults. Both of you. John, you even served briefly in the legislature, like Charles and Joseph. You had a chance to make something of yourself. What on earth happened?"

"I just didn't fit in at Milledgeville, Papa. It wasn't for me."

"You didn't even complete one term. Shame on you. It would have been good for the family to have a member in state government."

"I got elected only out of sympathy for Joseph's family. And I tried, Papa. I really did, but I just couldn't do it. I didn't have the education Charles and Joseph had, and I wasn't a lawyer. People would never have elected me a second time. I hated every minute of it and wanted nothing more than to get back home to Jekyl." John had never regretted his decision.

His father pressed his lips together, but he said nothing.

"Why don't you just sign the plantation over to us, Father?"

Henry suggested. "Then you wouldn't have to worry about it. You know you promised Mother it would be ours one day. And you never even lived here with Mary Aust. Why not do it now?"

"Not until I'm ready," he said sourly, "or until I think you're ready."

The younger Henry quaffed another large swill of whiskey, "So why did you come here today? Just to tell us what shirkers we are?"

"I came to make sure you were all right," his father said in a gentler voice. "You *are* my sons."

"We're fine, Papa." It was John who answered. He wanted to tell his father that Sylvia was expecting another baby, but he thought better of it. He wasn't even sure his father knew about Sylvia and their children. If he did, he would surely disapprove. But who was he to stand in judgment of anyone's behavior?

Henry made no response.

In the brief silence that followed, the old man squared his shoulders. "Well, then. You obviously don't need me since you're doing so well on your own," he said in a sarcastic tone. Any gentleness or affection in his voice had vanished. "I might as well be on my way."

"You haven't been here even an hour yet," John pointed out.

"So? Is there some reason I need to stay longer?" he asked, his voice edgy.

"Not that I can think of," Henry answered. "I'll be happy to walk you back to the landing."

"I don't need your help," his father responded. "I may be old, but I'm not helpless. I'll leave you two here, hoisted on your own petard. But try to remember—you're DuBignons. What you do will reflect on the family."

"As you should well know, Father," Henry said, his voice sarcastic.

That ended the discussion, as Henry Sr. and Henry Jr. glared at one another.

John offered once more, and in a more sincere tone than his brother, to walk his father back to the landing. "I can find my own way," the old man said shortly, as he put on his hat, picked up his silver-headed cane, and left, letting the door slam behind him.

CHAPTER 8

Brunswick, Georgia, early December 1859

When Félicité heard about the indictment of her brothers-in-law, she was distressed, but glad it had not happened while she and her family were still on the island. She hated to see the reputation of both the family and the island tarnished in this way, but she supposed it reflected more on the two men than on the island itself. At least, she hoped so.

It was not long until Christmas, and she was taking tea at the Hazlehursts with her sisters-in-law Catherine and Eliza. Both were upset by reports of the event and the subsequent hearings and felt the need to talk about it. All three women had followed the newspaper stories about the case of three crewmembers from the *Wanderer*, Captain Corrie and two Portuguese sailors who had been on the voyage. They were the first of the so-called "conspirators" to come up for trial, but they had been found not guilty on November 23rd by a jury of their white peers. That was encouraging, but the trials of John and Henry were still to come. Worst of all, it was such a public affair—followed in newspapers from Georgia to New York because it involved the controversial slave trade. The landing and its coverage only intensified the growing tensions between the North and the South.

"Oh my, Another family scandal. It's just so upsetting," Eliza said.

"Robert was embarrassed to be called to Savannah to testify," Catherine added, as she picked up her cup for another sip. "He's hoping he won't have to go again when John and Henry come up for trial,"

"I can't imagine what possessed our brothers to get involved in this mess," Eliza said. "And I can't believe our family name is being dragged through the mud this way. Not again! What were they thinking? As if Papa's transgressions were not enough shame for us to suffer—"

Félicité said nothing, but she hoped that no one would bring up the indictment at the wedding she was planning for her daughter Josephine. In the years since their move from the island, her children, especially her two oldest daughters, had blossomed into young women and taken advantage of a world of activity they had been denied while living on Jekyl. Brunswick had embraced them with open arms. They had been delighted to be welcomed into the social life of the town and had thrived on the parties and dinners and especially on the company of young people their own age.

She let her mind drift back to that most life-changing invitation, which had come well before the *Wanderer* incident. It was to a party after Easter a few years earlier at the home of a neighbor, Charles Schlatter, chief engineer and president of the Brunswick and

Florida Railroad, and his wife Frances. They had two children, an eight-year-old daughter named Frances for her mother, but known to everyone as Fannie. She was a pretty little thing about the same age as Félicité's youngest son, John Eugene. Both their mothers hoped that someday they might come to fancy one another, though that would have to wait, for they were not yet of an age even to come to the party. The Schlatters also had a son, Charles Jr., who, at eighteen, was clearly smitten with Josephine.

Félicité and her two oldest daughters had all been invited to attend, and they had looked forward to the party for weeks. Both girls were wearing becoming new dresses in the latest style, skirts with three-tiered flounces, a high neck, and pagoda sleeves for the occasion. Only the details and the fabrics differed. The spring twilight was lovely, and they enjoyed the short walk across Gloucester Street and up Union. All sorts of horse-drawn carriages, from broughams to buckboards, lined the street in front of the Schlatter house, the coachmen gathered outside to wait for their masters.

As Félicité and her daughters entered the large foyer, they surveyed the many guests who had already arrived. One of those, standing near the parlor fireplace, chatting with Charles Schlatter, was an attractive young man that none of the DuBignons recognized. Josephine spotted him right away—a handsome and rather dapper young man, with a tidy beard and light brown hair, neatly trimmed. As soon as Schlatter noticed their arrival, he rushed over to greet them, bringing the young gentleman with him.

"Madam DuBignon, I'm so delighted that you and your charming daughters were able to attend. We are always delighted to have you. Your presence is an honor."

Félicité smiled. "You are too kind, Charles. We are always pleased to see you, as you well know, and we have looked forward to your party with great anticipation." Both girls nodded in agreement.

He turned toward the young man. "Please allow me to present to you Mr. Newton Finney," he said. "He's a fellow northerner and a topographer with the U.S. Coast Survey team. They've been here since mid-February to survey the Turtle River and Brunswick Harbor. Perhaps you've noticed his ship, the *Meredith*, in these waters."

Finney bowed slightly in acknowledgment.

"Yes, I've seen it in the harbor," Félicité said with a smile to the young man. "And these," she added, "are my two oldest daughters, Mary Amelia and Josephine,"

"How do you do." Finney nodded courteously toward each of them, but his gaze lingered on the one called Josephine, transfixed by her deep, brown eyes and lovely oval face so perfectly framed by her thick dark hair.

"And where up north do you come from, Mr. Finney? Are you, like Mr. Schlatter, from Pennsylvania?" Félicité asked in a pleasant voice. He seemed an affable young man.

"I was born in New York, but my family now lives in Fond du Lac, Wisconsin," he replied with another quick glance at Josephine, who was smiling up at him in a most intriguing manner.

"You *are* a Yankee then," Félicité said, her tone teasing.

He grinned. "By birth only, Ma'am. I think I may be a southerner at heart."

"Indeed! And why is that?" she asked.

"Well, I've been working on the survey team since 1856, and

this is surely the most pleasant place I've encountered so far."

"Where all have you been?" she asked.

"I've worked on the coasts of New York, Virginia, Florida, and Georgia, but I like these Southern waters and warmer climes best of all. Living through a Wisconsin winter is something of an ordeal. The snow can be beautiful, but it's too cold to enjoy it."

"And you find our climate more tolerable?"

"Absolutely! Here, even in mid-winter, it's sometimes warm enough to be outside without a jacket. The vegetation is remarkable and—" He hesitated for a moment, then turned his eyes back to Josephine, "the ladies here are the most beautiful I've ever seen."

Josephine, who was hanging onto his every word, looked down coyly and smiled behind her lace fan, which she found especially useful at times like this.

"Mr. Finney was a West Point cadet before joining the survey team," Mr. Schlatter pointed out.

"Well, only for a short while, I'm afraid. I wasn't one of their stellar students, I must confess I frolicked a bit too much," Finney said, with an engaging grin.

Schlatter chuckled. "That's what youth is for. But one has to be excellent even to be admitted," he said. "Mr. Finney and my son Charles have become good friends, and I must say the entire family is quite taken with him."

"I can see why," Félicité said, returning the young man's grin with a warm smile.

"Now, my dear lady, let's leave the young people to get acquainted," said Mr. Schlatter. "I know my wife is eager to talk with you and will be cross if I don't deliver you to her at once." He gave her his arm to lead her across the room to where Frances

Schlatter was waiting.

Only a moment later, Charles Jr. joined the group of young people, making his adoration of Josephine all too obvious.

"May I get you a glass of punch, Josephine?" he asked.

"That would be lovely, Charlie. Could you bring one for my sister as well?"

"I'll go with you, Charlie," Mary Amelia said as she gave a merry nod to a friend across the room. "And then I'm going over to greet Georgia King, who just arrived. It was lovely to meet you, Mr. Finney."

"Likewise," he said with a nod.

Once young Charles and Mary Amelia had both headed toward the silver punch bowl, Newton Finney looked again at Josephine. "It would seem that you have an ardent admirer," he said.

"Oh, Charlie and I have known one another since we were children. We lost touch for a while after my father died and we moved back to Jekyl Island for a few years, but he's a good friend."

"You lived on that wonderful island? How delightful!"

"Yes, we all love it dearly, even though it was rather inconvenient for making friends on the mainland."

"Where do you live now?"

"On Union Street. Just on the other side of Gloucester."

"That's easy walking distance from the dock. Would it be too forward of me to ask permission to call on you sometime while I'm still here?" he asked.

"I'd be delighted," she said. "How long will you be in the area?"

"We're leaving very soon, I'm afraid. Our work here is finished for the season and we're only winding up a few details. But we'll be back for another phase next year. I'm just sorry we didn't meet sooner. It's yet another reason for me to thank Mr. Schlatter—for introducing us."

Josephine could feel herself blushing. "How did you make Mr. Schlatter's acquaintance?" she asked.

"One of my duties was to survey the city, including the railroad, which is how we met. He's been very helpful to me in my work."

Suddenly, Charlie was at her side again, holding out a cup of punch. She accepted it gracefully, wishing he would go away.

She and Newton had little time that evening to talk privately, but, before the party was over, they managed to find one more opportunity.

"May I call on you Sunday afternoon?" he asked. "It's my one day free."

"That would be delightful," she said.

"I'm very grateful. It's probably my only chance to call—at least for this year. We'll be heading to Florida by the beginning of next week."

"What a shame," she said.

"But we'll be returning next year about the same time, when I hope to continue our acquaintance."

"I'll look forward to it," she replied, already anticipating his Sunday call.

Josephine waited anxiously for Sunday to come. True to his word, Finney knocked on the door at precisely two o'clock in the afternoon, with a handful of sweet-smelling lilacs and an eager smile on his face. They had only that one glorious afternoon together. It was far too short, though Josephine's mother invited him to stay for supper, and he accepted without hesitation. By the time the evening came to an end, Josephine knew he was the man she wanted to marry.

December 2, 1859

The doorbell's raucous but familiar ring interrupted the quiet atmosphere of the DuBignon household on Union Street. As usual, the first person at the door was John Eugene, who, at almost ten now, was curious about everything—especially who had come to call.

"Mr. Finney's here!" he yelled, as soon as he spotted the visitor. It had been almost two years since Finney had first rung the doorbell. He had repeated it many times since.

"Johnny, old boy. I suspected it would be you who answered the door."

"Hi, Newt. Are those for me?" he asked with a smirk, pointing to the bouquet of camellias the young man was holding.

"Well... I tell you what. I'll give them to you if you promise to take them to your sister and tell her that she has a caller." It hadn't taken long for Newton Finney to become a fixture at the DuBignon house on Union Street whenever his ship was in port. And tonight was for him an especially important visit.

Johnny took the bouquet and raced up the stairs, as Newton watched. He'd always been amazed that camellias bloomed in the winter here. They didn't bloom at all in New York, so he thought it something of a beautiful miracle. At that point Mrs. DuBignon appeared.

"Hello, Newt. Welcome back. How long will you be in Brunswick this time?" she asked.

"Another week or so, I hope. I'm on my way back to the west coast of Florida for the coming season. We start in mid-December this year." He paused for a moment. "I hope you don't mind seeing me so often." Almost two years had passed since he and Josephine had met, but whenever his work brought him to the area, he called on her every single day.

"Not at all. You know you're always welcome, and I'm sure Josephine will be delighted as always to see you. She's upstairs getting ready for supper. She should be down in a moment. I'll have Beulah set another place for you."

"I don't want to be any trouble, Ma'am," he said quickly.

"It's no trouble at all. You know that Beulah always prepares enough food for your entire crew. I wouldn't be surprised if she's already put out another place setting the moment Johnny so delicately announced your arrival."

"I'd like to talk with you before supper, if—" Before he could finish his sentence, Josephine, bouquet in hand, came rushing down the stairs.

"Newton, thank you for the lovely camellias," she said, as he bent to kiss her hand.

"So continental," she said with a soft laugh. "I hate it that you're going to be here for such a short time."

He had already called every day since his ship came into port, but time was slipping by too fast for both of them.

"At least we have another week," he said. "I don't have to be in Florida until the middle of the month."

"That's not very long" she said.

"The season won't be long either. I'll be back by the end of March."

"How long will you stay then?"

"Well," he said, "that depends on you." They smiled at each other. Words were needless.

"Supper's ready," Beulah announced.

"Let's all go into the dining room," Félicité said. "There'll be plenty of time for you two to talk afterwards."

After supper, Josephine excused herself to freshen up, and Newton seized the moment to speak to her mother. "I wanted to talk to both you and Josephine. I know you haven't known me as long as you have some of her local suitors, but you must know by now that I love Josephine very much. I want to make her my wife, if she'll have me, and if you give your permission, of course." Newton's voice was earnest. "I don't think I can bear another year of separation."

"It's good of you to ask my permission, Newton, but the decision is entirely hers. You know by now that we're all very fond of you, and you've been nothing but a gentleman ever since we've known you. But that's only been a year and…what?…eight months? You haven't been together very much at all during that period. And what about your job with the Coast Survey?"

"I need to finish out this season. Then I was hoping that Mr. Schlatter might be able to help me find a position here in Brunswick. I know the time has been short, but during that time Josephine and I have come to know one another very well, better than most couples, I expect. We haven't been together many times, I know, but we've written to each other every week, almost every day lately. There's no better way, I think, to say what's in your heart, and I think hers is in accord with mine. Every time I see her, it's like coming home. Maybe it's not fair to ask her to commit herself until I have a new employment, but I do have a good deal of money saved up. There's not much to spend it on during these surveys, and I've been saving for almost four years now."

"You have my blessing, Newton, but it's her decision."

As soon as Josephine reappeared, her mother suddenly remembered some needlework that required her attention.

"Would you like to take a walk in the garden?" Newton asked. Josephine nodded. The evening was not as cool as December often was, but she would need a wrap. Taking her shawl from the coat rack that flanked the entrance and draping it around her shoulders, he touched her elbow to steer her toward the front porch and into the little garden at the side of the house. There he took her hand and drew her toward him to gaze into her eyes.

"Josephine," he said. "You know I never want to leave Brunswick as long as you're here. You know I love you, and I've already spoken to your mother. Now, I'm asking you. Will you be my wife?"

She searched his face. "And what about the survey?" she asked, her voice shaky.

"Well, I'll have to finish out this season, and I'm already committed for the next season—just for the southern part. That'll only be from December to March or early April of 1861. Then I'll find some sort of position here in Brunswick, I'll plan to stay here after that. But I don't want to wait another year to get married. I'd like us to marry this spring if you're willing. I can't bear to leave here again without knowing you'll be mine forever."

"I know you love your work. Are you sure you're willing to give it up?"

"You know I'm committed for one more year, but, if you can endure that, I'll give it up forever if you agree to be my wife."

"You know I will." She pulled his hand to her lips. "Yes, Newton, I'll marry you in the spring."

His smile lit up the garden. "As soon as possible. What about April 1st? It's a beautiful month here. My work in Florida for the season will be ended by then, and that's the earliest I can be sure to be back," he said.

"That's April fool's day. It would be bad luck. I'd prefer another date, but April would be wonderful."

"The sooner the better," he added, still smiling.

CHAPTER 9

Brunswick, Georgia, 1860

The earliest and most convenient time for the priest, Father O'Neill, to come from Savannah to perform the marriage ceremony after Newton's return from Florida was April 17th—a Tuesday. Not the best time for a wedding, perhaps, but since there was still no Catholic church in Brunswick, the diocese in Savannah did the best it could to oblige Catholics along the Georgia coast. Josephine and Newton didn't care, as long as they were married as soon as possible.

The only matter that marred the date was the upcoming trials of Josephine's uncles. Both she and her mother had fervently hoped they would all be over by mid-April and the memory of the *Wanderer* landing and the family's embarrassment, which had been hanging over their heads for almost a year and a half now, would be behind them. But when the scheduled trials were finally announced, they learned that they would not even begin until May. By then it was too late to reschedule the wedding, and Josephine and Newton were unwilling to put if off any longer.

Until shortly before their marriage, Newton was still at work on the Florida coast. He'd picked up where he had left off the previous season to survey the coastal area between Cedar Key and Bayport, as well as rivers in the area that emptied into the Gulf—the Waccasassa, the Withlacoochee, the Crystal, and the Homosassa. He had written Josephine to tell her that the survey team had dropped him off on December 1, with his sub-assistant, a small boat, camp fixtures, and surveying equipment. They had made camp about a mile north of the mouth of the Withlacoochee to begin their plane-table survey, which would include a study of both the coast and the river channels as much as three miles inland. What he didn't tell her about was the potential dangers in the rivers and marshy areas—especially alligators and occasional panthers or bears that roamed the region. Cane, corn, and cotton grew along some of the riverbanks, though most of the area from the Cedar Keys to the Anclote Keys and for miles into the interior was primarily wilderness. They encountered only small and occasional communities at the heads of rivers. The only one directly on the Gulf was a small cotton-shipping town called Bayport, which sported a small hotel and was the most convenient place for buying supplies.

While Newton and his assistant explored the wilds of the Gulf coast, Josephine and her mother spent their time in Brunswick and Savannah making plans for the marriage ceremony and selecting the fabric and pattern for Josephine's wedding dress. It was to be a pale blue silk with short sleeves, a tight tea bodice that came to a point at the waist, and a bounteous skirt that fit over a cage crinoline.

Josephine chose a bouquet of mixed spring flowers—lilacs, tulips, and lilies-of-the-valley, and, of course, if they could be found, late-blooming camellias the same color as the ones Newton had brought the day he proposed.

Their time of separation seemed long to both Josephine and Newton. But at the beginning of April, Newton finally wrapped up his Florida work, stored all his camp equipment near the mouth of the Homosassa River, and eagerly headed for Brunswick to be married.

The morning of the wedding dawned bright and florescent over the city of Brunswick. The landscape was ablaze with fiery azaleas and sunlit daffodils and the gardens fragrant with gardenias, jasmine, and promise. Nature itself seemed to be celebrating the upcoming event. By afternoon, as Félicité wove the last tendril of ivy among the array of spring flowers spread out on her parlor mantle and once more adjusted the palmetto fronds that stood in brass urns on either side of the wide doors that led into the dining room, she could only pray that the upcoming trials of her brothers-in-law would not arise as a topic of conversation to distract the guests from her daughter's happiness. Although Félicité was no longer close to her late husband's brothers, whatever they did reflected on her and her children. *Please, God*, she thought, *don't let anybody mention the trials*. The name DuBignon was distinctive in the area, and there was no way family members could not feel tainted by the actions of its other members, for they were all inevitably interconnected in people's minds. The whole unpleasant business nagged at her. She had so hoped it would all be behind them before then, but, like everyone else, she had been forced to accept the fact that it was not to be and that the incident would still be on people's mind.

By seven o'clock, the DuBignon parlor teemed with jovial guests—among them the Schlatters and the Darts, along with Félicité's married sisters-in-law and their husbands, with Eliza accompanying the Hazlehursts. While none of Newton's family had made the long trip from Wisconsin, the only missing relatives of the bride were the Charles DuBignons from Milledgeville, who had sent, with their regrets, congratulations and a silver pitcher, and John and Henry, who rarely left the island these days. Josephine was radiant in her blue silk gown, and nothing could wipe the broad grin from Newton's face.

The ceremony itself was relatively brief. Félicité smiled with contentment, wishing her husband could be here, as she watched their daughter's joyful expression throughout the sacrament. After the bridal couple exchanged their vows and received the nuptial blessings, they sealed their marriage with a rather impassioned kiss, which brought good-natured applause from the mostly non-Catholic guests.

When it was over, a florid-faced Father O'Neill cheerfully joined the bride and groom with their family and friends to sip champagne punch from silver cups and partake of the informal wedding supper that Beulah had prepared. Since neither Josephine nor Newton wanted a big to-do, Félicité had tried to keep it as simple as possible. Nevertheless, the dining room table was resplendent with food, loaded with large platters of ham biscuits, deviled eggs, crab puffs, and oyster pies. Bowls of fresh fruit and a three-tiered serving dish with an abundance of pastries added to the casual but copious wedding supper. The guests chatted cheerfully and celebrated the bride and groom with repeated toasts.

To Félicité's relief, not a single person mentioned the upcoming trials of John and Henry.

CHAPTER 10

Jekyl Island, Georgia, May 1860

The legal proceedings concerning the DuBignon brothers' involvement in the *Wanderer* episode were to begin in mid-May. To the brothers' disappointment, they were not to be tried together.

"It only drags it out all the longer," Henry complained, when he learned that it was Nelson Trowbridge, not himself, who was to share the first trial with John.

"It doesn't make a lot of sense, does it," John said, "but, given what happened in the earlier cases, I don't think either of us has a lot to worry about. Our roles were minor compared to those."

"I'd agree with you, but juries can be quirky, and our jurors will not be the same ones," Henry said.

Thus, John felt no sense of assurance as he sat apprehensively on the hard chair at the defense table in the Savannah courtroom and studied the grumpy faces of the stern-looking men filing into the jury box.

As the trial proceeded, it seemed to him as though the lawyers were discussing someone else, someone who bore little resemblance to him. The prosecutor tried to make him sound like a heartless slave master cruelly imprisoning helpless black prisoners for his own pleasure and profit, while the defense attorney depicted another man altogether, a benevolent fellow who merely provided shelter and safe harbor for the weary captives so long at sea, as any good southerner would have done. John felt as though he were neither of the people they described, but someone more complex, not all bad or all good, but a man who was just human and not so categorically definable. Fortunately, the trial was mercifully short.

The jury was excused to deliberate on the final afternoon of the trial, May 17. John did not have long to wait, for they returned in less than an hour with a clear verdict. Trowbridge's case, however, was not so simple and ended in a mistrial. He would have to face a new tribunal.

John had never been so happy as he was to return to the familiar and welcoming Jekyl Island and read aloud to Sylvia and the children his own judgment as it was reported in the *Daily Morning News*.

> *The case of the United States vs. JOHN DUBIGNON, charged with aiding and abetting in the landing of African negroes on Jekyl Island, was closed yesterday, and submitted to the jury about 2 o'clock, P.M. After a very few minutes absence they returned a verdict of "Not guilty."*

"Praise the Lord," Sylvia said, and both their sons nodded approval.

"Thank God it's over," John added. He was free and clear.

At long last the nightmare of the past year and a half had ended, at least for him. That night, with unspoken joy and without worry, he lay in Sylvia's familiar, comforting arms and savored the warmth of her body and the gentle quiet that pervaded the island.

Henry's trial was scheduled to take place almost two weeks later. Given John's rapid verdict, he felt assured that he too would be acquitted. However, as it happened, the trial did not even take place. In light of the previous judgments, the prosecutor, Hamilton Couper, decided it was pointless to continue and moved for a *nolle prosequi*, permission not to prosecute the remaining suspects, rather than waste his time trying cases he knew he would not win. Thus, the charges against all those who remained accused and were waiting for new trials, Brown, Trowbridge, Farnum, and Corrie, were also eventually dropped.

Charlie Lamar had been right after all, Henry thought. Apparently, a man of means on the Georgia coast could do whatever he wanted without penalty.

When the news of the acquittals arrived, Newton and Josephine were already back from their honeymoon trip to Charleston, where they had taken leisurely carriage rides around the city and strolled along the Battery toward White Point Garden. From there they could look out over the waters where the Ashley and Cooper rivers flowed together in the channel that led from the harbor to the Atlantic Ocean. They could see on the horizon the fortified walls of Fort Sumter, said to be ten feet thick. The federal fort, built over the last decade to protect the city was not yet fully armed and ready for coastal defense. Newton's gaze was fixed on the fort, but Josephine was more captivated by the aroma of gardenias wafting in the air, the many colors of azaleas blooming in the garden, and the gracious houses lining the Battery.

"It's such a romantic city," she said, snuggling closer to Newton, who put his arm around her, as they stood there gazing toward the open sea. "So beautiful."

"I think any city would seem romantic to us just now," Newton said with a soft laugh. "But it's historic too," he added, "older than Savannah."

"I think I would like to live in a larger city someday," she said. "Nothing ever happens in Brunswick, and I have seen so little of the world, unlike you. You've been everywhere."

He laughed. "Not everywhere. Only along the Atlantic coast and the Gulf. But you're right. I've seen more of the country than you have, and I want to show it all to you. Someday I'll take you North so you can see what life is like there."

"Is it so different?" she asked.

"Yes, it is. And growing more and more different from the South every day. Very few northern states still have any slaves at all. It doesn't depend on crops like cotton and rice."

She frowned slightly. "I thought you said you liked the South."

"Oh, I do," he said. "It's where I found you, so it's my favorite place in the whole world. But someday I'd like to show you what the rest of the country is like."

"Tell me how it's different."

"Life in New York is a lot busier. There are many stores and factories and new immigrants pouring into the city from places like

Germany and Ireland, all competing for work, but even so, to them America is the land of promise compared to where they came from. There are several theaters in the city and all sorts of people."

"It's exciting, I suppose, but it sounds awfully crowded."

"There's still open land. There's even a huge park recently established in the center of the city where nothing can be built."

"That sounds nice. But you're right. It also sounds busy."

"It is, compared to here," Newton said. "I rather like the slower pace of life in the South, but we could at least visit sometime and let you see for yourself."

"I'd like that," she said. "But now, I just want to enjoy Charleston and being Mrs. Newton Finney. Is that all right with you?"

"It's wonderful," he said. "Just perfect."

"Unfortunately," Josephine said sadly once they had returned to Brunswick, where they were occupying a room at her mother's house, "honeymoons don't last forever." She knew it would not be long before Newton would leave again to resume, for the last time, his commitment to the Coast Survey.

"Well, we'll just have to have another one as soon as I'm back for good," Newton said. "And then we'll find our own place to live."

He was staying in Brunswick as long as he possibly could, and it was there, on his mother-in-law's dining room table that he laid out all his sketches and notes to write his season's report. He delayed his departure as long as he could, doing as much preliminary work in Brunswick as possible, but by July he had no choice but to return north to prepare his final charts and get ready for the upcoming survey season back in Florida.

Josephine was in tears as he packed to leave.

"I'll only be gone a few months, before I'm back south again for the 1861 season." He had spent the month of June in Brunswick exploring opportunities to make a living there after he left the Coast Survey. He had talked with Charles Schlatter and various others about needs in the Brunswick area. They had all agreed that the one thing lacking in Brunswick was a good shipping company of some sort. Now, farmers and plantation owners had to take their products to Darien or Savannah for transport. Was that necessary, they wondered? Newton remembered the modest Florida shipping operation he had seen the previous year in the small town of Bayport. If a shipping line could make a go of it there, surely it could work in Brunswick, which had a better port and new possibilities of shipping by rail as well. It could save area plantation owners time, money, and labor. But it would also take time and money to set up such an endeavor. He had some money saved, but was it enough? It would be something to think about during his absence.

Josephine brushed her tears away as she watched him pack up his notes. She folded the jackets and shirts he had laid out, wanting to do whatever she could to help.

"I'm going to miss you so," she said with longing. If only she could go with him.

"I'll come back as soon as I can and I'll stop in Brunswick for as long as possible. It won't be long—really, only four months or so."

"It will seem like forever," Josephine said, as she smoothed the front of the shirt he had just placed in his valise. Tears stood in her eyes.

"I would take you with me if I could," he said, turning from his packing to take her in his arms. "Just be patient a little longer. It will only be a few months before I'm back in the South for good. Just wait and see. Then we'll have a long and happy life, just like in the fairy tales."

But life is never like the fairy tales, and things did not go as they planned. Josephine had never paid much attention to politics, but suddenly she had no choice but to take notice. The whole world was about to change, and she couldn't avoid the consequences.

On the morning of November 7, Josephine's brother Harry returned from an early walk bearing the news: "They elected Lincoln," he announced at breakfast. "I fear this will mean war."

"How awful," Félicité said. "Brunswick must be in an uproar." She knew that the so-called fire-eaters in the area had bitterly opposed Lincoln's election and favored their own nominee, a pro-slavery Southern Democrat named John C. Breckenridge. Lincoln, they thought, was the worst possible choice. He had tried to reassure southerners that he didn't intend to abolish slavery in the South, but they didn't trust him. Plantation owners up and down the coast were livid at his election. Tensions, already mounting between the North and the South, were bound to grow even worse.

"Excuse me, please." Josephine, her face pale at the news, rose from the breakfast table.

"What is it, my dear? Are you ill?"

"Mama, I just can't eat thinking that a war might break out before Newton gets back. You know that they're already clamoring for it down here. What if he gets stuck in the North? He'll have to choose sides, and if he's caught there—" She couldn't go on. Her face crumpled with worry.

"It's too soon to worry, Josephine. Try to look on the bright side. Perhaps nothing will happen before he's back. Perhaps nothing will happen at all."

"But she's right, Mama," Harry pointed out. "It will happen sooner or later. And he'll have to make a hard decision. His family and friends are up north, But his wife and *her* family members are all loyal southerners. I'd hate to be in his shoes." Harry himself was excited to think of the possibility of an upcoming war. He was seventeen now and eager to be a soldier. But he could understand his brother-in-law's dilemma. What a terrible choice he would be forced to confront.

"What do you think he'll do?" Mary Amelia asked her sister.

"I...I don't know," Josephine said before she turned to run up the hall stairs. That night and every night that followed, she knelt beside her bed and prayed that there would be no war.

"Newton's back," John Eugene shouted one afternoon in mid-November after he had raced to the front door at the first sound of the doorbell. He was twelve now, but no less eager to be there first. Newton tousled his hair and laughed.

"Hey, Johnny, how're you doing? You're a sight for sore eyes."

At the sound of his voice, Josephine jumped up from her chair, tossed aside the book she had been reading and ran down the stairs to fling herself into his arms. "Thank God you're home," she said, planting a barrage of kisses on his mouth, his cheeks, his eyelids, whatever she could reach.

"Ah, it's good to hold you again," he said with a long sigh of contentment.

"How long can you stay?" she asked.

"A few weeks at most. I'm due in Florida the first of December."

"Must you go?" she asked, clinging to him. "Things are so dangerous now."

"I'm afraid I must. But remember, after that it's all over, and I'll be back for good. You'll probably get tired of having me around."

"Never," she said.

By now her mother and all the other children had gathered in the foyer to greet Newton. Everyone was relieved to see him again. Even Beulah came out of the kitchen to give him a great big smile and a "Welcome home, Mr. Finney."

It was a rare time of intimacy, and Josephine was delirious with happiness. He was back in the South. He was her husband. He was hers forever. Whatever time the two weren't together, which was seldom, Newton would find himself in the parlor talking with her brother Harry, who was impatient for the war to start.

"Don't be so eager," Newton warned. "A war would be a terrible thing and it would tear our country apart."

"The South will win in a matter of weeks, I'm sure," Harry argued. "I know you're a Yankee, Newt, but surely you can see that. You'll have to choose sides, so I hope you'll go with the winning side."

"I hope I won't have to choose, Harry. I pray there will be no war."

"If there is, *when* there is, I'll sign up right away."

"Not so fast, young man. It's your life you're talking about here. I don't think your mother would approve."

"When I'm eighteen I can decide for myself."

"Let's hope it doesn't come to that," Newton said, ending the conversation.

On the first of December, Newton left again on a ship called the *Joseph Henry*, bound for the west coast of Florida to continue charting the coastline. But Josephine worried as national tensions went from bad to worse. Before Christmas, South Carolina seceded from the Union, and by the end of January, five more southern states had seceded, One of them was Florida.

Delegates of the seceded Southern states, she'd heard, were planning to meet in Alabama the following month to form the new Confederacy, and she'd heard that they planned elect Jefferson Davis as president. She wrote Newton of her concern.

He replied that "we are trying to ignore the national tensions and continue to work. So far no problems. We are basking in the winter weather in Florida and glad to be avoiding the snow and ice in New York. Please don't worry. There's no war going on, and I'll be home and back in your arms by the end of March. I can hardly wait."

The whole family was startled on February 18 to hear the doorbell ring and John Eugene's by-now familiar announcement, "Newton's back!"

Josephine rushed down the stairs, threw herself into his arms, and showered him with kisses. "You're home early! How did you manage that?" she asked, her voice excited.

"We had no choice. Things got a bit dangerous in Florida. In fact, I feel lucky to get home alive."

"What do you mean? What happened?" The entire family had gathered around by now to hear Newton's story.

"We'd been informed that the area was no longer safe after Florida seceded, so they recalled us early. My new assistant, a man named Nicholson, and I had already packed up all our survey equipment and delivered it back to the *John Henry*. All we had to do was come back, break camp, and get back to the ship. But then—"

Everyone waited breathlessly.

"As we were walking back to camp, I saw a steamboat approaching with about twenty men on board, and they didn't look friendly. They were all carrying guns, which they were pointing at Nicholson and me."

Josephine gasped and put her hand to her throat. "Oh, good heavens!"

John Eugene's eyes were sparkling with excitement at the story. "What happened then?" he asked eagerly.

"Well, as you might expect, since we were unarmed, there was nothing to do but raise our hands in surrender. We had a rifle back at camp in case of snakes and such, but without it, we were helpless. Then, the men got out of the boat and came toward us, guns still pointed. We didn't know what they intended. Finally one of them stepped forward and announced that they were the Bayport Safety Committee and he was its chairman. He was polite, but he informed us in no uncertain terms that our presence in Florida was unwelcome."

Newton paused to catch his breath. He could see that the entire family was drinking in his story. And he was enjoying telling it.

"I pointed out that no war had been declared that I knew of, and we weren't invading his territory, just doing a coastal survey. But he and his men didn't see it that way. To them we were hostile federal agents, treading in Confederate waters. 'What do you want us to do?' I asked."

"What did he say?" The story couldn't unwind fast enough for John Eugene.

"He said they'd come to confiscate all our equipment and make sure that we left Florida at once." At this point, Newton smiled. "He was so formal in all his proclamations. I would have found it amusing, except for the rifles still pointed in our direction. I decided it might not be wise to laugh. Instead, I kept my hands in the air and told him that our survey equipment was no longer here—only our tent and camping gear, and that we were already planning to leave. He looked disgruntled and turned to say to the man just behind him, 'I told you we should have come yesterday.' Thank God they didn't. I would have hated to see all that expensive equipment fall into their hands—our tide gauge, Gunter's chain, surveyor's compass, and all the rest. Those are expensive items, and I didn't want to be held responsible."

"How did the fellow react?" This time it was Harry who asked.

"They wanted the camping gear at least and made us pack it all up. Then, as they loaded it on their boat, I had the audacity to ask the chairman to sign a receipt for the camping equipment so I wouldn't be blamed for its loss."

Everyone laughed. "What was his reaction?" Harry asked.

"Well, he looked a bit startled at the request, but, being a gentleman, he signed it. That's how I learned his name—C. T. Jenkins. I thanked him and asked if we were free to go. He said 'Get in your boat, get out of here, and don't come back.' We didn't waste any time in hurrying to our boat and heading back to the *John Henry*. And here I am, safe and sound!"

"Thank God," said Josephine.

But they all suspected that the worst was yet to come.

CHAPTER 11

Brunswick, Georgia, April 12, 1861

The early months of 1861 remained tense and uncertain, as Southern states continued to secede from the Union to join the newly organized Confederacy. Newton had been back in Brunswick only six weeks when, in the early evening of April 12, the quiet of the town was disrupted by gunshots and whoops of joy coming from Gloucester Street.

Newton and Harry rushed out to see what was going on. The streets were filled with men, mostly young men, rushing about in celebration and sharing the news.

"What's happened?" Harry asked a tousle-haired young men wearing a broad grin and brandishing a pistol.

"The war has started!" he shouted. "We've attacked Fort Sumter." It was the last military stronghold in Charleston still in federal control. Men were slapping each other on the back and waving guns about, some of them shouting things like "We'll drive those Yankees into the dust," and "War at last," and "Praise the Lord."

Harry himself greeted the news with a shout of "Hallelujah" and joined the other men and boys celebrating in the streets.

Newton returned quietly to the house on Union Street in a somber mood. At twenty-five, and having had some training at West Point, he knew he was prime material to become an officer in the upcoming war. He had struggled with his situation but finally decided that, if war came, he would join the Confederate army. He suspected, though he did not know for sure, that his brother and his brother-in-law in Wisconsin would both fight for the Union. But he now had a Georgia family that vigorously supported the Southern cause. He knew that whatever he decided, he would feel that he was betraying someone he loved. He feared that his marriage would be over if he fought for the North. That would be the worst possible outcome, he thought. Thus, he had made a decision and taken action even before the war began, writing to the new Confederate States President, Jefferson Davis, in mid-March to request a commission should it be necessary.

"What is it, Newton? What's going on?" Josephine could see his gloomy expression, in stark contrast to the shouts of joy in the streets.

'The war has started," he said in a low voice.

"Oh no. So soon." She put her arms around him, knowing the conflict he felt inside, for they had talked about it. He had dreaded this war, even more than she did. But he would do his part.

Fort Sumter fell after a thirty-four-hour barrage. It was the first Confederate victory. The Southern states were jubilant and eager for the military glory they were certain the war would bring them.

Harry began at once begging his mother to let him join the army. He would be eighteen in June and he knew that then she could not refuse. But he was eager to enlist now. He wanted her blessing, but she still considered him a boy.

"You're too young, son. Don't enlist until you have to," his mother said, realizing his impatience but hoping, as some believed, that the war would be over before he reached his eighteenth birthday. He could only swallow his disappointment and begin to count the days until his birthday June 13, although he knew his mother would do everything she could to dissuade him even then. Shortly after his birthday, rumors circulated that a new Confederate unit was to be formed in Brunswick, and he had decided to wait until it was ready for volunteers.

The fighting only grew more intense. In late July, news reached Brunswick of the Southern victory at a place in Virginia they had never heard of. It was called Manassas Junction and stood along a little river named Bull Run. The Confederate Army had been outnumbered at the beginning of the battle 20,000 to 35,000 men. Still they persisted, and when reinforcements arrived and brought their numbers up to more or less equal those of the Yankees, they drove the Northern troops back toward Washington D.C. The victory heightened Southern enthusiasm and confidence that they could easily win this war. Names like P.G.T. Beauregard and Stonewall Jackson became familiar in every Brunswick household, and the outcome of that battle only spurred the eagerness of young men like Harry DuBignon who wanted to participate in the glory, and he was more eager than ever to join the military.

While the battle at Manassas inspired young men with dreams

of glory, it only made Félicité less eager to see her son go to war. The dangers were already apparent within the family. During a recent visit with her sister-in-law Eliza, a letter had arrived. Eliza opened it at once so they could share whatever news it contained.

"Oh, no!" she said as she read. "Archie has been seriously wounded." Their brother-in-law Archibald Burke, a captain who'd been assigned the command of company F of the Seventh Regiment of the Georgia Volunteer Infantry, had fought in the battle of Manassas. He'd been the first in their family to join the army.

"How bad is it?" Félicité asked, dreading the thought of such news.

"It's bad apparently. Eugenia says she fears for his life. She's going to Richmond to look after him."

"But what about the babies?" Eugenia had given birth to twins only a few weeks earlier.

"She's taking them with her, she says." Eliza wrinkled her brow.

"How awful and how difficult," Félicité said. "They're so young. And it's a dangerous trip. Is anyone going with her?"

"Only Julia."

"Julia?"

"You remember her. She was the girl who was part of Eugenia's dowry. She'll help look after the babies."

It was weeks before they heard from Eugenia again. She had remained in Richmond until, with her help and Julia's, her husband was able to travel. "He seems to be slowly recovering," Eugenia wrote, "but I'm afraid I have some other bad news. We're heartbroken that one of our twins died during the trip. I thank God that, at least, Archie and I are able to grieve together."

It didn't seem like much consolation to Félicité. The idea of losing one of her children chilled her to the bone. It made her more determined than ever to try to dissuade Harry from ever joining the army.

Now, the family had learned, Eugenia herself was not well.

"You see all the dreadful things that can happen?" she told Harry. But none of this bad news deterred his determination to join the army in the least. On the contrary, it only made him more resolute. He had even started to grow a beard to make himself look older.

"There's a new outfit that's being organized here in August, Mama," he told her for probably the fifth time. "I can wait until then. It's called the Glynn Guards and it will make up Company A of the 26th Infantry Volunteer Regiment of Georgia. I plan to enlist like most other young men in town. The whole Confederate coast is under Union blockade now. Yankee troops are stationed on ships right off our coast. Who knows when they might attack? I want to help defend our town."

"Oh, son, must you? Must you risk your life like that?" she persisted. "You're so young." She could imagine the horror of her son lying on some battlefield, wounded or even dead. But she already knew that her pleas were useless.

"Mother, I would be ashamed not to join up when so many others, like Uncle Archie, are making such sacrifices for the cause. I couldn't look my friends in the eye. I'll be careful, I promise. Besides, there's no fighting around here yet, and I probably won't even have to leave Brunswick, at least for a while. We'll most likely be stationed at Camp Semmes," he said, referring to the newly established military camp in south Brunswick.

Félicité could only pray. *Lord, let this war soon be over and may Harry never see combat.* But his siblings were supportive of his decision.

"I'm proud of you, Harry," Mary Amelia said. "I think you're very courageous."

"I agree," Josephine added.

"I wish I were old enough to fight. I'd join up with you." John Eugene sighed with envy.

"It will all be over by the time you're old enough, Johnny. We'll beat those Yankees soon enough," Harry said, cuffing his younger brother on the arm in a playful gesture. John Eugene grinned.

"Who's to be the commander of the new company?" Newton asked.

"George Dent of Hofwyl Plantation will be our captain," Harry said.

"He's a good man. I know he'll do what he can to keep his men safe," Newton tried to reassure his mother-in-law, who merely nodded, though she looked as though she were about to cry.

"I'm not the only one who's joining up, Mama. Charlie Schlatter plans to enlist in that same unit, and lots of other fellows my age."

She brushed back a lock of his dark hair, cupped his chin, and looked with earnest intensity into his eyes. "I know, son, but I'm your mother, and I can't help but worry."

Harry hugged her. "Don't worry, Mama. I'll be all right." He enlisted two weeks later, on August 14.

He was surprised to discover on the very day of his enlistment that he was not the only DuBignon eager to fight in the war. At the first roll call, Harry was startled to hear the name of another DuBignon on the roster. After the meeting was over, he sought out the other young man, who looked about his own age.

"You're a DuBignon?" asked Harry. "It's odd we've never met before Where are you from?"

"We've met before, Harry—a long time ago and only by chance. Your grandmother didn't approve."

Harry studied the young man standing before him. He bore a vague resemblance to his own younger brother, John Eugene, except that he wore a beard. They looked at each other with a certain apprehension.

"I'm from right here in Brunswick, just like you, and I know who you are. You're one of Joseph's boys. I know all about you. You can't live in a little town like this and not know things like that. I'm William Turner DuBignon. We were both born on Jekyl Island—about three months apart, as a matter of fact."

"Oh my God, I know you now. My family didn't talk about you and your family very much. You're one of Sarah Aust's sons."

"I am, and your grandfather is my father," said William.

Harry felt at a loss for words. The situation was awkward, but he managed to say the first thing that came to mind. "How's grandpa doing? I haven't seen him for a long time?"

"Well, he's gettin' old, but doing amazingly well for a man his age. Mary's pregnant again."

"Good grief! He never changes, does he?" said Harry. "How many does that make now?"

"This one will be the fifth." William chuckled, and Harry, still a bit uneasy, joined him. He suspected theirs would be an interesting relationship. They were bound to see each other daily for goodness knows how long, and he figured they might as well make the best of it. William seemed like a nice enough fellow, and neither of them was responsible for their family's bizarre entanglement.

"Well, we're in this unit together come hell or high water," Harry said. "I suppose we could carry on this family feud, but I'd much rather have a friend carrying a gun at my side. What do you say?" He held out his hand. William took it immediately.

"I agree. I guess I'm sort-of your uncle, and I'm supposed to look after you." He smiled broadly, trying to sound uncle-ish.

Harry laughed. "Let's just look out for each other."

CHAPTER 12

Jekyl Island, October 1861

A brisk knock on the door startled Henry and John, interrupting their dinner. A servant answered the door, and Henry DuBignon rose to greet the unexpected guest. As he entered the parlor, he was surprised to see Charlie Lamar, dressed in a Confederate officer's uniform, standing before him.

"Well, Charlie, I see you finally got the war you wanted. I hope you're satisfied," Henry said.

"As a matter of fact, I am, and I know I helped bring it about. Makes me proud," Lamar said with a grin, which was, at the same time, cheerful and arrogant.

"It would." Henry's voice was bitter. "What brings you here? We haven't seen you since—"

"I know. Since the *Wanderer* landed. This time I'm here on a very different mission. We're worried that there might be others trying to land here in the near future."

"You mean the Yankees? We've seen their ships blockading our coast, but so far, they haven't tried to come ashore."

"The commander thinks it's just a matter of time, and General Lee has ordered the fortification of the islands to protect the entrance to Brunswick harbor."

"You mean here at Jekyl?"

"Jekyl and St. Simons as well. Carey Styles is taking command at St. Simons. I've been ordered to undertake the task at Jekyl."

"Styles? The former mayor of Brunswick?"

"That's the one. He's a friend of mine, as I think you know. Lives over in Waresboro now and runs a newspaper there," Charlie answered.

"Will there be many troops on the island?" Henry asked, his annoyance evident.

"Three or four hundred at least—maybe more. I'm here to inform you that you have to evacuate—you and your brother. Take all your slaves and get off the island."

"What? Do you know how much trouble that is? And where would we go?"

"Inland someplace. I don't know. That's for you to figure out, but we need you all out of here by the end of the month."

"Good heavens, Lamar. That's asking a lot. What about our crops and our cattle? Maybe we could just stay here and work with you."

"You'd be in the way. We're going to occupy the entire island and save it from a Yankee invasion."

By this time, John, who had overheard snatches of the conversation from the dining room, was standing in the doorway, listening intensely. He did not look happy. "How can you drive us out of our home?"

"Government orders. We're going to build fortifications at the north end of the island to guard St. Simons Sound so Yankee ships can't get to Brunswick harbor."

"What if we refuse to leave?" John asked. "I was born here and I've spent my whole life here. I wouldn't know how to live anyplace else."

"You'll figure it out, John, and if you don't, I guess the government will have to move you out forcibly."

"You know, Lamar, you've never been anything but trouble to us," John grumbled. "You can't order us around, and I'm just not going to leave. This is *our* island."

"Don't make trouble for yourself, John. Just do what you're told. I don't want to have to force you out at gunpoint. We're doing the same thing on St. Simons. All the planters there are being told to leave as well. It's for your own protection, and we don't need any civilians in the way. Your only alternative is to join the army and send your slaves inland without you. If you don't and the Yankees land here, they'll set them all free—just like the British did in the War of 1812, I'm told."

That stung. The family had never recouped the losses from the English invasions of the island so many years ago. Many of their best slaves had left with the British. After the war ended, their grandfather had filed for reimbursement from the British government for almost $80,000, but he had been eventually compensated, they were told, with only a little more than $2,000, a tiny fraction of what they deemed the slaves were worth, much less all the valuables the British had stolen when they ransacked their home—not once, but twice. There hadn't been much left that was of any worth, mostly furniture which they couldn't carry. John had been only two years old when it happened and Henry not yet born, but they had both heard their father complain about it many times. They were certain they couldn't afford to lose any of their own slaves, for they had barely enough to work the plantation properly as it was. Those they had managed to keep from the *Wanderer* had certainly helped. Just when things had been going better, now this.

As for joining the military, John was nearly fifty, and while some men his age were volunteering, he had no intention of doing so. He was unaccustomed to military discipline, and the idea of leaving his family and living off the island with a group of strange men was a horrible thought. Nor did Henry plan to volunteer.

"I don't think the Confederates would want a one-eyed man," he said, reminding Lamar of the wound he had inflicted. "I wouldn't be of much use to them." His tone was bitter. "They've already got our brother-in-law, who was nearly killed at Manassas, as well as our older brother Charles and a couple of nephews. That should be enough sacrifices from one family."

Lamar laughed. "Charles is older than both of you, but I guess he couldn't resist the opportunity for glory, could he? Livin' up there in Milledgeville on his fancy plantation. I've heard he's in the Governor's Horse Guard now. Not likely to see much combat there." His voice was mocking.

"I wouldn't know." Henry said. They saw their brother very seldom. He never visited the island, and they never went to Milledgeville. They lived totally separate lives.

"When are your men coming?" Henry asked.

"They're already here—setting up camp at the north end of the island. It's a *fait accompli*, Henry, and there's no changing it. Just get your people together and leave the island with anything you need. I'm going to go now, so get to it." His voice was a command that ended the discussion. Lamar gave them a mock salute, turned smartly, and left the house.

They watched through the parlor window as he mounted his horse and rode north toward the Confederate camp.

"Where on earth can we go, John?" Henry asked.

"I have no idea. And I don't want to go," John said.

"We have no choice."

It was not an easy task. Most of the enslaved people didn't want to go into some indefinite future any more than their owners did. Some of them had never been off the island. Many had been born here. The graves of their ancestors were here. If they were being set free, they would have left the island joyfully, but to be sent into the unknown as slaves—perhaps to work on somebody else's plantation if their masters decided to hire them out—was a hardship. They didn't have much, but everything they had was here.

Sylvia was horrified when John told her what was happening. Like many of the others who were born into slavery, she had never been off the island, and the thought of leaving behind what had been her life for so long was frightening. She was afraid she might be separated from her children. And certainly, her relationship with John would never be accepted on the mainland—not the way it was here. None of this was her choice, but she had come to depend on him. What would it be like inland? Would they still live together or would she be hired out like everybody else to another slaveowner farther to the west? Who knew what hardships they would have to face in the days to come?

"John, can't we stay here—just you and me and the children? Them soldiers might never know we were here."

"I've thought of that, Sylvia, but I can't abandon my brother to do this all by himself, and I sure can't leave you and the children alone out here with hundreds of white men deprived of wives and sweethearts. Anything could happen." She shuddered at the thought. She had been violated only a few times in her life, and all those were by John himself. It still hurt to remember.

"But where will we go?"

"Henry is going to try and find some inland planters who might be willing to hire our slaves—maybe over near Waynesville or Waresboro. We won't get much for them, I'm sure, because other island planters will probably be trying to do the same thing. But they're expensive to buy, and it will be a good deal for the planters. At least it might keep the workers and their families all fed and make us enough to get through this fool war. We've got till the end of the month to figure it all out, but it's the only solution we can think of."

"You ain't gone hire me out, is you?"

"Of course not. You're my family. On the mainland, you'll just have to pass as our servant. I hear they don't take kindly to mixed families over there."

"What about the children?"

"Robert is sixteen now. He can take care of the horses or some such. Joseph is nearly seven. He can do chores. We'll all stay together."

"What about Caroline and George? They too young to help out."

"Well, you'll just have to take care of them, We'll keep 'em all safe, I promise."

Sylvia was crying now with all the uncertainty.

"What's the matter, Mama," George was tugging on her skirt, his face anxious.

"Don't you worry none, son," John said. "I'm gonna take care of you. Please don't cry, Sugar," he said to Sylvia. "You're scaring the children. We'll get through this. And then when this war is over, we'll all come back to Jekyl and life will be like it was before. I promise. And then we'll never leave the island again."

Sylvia tried to find reassurance in his voice, but it all looked bleak ahead. She laid her hand across her belly, thinking she had felt the baby move. She was pregnant again, as she had been much of the time since she and John had been together. What would happen when the baby came due? Would there be a midwife nearby?

It was terrifying to leave this little cabin, which had become their home. She remembered how determined John had been to build this little house—one where they could live together all the time if they wanted. Though he still planned to spend some time with his brother at the big house.

"You can plan the house," he had told her, "just like you want it. I'll see to it that you don't have to work in the fields or the cotton house anymore. We'll have a room for you and me and one for Robert and whatever other children come along. I'll get us a soft bed and a real cook stove, a table and chairs, and maybe even a settee. We'll have three or four rooms all to ourselves," he assured her. "You and Robert won't have to share a cabin with anyone else, except me, of course." She couldn't even imagine such a thing. She wasn't sure she wanted to move to some isolated part of the island away from the quarters, away from her mama and her brothers and sisters.

"But I'd be out there by myself," she said, not sure that, even with such a luxurious cabin as one that he had described, she could be happy. As if that mattered.

"You'll have me. And Robert and whatever other children we have will be with you. You can grow flowers and a vegetable garden. Robert can raise chickens, maybe a few pigs. We'd be on our own. It's something we can look forward to."

She had hated him at first, but over time she had grown accustomed to him and his ways, and she knew he was serious. Despite how it had all begun, she had slowly begun to see another side to John beyond the terrifying master who could do whatever he wanted to her. He was good to their children and to her, and most of the time he was a gentle man. All her life, she had lived in a one-room cabin with six or seven other people. All those rooms he described, with a separate room for children—to her it sounded like a mansion. The thought of never having to crank that gin or hull one more boll of cotton, the possibility of just sitting in the sun on occasional afternoons and watching the light grow golden in the waning afternoon, had a certain appeal.

She knew she had no choice anyhow. If he decided that's what he wanted, that's what would happen, and she might as well make the best of it. She tried to imagine what her life might have been like if he had never come riding down that twilit road so long ago. Had it not been for John, she thought, she might have gone on to jump the broom with one of the younger men in the quarters. She had noticed Cato and Moses both looking her over from time to time, and she liked them both, but they never dared touch her. She was the master's gal.

She wondered what it would be like to lie in the arms of a handsome man with dark, musky skin like her own, one who reminded her of her daddy before he got sold off. She remembered how happy he and her mama had been—at least happier than most folks in the quarters, who were so tired at night that all they could do was eat their boiled rice and bread and fall into their cornhusk beds. Her mama and daddy would work hard all day, trying not to do anything that would get them noticed, so they could come home at night, have supper together, talk or play for a while with their children, and then fall asleep in one another's arms. Even so, one of them would occasionally do something that would displease one of the whites and find themselves punished, even whipped. But that didn't happen often, for they worked hard and tried not to make trouble.

Sometimes at night the family would sit around a big log fire and tell stories or sing old hymns. Her daddy would strum on a banjo he had made himself. Some of the strings sounded better than others, but he could approximate a tune, especially with other folks singing. Then, when old man Henry sold him off, Sylvia's mama changed. She became sullen and silent. She never seemed to laugh anymore, and Sylvia could sometimes hear her crying in the night. They never heard from her pa again. Neither of her parents could read or write, but even if they could, there was not much way for them to get a letter from one plantation to another—even if they knew where he was. Maybe he had another wife by now. Maybe he was even dead. There was no way to know. But life was what it was, and there was nothing to do but accept the one God had given her, whatever it held or might hold in the future—even if it was on the mainland in the middle of a war.

Sylvia laid her hand across her belly, thinking she had felt the baby move. She had been pregnant much of the time since John had brought her here to live. Her mind drifted back to the beginning. How different her life might have been had she never gone out that evening, the only time she could ever remember when she was alone after dark on the road that led from the slave quarters to the beach.

She had worked alongside her mother all day in the cotton house, where they took turns separating the lobes from the fluffy bolls or cranking the gin to extract the seeds. She remembered that afternoon and how tired and hot she was. While her mother went to their cabin to fix supper, she decided to slip away from the quarters and go wading up to her knees in the ocean to cool off a bit. Her mama didn't want her to be out like that at night all alone, but her rebellious thirteen-year-old spirit had got the best of her, and she was determined to feel that cool water splashing against her legs and the sand moving under her feet.

Mama won't miss me for a little while. She'll think I'm just out playin' with some of the other young'uns in the quarters, she thought. It was not quite dark when she set out. She could see clearly, even as darkness fell, for the sandy roadway reflected the almost full, gibbous moon. She was more than halfway to the beach when suddenly she saw a man on horseback riding toward her. She moved to the side of the road to let him pass, but when he got close enough and she could see who it was, he was pulling back on his horse's reins.

"Whoa, Emmet," the man said.

She recognized the name of Master John's horse.

"What you doin' out here all by yourself, gal? You ought to be home helpin' your mama. Where you goin'?"

She was too frightened to speak. "I...I...was just—"

He dismounted. "I reckon I ought to send you on home now." He came toward her, looking her over. "Right pretty little thing, aren't you? You ought'n be out here all alone. No tellin' what could happen."

He reached out to take her arm. Then he hesitated, and his hand trailed down her back all the way to her buttocks. "Well now," he said, as his hands roamed around and upwards to her tiny buds of breasts. "Kind of little still, but you're almost a woman now." She saw his eyes narrow, and she was frightened. She had seen him looking at her like that before and with a funny little smile on his face that made her want to run and hide.

"My mama—" she started to say that her mama would be worried about her, but he knew as well as she did that her footsteps were turned away from home.

"You know the difference between a girl and a woman?" he asked.

She shook her head, eager to break away and run home to the safety of her family's cabin. She wished her daddy was here, but he was no longer on the island. He had been sold off two years earlier by Master John's father. He'd been a good picker, but the plantation needed a blacksmith since the old one had run off, and so her daddy was sold in a trade to get a new blacksmith. Sylvia remembered how her mama had cried and begged old man Henry to trade her and the young'uns too, but he just laughed. "Never you mind. I'll get you another man."

"Don't want no other man," she heard her mother mutter under her breath. Her mama hadn't been the same since. She continued to go to the cotton house every day, rain or shine, during picking season. But she had lost her laughter and what little joy she had once shared with her family.

"Well, I'll tell you the difference between a girl and a woman," John told her. "A girl doesn't know about what goes on between a woman and a man. But a woman does. I just bet you're about ready to be a woman, now aren't you." He chuckled, apparently thinking himself very clever.

She just stood there, frozen in fear, as he pulled a blanket from underneath the horse's saddle and spread it just beyond the roadway inside a palmetto thicket that shielded the spot.

"Come on, gal," he said, taking her hand and leading her to the blanket, where he laid her down, unbuttoned his pants, slid them down to his knees, then knelt over her. "Let me show you what makes a girl a woman."

She lay there stiffly as he spread her legs, lay on top of her, and started to explore her private parts with his fingers. Her eyes were wide with horror, and she could feel the hot tears streaming down her cheeks and her body trembling, but she didn't dare cry out, for fear he'd beat her.

"Now you just relax. You might like it," he said, as he began to rub his male member gently against her until it stood upright all on its own.

Her body grew rigid, and she closed her eyes as tight as she could, as he tried to penetrate her tiny body with his large appendage. Despite her fear, she struggled to stop the pain and get him off, but it was useless. He was a lot older than she was, and he was strong and determined. It took a lot of pushing and grunting on his part until he finally succeeded. She could hear herself crying in the darkness. Then he thrust into her again and again, until he finally moaned and rolled off of her, but still grasped her arm.

"Now," he said, when he was able to get himself under control again. "Reckon now you can call yourself a woman." He stood up again, wiped himself off with his handkerchief, and buttoned his pants. "You get on home now."

She struggled to her feet, sobbing now, and stumbled back toward the cabin in the dark. Something warm was trickling down her leg as she cut through a path that led to the slave quarters. She was never so glad to see the candles and lamps flickering through the small windows and cracks of the cabins. Before she went inside, she found a horse trough filled with water and cleaned herself as best she could. She brushed her skirt free of sand and pine needles and headed home. Her mother knew the moment she walked inside that something was wrong.

"What you been up to, girl?" her mama asked. But despite her mother's urging, she wouldn't tell. She was too ashamed.

After that he came looking for her—sometimes in mid-afternoon outside the cotton house when she had stepped outside to get a drink of water, sometimes in the corn field when she'd been sent to get a few ears for supper. Wherever she was and no matter what she was doing, he seemed to find her, and he would take her into the woods. She had tried to resist, but he was too strong for her, and she had given up and lay stiffly, trying to turn off her mind and hoping it would be over soon.

"Those little breasts of yours are growin'," he said with satisfaction before he entered her once again.

The following summer, she gave birth to a baby boy. Her mother took one look at the child and knew who his father was. His light brown hair and the gray eyes told her everything she needed to know. But she also knew it would do no good to complain to the master, whichever one it was. They had their way with slave women anytime they wanted. It had happened to her and to most of the women in the quarters, though not at such a young age.

"Ain't nothin' we can do about it," she said to her daughter. "Which one was it?"

"Massa John," Sylvia said, looking at the floor and feeling shame throughout her body. "I couldn't help it, Mama," she said.

"I know. I know how it is. All you can do now is try to take care of this baby and avoid that white man when you can." And for a while she succeeded. But only for a while.

All that was a long time ago when John was in his thirties. Over the years, she thought he had actually grown fond of her and tried in his own way to woo her. He had no truck with the other women in the quarters—at least none that she knew of. She was the only one. He would occasionally bring her little gifts—a piece of candy, a bead bracelet, sometimes a little bouquet of honeysuckle and marsh marigolds, and once, after Robert was born, an ivory comb. In time, she got used to him. She had no alternative. And she began to welcome the little gifts he offered her. The rest of the people in the quarters started to treat her with a certain deference. She was Master John's gal now, whether she liked it or not.

Now this war had come along. What would it bring? Would it change anything? She knew that John did not want to leave the island, but they had no choice, he said. This war was affecting everyone, and they were no different.

CHAPTER 13

Brunswick, Georgia, 1861

Newton complained to Josephine that he had not yet received a commission, but he was eager to do his part. She knew he would leave as soon as possible, but even before the commission was granted, he insisted on reporting to General Lee in Savannah, where, to her dismay, he was put to work by the Savannah Engineer Department to serve as assistant engineer, clerk, and draftsman.

She suggested that he write a letter to his family in Wisconsin to let them know of his decision, justifying his choice. He let her read it before he mailed it. "I am part of a Southern family now," he wrote, "and I pray that I will never encounter a battle between my old friends in the North and my new friends here, but this is the family I will live with for the rest of my life. I hope you will understand why I have decided to serve the Confederacy." They did not respond, and she never knew whether they had received his letter or not, given the circumstances.

Finally, on October 25, he let her know that he had received his commission as First Lieutenant in the Corps Artillery, and in late January, he was assigned to a new post as ordnance officer at the Confederate Arsenal in Augusta, Georgia. He reported for duty on January 28. As ordnance officer, he was responsible for keeping the equipment secure, in perfect working condition, and ready to be shipped out at any time to troops in the field.

When he told Josephine about his new assignment, she was delighted, for he would still be in Georgia, close enough to visit from time to time, and this was not a fighting unit, but rather a maintenance and supply post. He was pleased as well since it was unlikely that he would ever have to go into combat against any of his northern relatives. Augusta bordered the Savannah River, which divided Georgia from South Carolina, and since it was not a coastal city, for now it was secure from Union attack.

"Best of all," he said with a grin, "I think it's safe enough, for the time being at least, for you to come there and live with me."

Josephine squealed with excitement when he told her. She loved Augusta already. She'd felt lost without Newton. She was proud of him, of course, and delighted that he had decided to join the Confederate army, which she felt expressed in a profound way his commitment to her and their marriage. But the very thought of being without him for what could be years had spread before her like a ribbon of darkness.

When Newton reached Augusta, he began immediately to look for a suitable place for his wife and himself to live together. As soon as he located a little house to rent, he wrote to Josephine, asking her to come and join him there.

"I miss you terribly," he wrote.

Without hesitation, she took the first train she could get to go to him. Their new house was small, but it was convenient to the Arsenal, and it was the first home they had shared apart from her family. She was ecstatic.

Throughout the first months of the war, the South seemed to be doing well. The great victory at Manassas that sent the Northern army into a panicky retreat had convinced southerners that the Confederates would have an easy victory. News of smaller victories at places like Wilson's Creek in Missouri and Ball's Bluff in Virginia reassured the populace that the South would quickly prevail. But by early 1862, all that had changed.

Back-to-back Confederate losses at places like Tennessee's Fort Henry and Fort Donelson, and Roanoke Island in North Carolina had altered everyone's perception that this would be an easy war. The battle of Shiloh in April would only confirm that.

Félicité could only worry about her son Harry. The family rarely saw him now, for his unit was frequently on the move. They tried to keep track of the Glynn Guards, but it was harder now that they were no longer at home. Every day Josephine prayed for her son's safety, for news about the war was not good.

Despite the menacing presence of the federal blockade in coastal waters, Brunswick had seemed relatively safe until then. Jekyl and St. Simons Islands had been well fortified with Confederate batteries to protect the town's harbor, but in early 1862, all that changed. General Lee decided that the dangers were even greater in Savannah, and in spite of all the work that the troops had done, he ordered the islands abandoned, leaving Brunswick completely vulnerable to Union attack. To keep the population safe, the military ordered local citizens to evacuate the town and move farther inland.

Like everyone else, Félicité's family was compelled to pack up whatever belongings they were able to take with them and find another place to live farther away from the coastal area.

"Where will we go, Mama?" Mary Amelia asked.

"I'm not sure yet, but we'll find someplace safe," Félicité replied, with little certainty in her voice.

No one was eager to give up their homes and leave behind so many things they loved. The frenzy of deciding what to pack and finding a place of refuge upset the entire DuBignon household. Félicité decided that the best option for her family was to take refuge in Waynesville, some twenty miles to the west, as most other Brunswick citizens were doing. Keeping her children safe was her main priority.

"Evacuation is hard, isn't it, Mama?" Johnny said as he toted his sisters' valises to the wagon.

"Yes, it is, son, but I fear it's necessary."

They couldn't take everything, so she let each of her children select the things they felt they most needed, while she chose certain household and jewelry items that she prized most of all, most of them gifts from Joseph. She could only pray over the rest and hope it would still be there when they returned. They stuffed the carriage full and hired a wagon as well. Their cook, Beulah, drove the wagon and John Eugene rode beside her, while their coachman, Moses, manned the carriage carrying Félicité and her daughters. It was difficult, as Johnny had noted, but, as was typical of his mother, she garnered enough strength to do all that needed to be done to get her family out of harm's way.

As the war continued, matters did not improve for the South. But in 1863, Newton and Josephine were far more focused on her first pregnancy than on following the battles.

"You're a tender father-to-be," Josephine said, as they lay in bed at night. He was holding her gently, spoon-fashion, his hands on her belly, where he could feel the baby moving inside her.

"I want to be the best father ever, because I know you'll be the best mother." The name they had selected for the child, if it was a boy, was to be Joseph Erasmus, for the baby's two grandfathers. They had not yet selected a name for a girl, for Newton was determined it would be a son. Josephine was ready nonetheless. She knew that her own mother's name, Félicité, would be a part of it.

Josephine and Newton were as happy as any young couple could be in the midst of a war. But they were both aware that it might not last. When the war ended, whatever the outcome, their lives would be forever changed. All the destruction, all the regional hatred, all the terrible losses would undoubtedly haunt the nation, whether they were two countries or one, for many years to come. Now that he was going to be a father, Newton was giving even more thought than usual to the future. He had been investing heavily, putting to use all those savings he had accumulated as a member of the Coast Survey, speculating on various commodities, hoping he could emerge from this war comfortable if not a wealthy man. Josephine was happy at the thought of focusing on the future with a new baby. She had everything a young woman could want—except peace and certainty.

She awoke on October 2 with labor pains. Newton, who had not yet left for the Arsenal, was in a panic.

"What should I do? What should I do?" he asked, like a helpless boy.

"I think the best thing would be to fetch the midwife," said Josephine in a calm voice, smiling between contractions. "Then I want you to go do your duty."

"At the Arsenal? And leave you here alone?" He was incredulous.

"I won't be alone. The midwife will be here, and you would be completely useless at such a time. I'll have someone come for you as soon as the baby is born."

"You're so brave," he said, leaning over for a delicate kiss, for she seemed so fragile.

"Now go find Maum Isabel and bring her here. I'm going to need her." She drew in her breath as she felt the beginning of another birth pang,

Newton threw on his clothes, rushed out the door to saddle his horse, and rode away like a madman. Once he had returned with the midwife, he refused to go to work. Instead, he paced the yard in front of the house, terrified and worried by Josephine's cries of pain. By 3 o'clock he was inside his home again beside his wife, holding his baby son in his arms.

In late August of 1864, Josephine was rocking ten-month-old

Joey, smiling down at the child who was almost asleep in her arms, when they were both startled by a deafening explosion. The baby stiffened at the sound, and her heart leapt. *Dear God*, she thought, *are we under attack?* Usually news of approaching enemy troops could not be kept secret, but she supposed it could happen. She covered her baby with her own body to prepare for the next assault. But it did not come.

What was happening? There was only one equally horrible possibility. Something had exploded at the Arsenal's powder works. She and Newton were both aware of the dangers of working with the gunpowder that was being produced at the Arsenal in huge quantities, 7,000 pounds a day she had heard Newton say. To protect the workers from utter disaster, the commanding officer, Col. Rains, had constructed the powder works in a dozen or so separate buildings stretched about two miles along the Augusta canal. He thought it unsafe to produce it all in a single location. Even so, gunpower was dangerous, and she knew it.

With Joey now wailing in her arms, she rushed outside and peered in the direction of the Arsenal. Sure enough, black smoke was rising from that direction.

"Oh, my God," she said, her hand at her throat. She could only pray that her husband was nowhere near where the explosion took place. She held her breath for what seemed like forever, peering down the road toward the Arsenal. Finally, she saw Newton in the distance, riding toward the house, toward her, still standing in the yard, too frightened to move, and little Joey still whimpering. Newton got off his horse and took the baby from her arms. Her face was as white as the clouds overhead

"Newton, thank God," she said, collapsing into his arms and

snuggling as close as she could get with the baby between them. She was breathing deeply for the first time since the explosion.

"I knew you'd be worried, so I got permission to come home to let you know I was safe," Newton said, embracing both her and the baby.

"I thank God you did. I was dying of fright. Was anyone hurt?"

"I'm afraid so—nine dead in all," he said grimly, glancing at his son.

"Do you know what happened?"

"It appears that some fool thought he might sneak a smoke while his supervisor was not on duty. It killed seven men in the Arsenal, the sentry outside, and a boy just walking by with his mule. What a disaster!"

"I'm so sorry, darling. I'm just glad that you're not hurt."

"Thank God for Col. Rains's foresight. Building the Arsenal the way he did was costly, but it saved lives today." It was the worst day of the war for Josephine, and there had not even been a battle.

CHAPTER 14

Rural Georgia, late 1862

By the time Brunswick was evacuated, John and Henry had already left the area. It had not been easy for them to find places for their slaves during the war, but they had no choice. There was no way to feed them all with no money coming in. They had managed to hire out most of them at places farther inland, which was a godsend. At least those workers would be fed and housed, although the compensation the brothers received for their workers' labor was far less than it would have been before the war. The army requisitioned the strongest of the men to do the work white soldiers refused to do. And a few of them found opportunities to run away to seek help from Union troops, if they could find them.

Not long after the first of the year, rumors began to circulate about the President's proclamation freeing people held as slaves, even in Confederate states. Word of mouth carried it among the enslaved people, who saw the South's losses as a hope for future liberation. They would be free only if the North won the war. To Henry's dismay, that was looking ever more likely.

John, on the other hand, was too busy trying to keep his family together to worry about the outcome. They couldn't live in town, of course, but he had found a dilapidated and abandoned house in the woods about four miles west of Waynesville where they wouldn't be bothered by townspeople. He and his sons repaired what they could, so rain wouldn't leak in or wind blow through the cracks. Henry refused John's invitation to live with them. He thought it demeaning to live in such a shack along with colored people. Instead, he found shelter with his sisters Eliza and Catherine in a plantation house near Tebeauville that belonged to a member of the Hazlehurst family, an option not open to John and his family. Nonetheless, the brothers kept in touch.

It was almost spring when one day Henry surprised John and Sylvia by riding up to their cabin in mid-afternoon. They were sitting on their run-down front porch and John was whittling on a whistle for his youngest son. Sylvia was nursing Cecilia, who'd been born only months after they left the island, She quickly covered her breast as John dismounted.

"Well, howdy, Brother, what brings you here?" John said.

Sylvia rose, nodding at Henry, taking the baby inside to finish her feeding. The brothers, she knew, would prefer to talk alone. And she never felt welcome when Henry was around.

Henry took off his hat as he climbed the wooden porch steps to sit on the plank bench she had vacated. "Well, I see you have another one."

"You mean Cecilia? She was born a year after the war started. Sylvia was already expecting when we left Jekyl. There was another one as well, Selina, a twin, who died not long after they were born." Henry did not react.

"What are you going to do after the war if they're all free?"

"We'll cross that bridge when the time comes," John answered, but there was uncertainty in his eyes. If the South won the war, Mr. Lincoln's proclamation wouldn't be worth the paper it was written on. If the North won, he had no idea what the future might hold. He knew that keeping his family members as slaves was the only way he could be sure they would stay. He hoped Sylvia had come to care for him, but they never talked of such things, and John did not ask. He never wanted her to feel compelled to say anything she did not mean in her heart. At the moment, the Yankees seemed to be winning, and things were looking far more uncertain than they had in earlier years. He shook the thought away.

"Now what brings you here?" John asked his brother. "You've never visited before. Letters, but no visits."

His brother leaned forward in his chair and looked John in the eye. "I've decided it's time we confront our father about Jekyl Island. I think this would be a good time. I 'speck it's overrun with Yankees now and surely of no use to him. Besides, he's gettin' old. I think it's probably now or never."

"What do you propose we do?" John asked.

"Go to Ellis Point and demand that he deed it over to us."

"I don't think that *demanding* something of our father will have much success."

"Well," said Henry. "Maybe that's too strong a word. How

about 'convince'?"

"Henry, you know that you and Papa are like two bulls in rutting season. I'd go for words like 'urge' or 'persuade' or even 'ask.'"

"Do you think that would work?"

"Better than demanding by a long shot," John said.

"Well then, let's do it. When can we leave?"

"I'll go on one condition. You let me do the talkin'."

Henry frowned and started to protest, but his brother interrupted. "I mean it, Henry. You have a temper on you."

Henry finally agreed. He knew John was right, but he also knew it would be hard for him to hold his peace.

They left the following morning. As they rode side by side along the road toward Brunswick, Henry turned to his brother and said, "You know, John, this will be the first time we've ever visited our father and his new wife."

"Not so new," John observed. "They've been married ten years now—goin' on eleven. And they've got a passle of daughters to prove it."

It was a long ride, but their father's house was a few miles west of town, and closer to Waynesville than Brunswick was. Their father and his new family had not evacuated, thinking it too difficult with all their young daughters. Both John and Henry felt some apprehension as they approached.

Only three little girls were playing in the yard, but the two brothers approached the house with a bit of apprehension. They had deemed it safe enough to travel in that part of Georgia, but they had not notified their father that they were coming. He might have a shotgun ready. But he'd seen them approaching and greeted them at the door. They were both shocked by his appearance. They hadn't laid eyes on him for five years, and during that time, his beard had grown longer, and his hair was entirely white now. His wrinkles were deeper and his face seemed to have settled into a perpetual scowl.

John Couper peered inside the house. He could see that it was simply furnished and tidy, but their father did not invite them in.

"Well," Henry Sr. said. "This is an unexpected visit."

"We didn't have time to let you know that we were coming," said John.

"I might not have got the letter anyhow. You never know these days. What brings you here?"

"Can't sons visit their father occasionally?" Henry Jr. said, his voice curt. John gave him a warning look.

"Of course," said their father. "It's just that you've never come before, so I assume you must have a motive beyond a simple filial visit."

"Can we come in?" asked John. "We'd like to talk with you."

"Let's sit on the porch," his father said. "Mary," he called out, "bring us three glasses of lemonade."

"You may want something stronger," said Henry Jr.

"Lemonade will do," his father said, setting his jaw.

Once they were settled into the porch chairs, it was John who opened the conversation. "We wanted to talk with you about the island, Papa."

"What about the island? I assume no one is there now. I hear the Yankees have left."

"Have they? Well, that's good." John cleared his throat. "Papa, Henry and I have been working the plantation for ten years now, and we both think, in the interest of good will, that it's time you deed it over to us."

"And why should I do that?"

"Well, as I said, we've been doing all the work there for a decade, and it was part of your marriage agreement with our mother that it should pass along to your children—yours and hers. You're getting older now, and we want the matter settled before your death. Anything could happen after that. We think it would be best for everyone if the matter were settled now." John could see his brother nervously clenching and unclenching his fist. It was hard for Henry to remain quiet when he felt so strongly about a matter. But John had reminded him before they arrived that any show of his obstinate temper would only cause their father to dig in his heels. As for himself, he was able to maintain a more moderate tone.

"I have other children, you know," his father said. They were well aware of that, and in their brief glimpse of Mary when she brought out the lemonade, John thought she looked as though she might be pregnant yet again.

She had tried to sweeten the lemonade with honey, but it was still not like the lemonade of old. "Five girls by Mary and two sons and a daughter by Sarah," he reminded them.

"We know that, Papa, and you can leave something else to them. After this war, who knows what shape the island will be in? It may even be lost to the Yankees altogether. It's not bringin' in any income now, and who knows after the war?"

"Then why do you want it, if it's no use to anyone?" his father asked.

Henry Jr. opened his mouth to speak, but John interrupted. "Let's let Papa think it over, Henry," he said. Any sign of animosity would only cause their father to harden his stance. He had only become more stubborn over the years and had clearly grown old. He seemed strong enough for a man of almost seventy-six, but his age had become a primary factor in his sons' determination to get the matter settled now.

"I repeat, why do you want it if it's of no use to anyone?"

"Well, Papa, as I said, it's our home and, we feel, our legacy. We were born there and have spent our entire lives there. We love that island, and we hope to go back if this infernal war ever ends. I, for one, want to live there until I die. None of your other children has the same connections that Henry and I do."

Henry Sr. said nothing for a few moments. Both of his sons sat silent, waiting.

Finally, after what seemed an endless moment, their father said, "Give me until tomorrow to think it over?"

"Of course, thank you for considering it. We'll look forward to seeing you again tomorrow," John replied. He hoped their father might offer them a bed for the night, but he didn't.

When Henry Sr. stood up, both his sons stood as well. He stretched out his hand to shake, first with John, then with his namesake. "You make a good case, son," he said to John. "But I have to think about it. I have others to consider. Come back about nine tomorrow morning and I'll give you an answer."

The two brothers mounted their horses and rode away as though they knew where they were going, though of course there was no hotel or inn available anywhere close by. Once out of sight of their father's house, Henry turned to his brother.

"I thought you made a good case, John, and you were probably right not to let me speak."

"I hope I didn't make you mad back there when I interrupted you, but I know what it's like when you and Papa lock horns. I really meant it when I said I want to spend the rest of my life at Jekyl—until my death."

"I know you did," Henry answered. "But the most important question now is where are we going to spend the night?" He was always the more practical one.

"We'll camp out, like we did when we were boys. Come on, let's find a good spot."

When they returned the next day, to their surprise, their father invited them in for breakfast. They both welcomed it, for their rations had been slight, and they were hungry. Their father even seemed to be in a cheerful mood, which John took as a good sign. Mary did not join them at the table, but she served them amply with unsalted eggs and grits, and a fried pullet. Salt was scarce, and the household had long since exhausted supplies of any other meats, but chickens were easy to raise and they needed the eggs. Mary had used the last of the flour to make biscuits, and she had made "coffee" with ground okra seeds. It was the best meal they'd had since they left Waynesville.

"I hope you boys had a restful night," Henry Sr. said.

"We're fine, Papa. I hope you had the same," John answered. He paused a moment, then said, "Have you made a decision?"

"Let's enjoy our breakfast and talk about that later," Henry Sr. answered. The two brothers looked at each other, unsure of what that portended. In any case, they finished their breakfast discussing only news of the war and the scarcity of commodities like salt and coffee.

When the meal was done, their father led them once again to the front porch.

"We enjoyed the breakfast," Henry Jr. said, clearly trying his best to be amiable.

"Glad you did," said his father. "Now let's get down to the question you asked me yesterday."

Both Henry Jr. and John said nothing, waiting for the old man to speak.

"Here's what I've decided. I've thought about it overnight, and I think you're right that the island should stay with my children born to Amelia. I want to keep it all together in the family—not sold off in pieces to strangers. But I can't leave it to just the two of you. I'll take care of drawing up the legal papers right away, but I will include your brother Charles and your unmarried sister Eliza in the transfer. I know you boys have been taking care of things, but I wouldn't feel right to leave them out. Here's what I plan to do." He took a piece of paper out of his shirt pocket and unfolded it. It was a crude drawing of the island, which he had divided into portions. He pointed to the southernmost division.

"I'm going to deed this part of the island to Charles. It's the least cleared and cultivated. He probably won't work it, but at least he'll own a share." Then he pointed to the middle and most productive section. "John, this part will be yours, and Henry," he said, indicating the northern end, "this section north of Rock Bois will go to you. I've also thought about Eliza. Since she's unmarried and has no husband to care for her, I'm also leaving her a small portion of the island. She will have no means of cultivating it without your help, so she won't need as much land. Anyhow, I'm giving her thirty acres—that part we used to call Bryan's Old Field. It's fertile enough, if anybody wants to work it, but I'll also be leaving her some other property, including some of my railroad stock. She'll manage well enough. I'll get the papers drawn up next week."

"What about Joseph and his family?" John asked.

"He's dead," Henry Jr. reminded his brother shortly. "Papa wants to leave it to his living children."

"But—" John began again.

"No, I think Henry's right. It should go to my living heirs," their father said.

"But Joseph has sons who—" John began.

"I've made up my mind," their father said sharply.

John said no more. It was better, he thought, to let it drop.

Henry Jr. couldn't believe it had been this easy. "Thank you, Papa. We both appreciate it, and we'll take good care of the island, if we can ever return."

As they rode away, both men had a deep feeling of satisfaction. At long last, the island would be theirs and proof that their father still cared about the well-being of his first family. A guarantee for the future. It was a dream come true.

CHAPTER 15

Coastal Georgia, 1863

The quick victory the Confederates had once hoped for did not happen, and it looked as though the war might drag on far longer than they had all believed. Harry DuBignon and William, his comrade and half-uncle, had spent their first year of service close to home as part of the Glynn Guards, both reenlisting when their term was up. In early 1862, the Guards had been incorporated into an artillery unit and later into the Georgia Volunteer Cavalry in what eventually came to be known as Clinch's Cavalry, under the command of Major Duncan L. Clinch, Jr.

Their duties still lay for the most part between the Altamaha River and the St. Mary's—a part of Georgia that was difficult to defend because of the porous vulnerability of its islands, rivers, and estuaries. When the Confederacy had transferred the troops from Jekyl Island and St. Simons to Savannah, they'd left Brunswick virtually undefended. As a consequence, the Union military sought to undermine such things as brickyards, salt works, and sawmills in the area. They were not major battles, perhaps, but the Glynn Guards took part in various skirmishes to defend them.

In many ways, Harry and William were lucky, though they had not viewed it as such at the time, for they were eager to fight. Their company had been passed over the first time in the summer of 1862, when a part of their regiment was selected to go north to join the Army of Northern Virginia, which would fight in some of the most deadly battles of the war, Fredericksburg, Chancellorsville, Antietam, and the Second Battle of Bull Run. Although they were annoyed to be overlooked, it may have saved both their lives, for the casualties in those battles were staggering.

Then, in March 1863, part of their regiment had been ordered to northern Florida to shore up the defense of that region, but Colonel Clinch took only five companies with him. Once again William and Harry's unit was left behind to guard the southeastern part of Georgia.

They hadn't seen any major incursions by the enemy, any big battles to that point, though there were frequent skirmishes and some casualties—more resulting from a typhoid epidemic that ravaged their camp in 1863 than from the war. The Federals used St. Simons and Fernandina as their primary bases of operation, and the Glynn Guards were sent on raids to those islands more to disrupt Union activities and create chaos than to engage in combat. They were successful in burning the wharf and warehouses at the south end of St. Simons and destroying stores of coal as well as supplies of both the commissary and the quartermaster, thus crippling the operations from that island, at least for a while. In short, they made their presence felt in the area.

Again, in 1864, Clinch's Cavalry was called to the defense of northern Florida, where in mid-February, both Harry and William took part in the battle of Olustee, but the wounding of Colonel Clinch removed their unit from the rest of the fight, which the Confederates won. Their worst losses of the day resulted when the Cavalry attempted to cross a bog, which proved to be quicksand, causing the loss of several panicked horses.

The Cavalry remained in northern Florida under new command until April 23, when they returned to Georgia, where their most challenging assignment north of the Altamaha still awaited them—the defense of Atlanta. Colonel Clinch returned to resume command on July 5, when he split his troops into two units—one deployed to Charleston, the other to Atlanta. Harry and William found their company headed for Atlanta, where they saw the worst fighting they had faced in the war. Fortunately neither was wounded, and by mid-November, it was over, and Sherman began his infamous March to the Sea.

Still both men survived and were eager to go to the defense of Savannah. Throughout the skirmishes, the occasional battles, and the long nights with little sleep and less food, Harry and William became close friends, depending on one another, and fighting side-by-side. In their leisure time, they would sit around campfires and reminisce about home—about Jekyl Island, the one place they had in common and where they had both spent much of their boyhoods. Although they talked occasionally about the entanglement of their families, neither of them had anything to do with those problems and they made for uncomfortable conversation. As the war dragged on and they shared more experiences, they talked less about their family's past and more about the island itself and how they longed to go back. Their young lives spent in that peaceful place were such a contrast to the horror and death they now experienced.

In a sense, it was that memory of home that they were fighting for—to protect the simple life they had known when they were boys. It wasn't about slavery for either of them, for neither of them was a planter, and they would have been happy enough to see their dark-skinned friends from childhood free to enjoy their own lives. They had all played together when they were young—fishing in Jekyl's tidal creeks, wandering the beach to watch for dolphins, looking for turtle nests, and enjoying occasional splashes in the surf, but as soon as their black friends turned seven or so, they were sent to the fields, and things were no longer the same. They both knew it wasn't fair. But their family didn't seem to know how to run a plantation any other way.

Once they knew they could completely trust one another, William dared to share another topic of conversation with Harry—a secret he had harbored for many months. One evening, everyone else had crawled into their tents and they were the last two soldiers left around the campfire

"I want to show you something," William said, pulling from his pocket an ambrotype in a leather case worn around the edges. It contained the image of a girl—almost a woman. William held it out shyly to show it to Harry. He could see she was pretty, but he couldn't tell from the faded sepia photo what color her hair was or her eyes. He could tell, however, that William thought her very special.

"Lovely," Harry said. "Who is she?"

"Her name is Lottie. Well, it's really Charlotte, but everyone calls her Lottie. She lives in Tallahassee."

"I gather she's someone you're fond of. How did you meet her?"

"We met when we were stationed in Florida. We corresponded for a while, but I haven't heard from her in recent months. It's hard to keep up, what with all the changes. After the war, I'd like to see her again. In fact, I think—" He hesitated. I think she's the girl I want to marry."

"And I think you're in love, my friend," Harry teased.

"I don't know how she feels, but I decided that when, or if, this war ever ends and I'm still alive, I'm going to Tallahassee and find her."

"I think that's a wonderful idea. I wish I had a girl I wanted to go back to. You're lucky, Billy." William never let anyone use that nickname except Harry, and then, only in the most private moments. He didn't much like it, but somehow Harry said it with such affection that it sounded like a title of honor."

"Wish me luck," William said.

"You have all my best wishes, but you know that already. Does she have a sister?"

"Darned if I know, but if she does, I'll let you know." Both men laughed softly.

With the fall of Atlanta, the men of Clinch's Cavalry, or what was left of them, were rushed to Savannah in a vain effort to hold it against Sherman's men. Some of them were sent to the defense of Fort McAllister, which stood near the mouth of the Ogeechee River and protected the main waterway approach to Savannah from inland. Once again, the company of Harry and William was not selected. As it turned out, it was a stroke of luck, for most of those assigned to the mission were killed or captured. And once again, Colonel Clinch was wounded. But the two young soldiers seemed to be leading charmed lives. Maybe God had something more important for them to do. Whatever it was, it was clear to both of them that the war was almost over and the South was going to lose.

By the time it finally ended in April 1865, both Harry and William had been promoted to the rank of sergeant, with Harry holding the dangerous but honored position as color sergeant for his unit. They had both served well and long, and they were tired but alive. They could return home and start again. Unlike so many others, they had survived to help try to reshape the region of their birth into a better world.

Once the peace was signed, the two men parted as friends. William had asked to be furloughed in Tallahassee, while Harry chose to go home to Brunswick.

Harry clapped William on the back. "My only regret is that we won't be able to return to Brunswick together as comrades. We won't get to see the shock on the faces of all the busybodies who have gossiped about our family for so many years."

William grinned. "I'd like to see that too. Greet them all for me, won't you?"

"Not if I can avoid them," Harry laughed.

Then, after so many months of training and fighting side-by-side, the two men shook hands and went their separate ways.

There was no longer a train line into Brunswick and the docks were crowded with people, so Harry decided to walk home. It was not that far, only a little more than eighty miles, and the spring weather was invigorating. He figured he could do it in four days, maybe even three. Although he had almost no money, he trusted that he could rely on the kindness of some farmer's wife who might give him a hot meal now and then. Many men and boys on the road just like him were trying to get back to their families. Sometimes they filched from a farmer's field of beans or corn, and occasionally they found wild berries that were beginning to ripen. The men who had taken their own rifles into the war sometimes managed to shoot a rabbit or some other small game. These, they would roast on a spit and share with a few comrades. In normal times, had they not been so spent, it might have been a challenging and even pleasant hike, but not now. It was an ordeal, and most of the men, like Harry, longed for a soft bed and a home-cooked meal at the family table.

CHAPTER 16

Late April, 1865

"It's over, Sylvia. We're going home," John said, after news of General Lee's surrender at Appomattox reached Tebeauville. He had mixed feelings, gladness that the war was over and that they could return to Jekyl, but dread for what he might lose now that the North had won. He had for many years, almost since the birth of their firstborn, Robert, viewed this pretty, dark-skinned woman, his Sylvia, as his common-law wife, and he would have married her in a church if the law allowed, but marriage between the races was forbidden, and he knew that their relationship was considered a scandal in Georgia and throughout the South. It didn't matter. She was the only woman he had ever really known and who had known him so well. He was in his fifties now and Sylvia still in her thirties, but they had six children that bound them together—Robert, Joseph, Caroline, George, and two new ones who had been born during the war, Cecilia in 1862 and

Cornelia in 1864. Their oldest son, Robert, was already in his early twenties and would, John suspected, soon want to find his own wife and settle in his own home.

Sylvia greeted the news of the war's end with her usual placidity, although he thought he detected the barest trace of a smile on her dark lips. Her fears of separation had not come to pass, and they were all still together at the old house in the woods. The older children cheered, for they were eager to get back to Jekyl. They had adapted to the makeshift life they had been compelled to lead during the war, but, like their father, they always thought of Jekyl as their real home.

John stood silent for a moment, watching the shifting shadows cross Sylvia's face. He was never sure what she was thinking, but he felt he needed to say what he suspected was on both their minds.

"You know, Sylvia, you're free now. You and the children—you're all free. You don't have to come with me if you don't want to," John reluctantly reminded her. "You can do whatever you want now, but I'm hoping you'll come back to the island where we can live out the rest of our lives together. I thought our life was good there. People left us alone and we were happy. At least I was, and I hope you were too. I would miss you and the children somethin' awful if you decided to leave." He didn't have to say it perhaps, since she already knew she was free now. But he wanted her to know that he was well aware of the fact that she was no longer his property and that she didn't have to stay. Nevertheless, he hoped fervently that she would choose to remain with him, in spite of her new freedom. Even their children had been legally his slaves. Although they were his own flesh and blood, the fact that their mother had been a slave had made them slaves by law.

John viewed her now as the wife of his heart, and he had come to regret how it had all begun when she was so young. He wasn't sure whether she still harbored ill will toward him about all that. He knew she did at first. He had tried to be more gentle after the first few times, but she was so small. He must have hurt her. He remembered how she had cried, as though her heart were breaking. He hoped that she had forgotten all that and forgiven him. But there were still lingering uncertainties. He had taken her against her will and, as far as he knew, he was the only man she'd ever known in a Biblical way. He hoped his years of caring for her and the children counted for something with her.

"It's your decision," he said. Although she was free and no longer obligated to stay with him, he was also aware that she didn't have a lot of choices, for she had no other means of support.

She stood silent for a moment, as though she were thinking it over. Tears glistened in her eyes as she reached out for his hand. Was she happy? *Had she been happy?* It was not something an enslaved woman could give herself the luxury of thinking about. Now that she was free, she considered his question, but even she wasn't sure of the answer.

"I thank you for sayin' that, John," she said. "I've wanted my freedom all my life. And if I'd had it at the start...." Her voice trailed off. "But we been together now, havin' babies to care for, ever since I was fourteen. We been makin' a family for more'n twenty years now, and we know each other right well. I reckon I can put up with you a little longer."

His shoulders relaxed, and his tensions vanished. It was the closest to a declaration of love either of them had ever shared.

Whatever they may have felt, they both knew that it was now a lifelong commitment, despite the new freedom laws.

"Well then," he said with a grin, "let's go home."

Their return to the island was, for John and Henry, a joyful homecoming. It was theirs now. At long last, they finally owned Jekyl Island, along with their brother Charles in Milledgeville, who took no interest in it, and their sister Eliza. Now that they knew for certain they would not lose their homeplace to their father's new and growing family, that was one worry they would never have to face again.

Once they were back on the island, the first thing John did was to inspect the cabin he had built for his family. He was pleased to find it still standing, though it was overgrown with weeds and vines and in need of repairs. Raccoons had invaded, and it required a thorough cleaning. Still, it was better than the dilapidated old house in the middle of the pine forest they had just left. And it was good to be back. *My boys and I can fix it up again,* John thought. Robert and Joseph were both old enough to help now, and they seemed always willing. He was right proud of them.

John had found in this little house in the woods far more happiness than he'd ever known anywhere else. He didn't need or want all the fancy woodwork, the wallpaper, and the shiny floors that his brother craved and enjoyed in the old family homeplace. His cabin and Sylvia's, as he thought of it, was a simple abode, but it suited them. He could relax there as he never had been able to do at his parents' home—at least since his mother's death. Here he could do whatever he pleased. Even the children could be themselves without fear of damaging some special heirloom his grandparents had brought from France. They could find freedom here that they had found no place else. *There are different kinds of freedom,* he thought. Sylvia received one kind when the war ended. Here they could have another—independence from interference and judgment. Here they had absolute sovereignty over their life choices. He hoped she would savor it as he did.

After supper, when she had finished washing and putting away the dishes, Sylvia walked out to the front porch to sit for a while and watch her two younger boys playing soldiers, using sticks they had picked up in the woods for guns. They knew that black soldiers, once boys like them, had fought in the war. And they wanted to fight too. She was glad they were too young when the war came along.

Things were supposed to be different now. But even though they weren't slaves anymore, nothing had really changed in her life. She remembered the day John had asked her whether she would return to Jekyl with him. With six children by now, what choice did she have? She knew that, in many ways, he treated her better than a lot of men treated their legal wives. Still, without the children, she would have considered trying to live on her own. Perhaps she could have gotten a job as a housemaid in Brunswick or Savannah. Perhaps. But she had heard that those jobs were hard to find now, for most women like her no longer worked in the fields. They sought domestic work instead. But this was not an option for her. With the small amount she might be able to earn, how could she support six children?

In the end, she thought she had made the right choice in coming back. John treated her well enough, and she could do a whole lot worse, she supposed. Despite the way it had begun, it was a fairly decent life. He had kept them all safe and provided for during the war, and he seemed to care about her and their children, even building them their own cabin, larger than any other she had ever lived in. She would never know what her life could have been like, had she taken the children and refused to return. But she had decided to stay, and they would still be a family.

In the days after their return to the island, Henry and John set out to inspect the damage that had been done since their eviction by Charlie Lamar. They had heard about his death in Columbus in the last big battle of the war, one that took place after the peace had been signed at Appomattox and the war was virtually over. But word of the surrender had not reached the troops there, and, as it turned out, Lamar was said to be the last Confederate officer of significant rank to be killed in the war.

"If he had to die," Henry said when they learned the news, "I think he would have been pleased to know that he had fought to the bitter end and beyond. He was a true southern patriot."

"I expect you're right," John said. "But he wanted this war, and it killed a lot of other men besides him, so I don't have much sympathy for him."

As they toured what was left of the plantation after four years of intermittent occupation and neglect, John's oldest son, Robert, accompanied them. As they rode through the barren fields, they talked about how they could organize a new work force.

"Maybe we could persuade some of our people to come back and help," Henry said.

"What do you think, Robert? Do you think anybody would be willing to return?" his father asked.

"I don't know," Robert said. "They're free men now—not slaves. Most of 'em were unhappy before the war. And a lot of folks, now that they're free, they think they don't have to work no more."

"How do they think they're going to feed their families?" Henry asked.

"I don't reckon they've rightly thought about that. Food and clothes was always provided for 'em. Some of 'em don't understand that now they got to work to pay for those things."

"Surely they'll come back. Some of them at least. We were good masters. We treated 'em right," Henry protested.

Robert looked skeptical, remembering a different past of mistrust and occasional beatings "But you was still masters. And for them, there weren't no such thing as a good master. Nobody wanted to be a slave. I don't reckon you can understand that."

"They might be less reluctant to return if it was you who tried try to persuade them, instead of Henry or me," his father said. "Would you be willing to go off the island and see if you could find any of them? You could tell 'em that they would be welcomed back."

"On what terms?" Robert asked. "They's free men now. None of 'em gonna be willin' to work without pay. And a lot of 'em don't live around here no more."

"Son, you know we have no means to pay anyone right now. But we could promise them a share of the crop and whatever income they could derive from it."

"I don't 'spec they'll be willin' to work for nothin' but a promise. What else is you willin' to offer? You got to remember. They ain't slaves no more. They're free men," he said again.

Henry spoke up. "They can live in their old cabins, rent free, and have their own little plots of land—maybe two or three acres. They can grow their own gardens and raise their own pigs and chickens. They can hunt and fish on the island. At least they'd have a roof over their heads and food for their families. And they'd have a cash crop at the end of the growin' season.

Robert agreed to try.

However, despite a month-long effort to persuade any former slaves he could find to come back, most of them refused. They had made other plans—moved in with family members or found work on the docks or at other plantations or farms farther west where they could count on a small income. They didn't want to be reminded of their life as slaves. Some even chose to exercise their new freedom, at least for a while, by doing nothing at all.

Even so, Robert managed to get a few of them to agree to return. It was the only home some of them knew. Like him, they had been born on Jekyl. And they had no other good options. Not at the moment at least.

"Ever'thing'll be better now. Ain't nobody gonna force you to work from sunup to sundown, like they used to," he assured them. It was a new start, he told them in his youthful optimism, on fairer and more equal terms. He hoped with all his heart it was true.

CHAPTER 17

Brunswick, Georgia, April 1865

Now that the dangers had ended, the townspeople of Brunswick were both eager and apprehensive to return home. They weren't sure what to expect. They had heard rumors of much devastation there, but they couldn't be sure. The railroad line between Waynesville and Brunswick was entirely gone, the rails having been removed and used for defense purposes by the Confederate Army. Thus, it was not by train, but in an old farm wagon, that Félicité and her children, with John Eugene driving the horses and her youngest daughters Louise and Cité perched beside him, returned to Brunswick. Félicité and Mary Amelia made themselves as comfortable as possible in the back. They had sold their carriage to pay for necessities and were grateful to have the old wagon, which was large enough to carry them all, for almost every conveyance of any type was in service to bring people and their possessions home. As the wagon pulled into Gloucester

Street, they looked around in dismay and disbelief. The town was nothing like it had been when they had left.

"Oh, Mama," Félicité heard the anguished voice of Mary Amelia and the discouraged groans of her younger children as they looked about. They reflected her own feelings, and no doubt those of everyone coming home. She could hardly believe her eyes. The town lay in a state of desolation. The houses that still stood were in ruin, overgrown with vines and showing signs of rot, the skeletal remains of dead tree limbs lay on crushed roofs. Some of the houses had been fairly new, like her own, and she was shocked that four years of neglect could cause such damage, even though she was aware that in the coastal area, fierce autumn storms and the desiccating heat of summer, things deteriorated much more rapidly than inland. But it wasn't only neglect. They had all heard about the burnings by the Confederates and the bombardment by the Yankees, but seeing the reality of all the damage was quite another matter. Her own house and the one that her sister-in-law Eliza had built next door, would both have to be reconstructed, if not from scratch, at least with major repairs and restoration. She felt overwhelmed by the enormity of the work ahead.

The war had been hard on all the family, but especially on Félicité. The hardships she and her children had faced, the worry for her son and son-in-law in the army, the death of so many good young people—all had crushed her spirits. Her bones ached from the long wagon ride, and she could feel how much she had aged in the past four years. Now, she was thin, weary, and in ill health. Her heart was heavy as she looked over the city, finding it hard to believe the devastation before her eyes. She remembered the story that had been told by a young soldier whose name she could no longer recall, but who had served with the Piscola Volunteers. He had been convalescing in Waynesville after being wounded. The boy was one of those who had seen the destruction firsthand and was eager to talk about it. She already knew that, as soon as the townspeople had evacuated in the early months of 1862, the Confederates had burned the dock and the railroad station to keep the Yankees from using them. But the young soldier also brought new information about Brunswick.

"There's not much left of it, I'm afraid," he had said. He couldn't have been more than nineteen, but his eyes were already haunted by wartime memories. A crowd gathered as he described what he had seen.

"It was only a brief skirmish, or so we thought," he said. "Our unit came across a Union barge at anchor in sight of Brunswick's Camp Semmes. Like the town, it too was deserted. When we got there, we could see Yankee sailors on a sand bar in the Turtle River. We couldn't tell what they were doing, but it looked like they were gathering oysters. We fired on them, and I'm pretty sure we killed a couple. The rest made it back to a larger ship and got away. We thought it was all over, but we soon learned better. The Yankees got back at us by shelling the town. It was awful."

Now, here in front of them, was proof of his words. All that remained were mostly empty hulks of the fine old houses that had once so proudly lined the shaded streets. Now the area was filled with rubble left by the shelling. Almost a century earlier, Brunswick, like Savannah, had been laid out around a series of public squares adorned with fountains and benches, with tall trees and well-tended bushes that in the spring would explode with fragrance and color. How pleasant it had been. She could not hold back her tears.

"Don't worry, Mama, we can rebuild." Mary Amelia put her arm around her mother. Her voice was soft and encouraging, but Félicité knew that her daughter's heart was as heavy as her own, not just from seeing the town in a shambles, but also from the recent death in the battle of Atlanta of a handsome soldier named Jim whom Mary Amelia had met and loved so briefly in Waynesville. They had seemed meant for each other, but in wartime, nothing was as it should be. Her broken-hearted daughter had bravely dried her tears and said, "Perhaps...," her voice hesitating, "perhaps as the oldest daughter, it is my destiny, like Aunt Eliza, never to marry, but to be the maiden lady who looks after everyone else."

Her comment broke Félicité's heart. She had seen Josephine's joy since her marriage, and she knew that Mary Amelia longed for such happiness. But she feared it was not to be. Mary Amelia had loved the young man deeply, but they'd had so little time together, and when news of his death arrived, her daughter's heartbreak was palpable. Félicité embraced her with all a mother's tenderness and love, wondering why God would let such tragedies happen.

Now, with the war ended, there were new things to worry about. What was to be done? Where would they stay? Félicité had no siblings, and her sisters-in-law in Brunswick had also lost their homes.

It was her brother-in-law Henry who unexpectedly came to their rescue. Now that the brief Yankee occupation of Jekyl Island and any further threats had ended, he and John Couper had been among the first to return home.

"By some miracle," Henry told Félicité when he'd heard the family was back in Brunswick and came to find them, "the Yankees didn't burn the big house, despite rumors to the contrary. Thank God for that. Your old house on the island, I'm afraid, is ruined, but you can stay with me until you are able to rebuild." He would be glad for the company, he said. John never stayed there anymore, and there were four bedrooms in the big house.

"If you don't mind sharing, there'll be plenty of space. And we can all support each other through the difficult days ahead. Most of the slaves are gone for good, I'm afraid, but we hope that some of them might come back and be willing to help out," Henry said.

Going back to Jekyl sounded like paradise. Félicité remembered it as a place of peace and healing as it had been for her after Joseph's death. There had been no fighting there and little to remind them of the war, except for the fortifications that had been built. But there were also practical considerations.

"How will we all live, Henry?" Félicité asked. "For now at least we have no income."

"There are stray cattle left and deer and other game on the island, so we'll have meat. And we'll plant some corn and a vegetable garden. We'll manage. I'm even going to try to grow a little cotton. Your children are all old enough to help out now." She had a passing concern that his motive was less altruistic and more practical as he sought help in what was probably a hopeless endeavor. But she quickly brushed it aside. He only wanted to help his brother's family, she was sure. All of them were adults or almost adults now. Though three of them were not yet twenty-one, they were strong and hearty. Even John Eugene, at only fifteen, could almost pass for a twin of his older brother, except for the beard. He had grown nearly to the height of a man and learned by wartime necessity to do what men did. Until his brother's return, he considered himself the man of the family. But there were still so many things to worry about.

"What about your sisters—Catherine, Sarah, and Eliza?" she asked her brother-in-law.

"They have their husbands' families to depend on—all but Eliza. They'll be fine. Eliza can come too, unless she decides to stay with Catherine, but it's mostly you and your children I'm worried about."

She was grateful. Henry could be prickly at times, but he had loved his brother Joseph, and she felt sure that, deep down, he and John would do whatever they could to help their family. Thus, the decision was made. *It's amazing,* Félicité thought, *how Jekyl Island always seems to be our refuge when we need it.* And they needed it now.

Before they left for the island, Félicité and her children picked through the remains of their Brunswick house to see what they could salvage that might be useful at Jekyl, but there was almost nothing left that wasn't ruined by canon fire, rot, or exposure to rain. They had little more than the belongings they had been able to take with them when they first evacuated, and there hadn't been room in the wagon for all of those.

Thus, that sunny day in early summer, when they boarded the boat to make their way through the marshes, already greening to their springtime hue, her family had little to offer, except themselves. Félicité knew that she personally wouldn't be of much use, in her condition, but Henry was right. The children could help, and she would do what she could. Compared to what they had been through and what they faced in Brunswick, Jekyl sounded like paradise.

CHAPTER 18

On the road from Savannah to Brunswick, Georgia, April 1865

It took four and a half days to walk home. Harry had developed blisters on both feet, but he was nearly there. He had slept in barns and in the open air, occasionally bathing in a cold stream along the way when he could stand his own stench no longer. Now finally, weary and footsore, he was almost to Brunswick, and he felt his spirits rise. He hoped William had made it safely to Tallahassee and that he would find his Lottie there waiting to welcome him home.

Harry tried to imagine the surprised reaction of anyone who knew both young men if they had seen them limping together back into Brunswick in their filthy uniforms. The very thought made him laugh. Everyone in town, it seemed, knew of the infamous affair between Harry's grandfather and William's mother, Sarah Aust, and then, after the death of his wife Amelia, how his grandfather had shocked the community once again by not marrying Sarah, his mistress of ten years, but rather her twenty-year-old daughter, Mary, from an earlier marriage. That alone would have been enough to start tongues wagging, but the fact that he was in his sixties and she was pregnant with his child only added greater indignation to community gossip.

Any friendship between William and Harry would have been unthinkable before the war, for despite their blood relationship, their families had nothing to do with each other. *War can make strange bedfellows,* Harry thought with a smile. His friendship with William had caught them both unaware when they found themselves together as new recruits in the Glynn Guards, but in retrospect, he thought it made sense. They not only shared a bloodline. They had mustered in on the same day. They were the same age, both born on Jekyl Island only months apart in 1843. As two of the youngest men in the company, they had bonded easily. As comrades-in-arms, they trained together, marched together, and fought side-by-side, discovering in the process that they had much more in common than disreputable family connections.

Perhaps the most pleasant thing they shared was their memory of the island, where they had spent much of their childhoods. It was the place where they had walked the same beaches and scoured the same land for Indian relics. They had swum in Jekyl's ocean surf and fished in its creeks. And they had known many of the same people, black and white alike, as they were growing up. Then, they had risked their lives together and, in the process, come to like and trust one another. It seemed so natural.

As he entered the town of Brunswick, Harry was shocked to see his home and his town almost in ruins. He had heard about the skirmish in 1862 between Confederate and Union troops that had resulted in the Yankees' burning of a railroad bridge nearby, but he had not known about the shelling of the town. He suspected that it looked even worse since it had been neglected for so long during the years when all the residents had taken refuge elsewhere. Given the condition of the town, he was crestfallen. He had looked forward to joyful greetings from his family, the good food of home, and sleeping in his own bed. Now he faced only disappointment and uncertainty.

He was somewhat heartened to see that a few people were already making efforts toward recovery—neighbors helping neighbors to remove the rubble so they could begin to rebuild. But it was obvious that no one was working on his own family's home on Union Street, the house his mother had built just before they moved back to Brunswick after his father's death. He'd make sure they saw to it right away.

He stood there, dismayed, before its empty devastation. Some of it was still standing, but it was in dire need of reconstruction. Suddenly he caught sight of the familiar face of their old neighbor Urbanus Dart, who was giving instructions to the workers clearing debris away from his property. He seemed many years older now, more stooped than the proud upright man he remembered. When the old man caught sight of him, he hurried over.

"I'm glad to see you back safe and sound, Harry."

"I hear you served as well."

"Well, at my age there wasn't much I could do, but I did what I could."

"Has your son made it home yet?"

"He has, I'm happy to say. And we welcomed him back with open arms, and a few joyful tears from the ladyfolk. Our families were among the lucky ones." He grinned. "Speaking of which, are you looking for your family?"

"I am. Do you know where they are?" the young man asked.

"I believe they're staying on Jekyl Island with your uncles," Dart said.

"Really? I'm glad to hear they're safe. Thank you so much, Mr. Dart. Do you have any idea where I might find a boat to take me there?"

"There are freedmen swarming the docks who'll be pleased to row you to the island—for a sum, of course. Do you have any money at all?" He eyed Harry's dirty, well-worn uniform with skepticism.

"I'm afraid not. I had only a little when I mustered out, but it's all gone now. Most of the time, good farm ladies would feed me for free, but sometimes not."

"Well," said Dart, reaching into his pocket. "Maybe this will help." He held out to him a handful of silver coins—not Confederate money, but U.S. currency saved from before the war.

"I can't thank you enough, Mr. Dart. And it's only a loan. I'll pay it back as soon as I get settled."

"Don't worry about it, son. I'm just glad to see you home safely. I hope you find your family in good shape. Give them my regards."

When Harry stepped out of the cypress pirogue at Jekyl and paid the black boatmen, he felt he had come home. The first person he saw near the dock was his uncle Henry, who greeted him warmly.

"Is that you, my boy?" his uncle asked. "I wouldn't have recognized you anywhere else. You've changed."

The young man nodded. How different he must look, for now he had a full beard, a rather scraggly one after his time on the road. He had seen a lot of terrible things during his years in the army, and he was no longer the naïve young man he had been when he first went away.

"Well, I'm four years older, but you look just the same, Uncle Henry. It's good to see you. I've been told that my mother is here, with my brother and sisters. Do you know where they're staying?"

"They're with me, of course, at the big house. Your old house was all but demolished by Yankee soldiers living there. Damn pigs, those Yankees. So how're you doing, my boy? You look fit enough, though a bit thin. But we can fatten you up and have you right as rain in no time."

Harry grinned. "I'll count on that, Uncle Henry. Now, I'd mainly like to see my family."

"Well, I reckon they'd like to see you as well. Your mama has been worried that she hadn't heard from you in a month of Sundays."

"Well, we kept moving around. It was hard to find time to write. Then I had to walk home from Savannah."

"Well, let's get on back to the house and see if we can find them."

As they made their way toward the big house, Harry savored every pine tree, every live oak, the wildflowers that dotted the roadway, and the earthy smell of the plough mud and marsh grass swaying near the shore. How he had missed this island. It flooded him with joyful memories of his childhood, his father, the happy times and the melancholy times his family had spent here when he was a boy. He thought of those Sunday walks to the north-end cemetery and the sweet moments he had shared there with his mother, sisters, and little brother. Not many boys could claim the wonders he had known on these shores and in the woods and along the inland waterways so rich in life and so nourishing to the spirit. Perhaps once again, now that this horrible war had ended, he could find true peace here.

His feeling of well-being was shattered, however, when he saw the ravaged face and bent form of his mother. When he had left to join the army, she had been still pretty, young-looking despite her fifty years, and vibrant with life. Now she was a shadow of her former self. Her hair was gray. Her cheeks were sunken, her face pale, with wrinkles etched around her eyes and mouth. She was thin and frail and looked nothing like the mother he had left behind.

"Are you all right, Mama?" he asked.

"I'm fine, son, and even finer now that I see you home again, alive and well." His sisters smothered him in enthusiastic embraces and kisses, while his brother stood back to wait his turn.

"Good grief, John Eugene," Harry said. "Is that you? What happened to little Johnny? You've grown a foot. You're as tall as I am now."

"Welcome home, brother," the boy said, grinning broadly. "I'm glad you're back. We've missed you." They gave each other friendly slaps on the back and finally a hug.

Later in the day, after all the initial fuss was over, Harry walked with his sister, Mary Amelia, to the front porch overlooking the marsh and out of hearing from the others.

"What's wrong with Mama?" he asked.

"Well, at first I thought it was just worry over the war, the uncertainty, all the loss that was wearing her down, but now, to be truthful, I think she may be really ill. It just seems to eat away at her, and she's getting weaker and weaker."

"Has she seen a doctor?"

"I tried to persuade her, but she didn't want to bother any doctor in Waynesville when there were so many wounded soldiers to care for. She's grown worse in the past year. And she seems to have lost her will to live. I hope she'll improve now that you and Newton are both home safely. She can stop worrying so much. And I'm sure Uncle Robert will insist on examining her when the Hazlehursts return from the plantation where they took refuge."

"So Newton made it home already?" His sister nodded.

Harry knew his brother-in-law had enjoyed a fairly easy assignment during the war. He not been compelled to leave Georgia in his service, though once, as they feared Sherman was about to invade Augusta, his commander had ordered the arsenal moved to Savannah. As it turned out, however, Sherman avoided Augusta altogether and went straight to Savannah instead.

"I heard about that terrible explosion in the munitions factory at the Augusta Arsenal several years back," Harry said, "but when I didn't hear from the family, I assumed Newton was all right."

Mary Amelia laughed. "It scared Josephine to death, of course. The explosion killed some people, but Newton's fine. She spent a lot of her time in Augusta with her husband, but when Sherman left Atlanta and began to head in their direction, he sent her and their baby to us in Waynesville.

"Baby? You mean I'm an uncle?"

"You sure are. To the cutest baby boy, born last August. They named him Joseph for Papa. We call him Joey." Mary Amelia smiled, a proud aunt. "As soon as the war ended, Newton turned over the Arsenal to a Yankee General, a fellow named Steadman from Ohio. Then he came home to fetch Josephine and the baby. Now they're back in Savannah. I'm hoping they'll come home before long. But I expect they're just enjoying the peace and quiet for a few months."

"They're still there?"

"They wanted a second honeymoon and talked about going back to Charleston, but Newton warned her that the awful fire there in 1861 had destroyed much of the city. He thought it would be disheartening to go there again. He said, 'Let's just keep our wonderful memories intact.' Then he suggested they go to Savannah instead, where he had some business to attend to."

"I've heard there was a fire this year in Savannah too—back in January, I think."

"That's true, but the damage was not as great as the one in Charleston, or so I'm told, and it was limited to the western part of the city. They say the main part of the town is still intact."

"I hope that's true," Harry said. "I guess Newton will start looking for a new career when they get back. Maybe that's what he's doing now. I don't think anyone will do well as a planter anymore. But he's smart, and he'll have plenty of good ideas. I guess I'll need to give it some thought myself."

"Probably. He and Josephine will also be trying to find a new place to live, I imagine, and maybe even add to their family."

"What about you?" her brother asked, with a teasing smile and raised eyebrows. "Any prospects along those lines?" He had always thought her as pretty as Josephine with her dark blue eyes and sandy hair, but as far as he knew, she had not had a serious beau.

Her eyes suddenly filled with tears. "I lost the only prospect I ever wanted in the battle of Atlanta."

"Oh, Mary Amelia, I'm so sorry. I should keep my big mouth shut."

"No, it's all right. There are a lot of grieving women and widows now. I fit right in."

"Will you tell me about him sometime?"

She tried to smile. "Sometime maybe. But not today. You've just come home, and we all want to be happy for a change."

It was at dinner that night when they learned that their grandfather had signed the island over to his three living sons and his unmarried daughter. The matter came up during a conversation about what they all hoped to accomplish now that the war was over.

"Now that John and I each own our section of the island," Henry Jr. said cheerfully, "we are hoping to manage even better."

The young people sat in silence for a moment, exchanging looks of shock and surprise. It was Harry, his face pale, who finally spoke, "You own it? Our grandfather has turned over ownership of the island to you?"

"Well, not just us. A part of it belongs to your uncle Charles and to your aunt Eliza."

"When did that happen? And how?" Harry asked.

"John and I went to visit him in 1863 and convinced him that it was the right thing to do. After all, we took care of the plantation for well over a decade," Henry said, a bit defensively.

"There is no plantation anymore, Uncle Henry," Harry reminded him. "You have slaves no more. The entire system has vanished. We thought the land would be divided at his death among all his children."

"He thought that only his sons should inherit, for the daughters are married and have someone else to take care of them—all but Eliza, of course. And he signed over thirty acres to her."

"Our father was his son as well. We'd all hoped *his* share would be divided among his children," Harry said. "The island is certainly large enough, and we all feel attached to it."

His uncle Henry's jaw tightened and he looked annoyed by Harry's words. "He chose to divide it among his *living* children," he finally said.

"I see," said Harry, trying hard to keep disappointment out of his voice, as he remembered the almost-magical feeling of watching the moon rise over the ocean and the kiss of the gentle surf on his bare feet. At such moments, he had felt it all belonged to him. The island had always been his true family home. He remembered how his spirits had been crushed when his mother had told him they were leaving the island and moving into Brunswick. John Eugene had been equally upset. Now they were losing it again.

A long moment of silence settled around the table. Then, John Eugene laid his napkin beside his plate, and stood up, fighting off tears that were trying to form in his eyes. His jaw was set, and his face was flushed.

"Please excuse me," he said. His mother nodded, even though his plate was still half full. He let himself quietly out the front door and went outside to walk in the darkness.

Félicité and her children returned to Brunswick as soon as possible. They all agreed that while the situation was not the fault of their uncles, but rather the result of their grandfather's indifference, nonetheless they felt less welcome now that the family home belonged to Uncle Henry. Harry and John Eugene were far more upset than their sisters, who were quite content to move back to Brunswick. But the two of them had never wanted to leave, not even now. As boys, they had wanted to stay and grow up in the freedom and beauty of the island, as their father had. Harry, like all his sisters, had been born there, and John Eugene, despite the fact of his birth in Brunswick, was so fiercely attached to Jekyl that he always claimed that he too had been born on the island. It was where their earliest childhood memories lay. He remembered how he and his brother had looked for sea turtles on the beach and alligators in the ponds. And how they had seen baby turtles dig their way out of the sand and scurry toward the ocean. It was a place of enchantment for them both as ever-curious little boys, and it stung that his family had been cut out of any share of the island by his grandfather. *It just isn't fair,* he thought. He remembered how John Eugene had looked when the two of them had discussed it all. And he would never forget the determination on his brother's young face when he said, sounding older than his years, "Someday, somehow, you and I, we'll rectify all this."

Fine houses were beginning to rise again on the streets of Old Town. Félicité wanted to restore their home right away, but she was just too tired to do what needed to be done. She turned the matter over to her oldest son and daughter, Harry and Mary Amelia, who set out to have it built back just as it was before.

When the Hazlehursts returned to Brunswick, and Robert had a chance to examine Félicité, he could only shake his head.

"There's nothing I can do," he informed her family. "It looks like a cancer, and it's only a matter of time, I'm afraid. She's in God's hands." He and Catherine both insisted that Félicité come and live with them so that he could care for her more easily. Mary Amelia stayed there with her mother and her aunts Catherine and Eliza, while the others went to live in their partially restored house. Josephine and Newton had returned immediately with baby Joey as soon as they learned of her mother's illness. He was Félicité's only grandchild, and they knew she would want to enjoy a little time with him.

Her condition worsened day by day. As death drew near, her sons and daughters all gathered around her bed at the Hazlehurst home to say their last goodbyes. The last thing she saw was the tear-glazed eyes of her children. Her final words were, "No tears now. Be happy for me. I'm going to be with your father." But they could not help the tears that flowed despite her wishes.

"She was such a good mother," Josephine said, wiping her eyes. "I only hope I can be half as good a mother as she was."

Newton put his arm around her. "Of course you will," he whispered.

Mary Amelia said to her sister, "After Papa died, I can remember how she grieved. At least now they're together," she said.

"But she was so young—just fifty-four," Josephine said in a teary voice. "It breaks my heart that she didn't even live to see all of us grow up."

"She'll still be watching over us, and we'll look after the younger ones and make sure they're all taken care of," her sister Mary Amelia assured her. Three of them had not yet reached the age of twenty-one— Cité, Louise, and John Eugene, who was the youngest at only sixteen.

They buried their mother in Oak Grove cemetery, not far from the center of town and within easy walking distance of the home they were rebuilding. They had considered burying her at Jekyl Island, where her husband lay, but they no longer had the freedom to do so without seeking permission from an uncle. In the end, they decided instead to lay her to rest in Brunswick, where most of them would likely be buried one day as well. It rained the day of the funeral, as though the skies were weeping with her family. It was impossible to tell the raindrops on their faces from their tears.

CHAPTER 19

Brunswick, Georgia, October 1865

Even as Félicité's children mourned their mother, they could see Brunswick coming to life once more. The war was over, and a new world was being born in Georgia. They were all young and eager to put the painful years of the past behind them. They only wished their mother were still alive to give them advice and spur them along, Harry in particular. He felt torn in two. He was inconsolable over the loss of his mother, and it was difficult for him to find his way again. Along with his brother and sisters, his brother-in-law Newton made an effort to cheer him up.

"I know it's hard, Harry, but look at all the opportunities of this new era we live in," Newton said. "You need to consider your options. We all have to start over. The question is how. I've thought about it a lot, and with all the building going on around here, I've decided to start a new lumber company. Look at all the virgin pine trees in this area. It's a clear opportunity. You can work for me if you like, at least until you figure out what you want to do." Perhaps giving the young man something constructive to do would lift his spirits. Newton had made many investments during the war, but he had lost most of them when the Yankees took over. He was eager to get a new start and always optimistic that he would succeed.

Harry took the job, but he was still having a hard time getting over the loss of his mother. He had seen so much death and dying in the past four years that he had hoped to be spared all that once he came home. Yet he had barely returned before he was compelled to witness the last stages of the slow and painful process of his mother's dying. He took it harder than anyone else in the family, because he had been away for so long and had missed her last good years. Even those years hadn't really been good, for she had constant worries, he knew, about the war and the survival of her family. Like everyone else, he longed for the way things used to be, when all her children were with her and they were all safe. He felt that he had contributed to her demise by his insistence on enlisting so early in the war, but he had thought it his duty. Now he felt conflicted and even a bit guilty, ashamed of the fact that he mourned the loss of Jekyl almost as much as he mourned his mother's death. He had fallen into a state of depression that he was having a hard time casting off.

All his sisters were eager to cheer Harry up and see him get on with his life. They were sad as well, but not morose, as he seemed to be. They were determined to help him find happiness in life again, just as they were eager to do for themselves. His two younger sisters, Louise and Cité, whose name was a shortened version of her mother's, were both eager to seek the kinds of pleasures they thought young women should have—parties, dances, pretty dresses—all of which they had been too young to enjoy before the war. Now that

Louise was nineteen and Cité seventeen and the world was at peace again, they felt their time had come.

Thus, when they were invited in the spring of 1866 to visit a friend in Savannah, they were excited and eager to go. They were tired of the ruins, tired of all the noise of the building that was going on throughout the neighborhood, and tired of missing out on all the diversions and delights young people should experience, but which were still rare in Brunswick. They pleaded with Mary Amelia, who had taken over as a mother-figure for her younger siblings. She finally allowed them to go, if only so they would stop pestering her. She understood their longing to be carefree in their youth.

While they were in Savannah, the sisters enjoyed parties and balls celebrating the end of the war, though Savannah too was filled with the noise of rebuilding. At one of the fashionable *soirées* they attended during their stay, they met a vivacious young woman about their age by the name of Alice Symons, though her friends all called her Bama. The two sisters were quite charmed by their new friend, who had been born in Brunswick but had moved to Savannah as a young girl. The three quickly became fast friends, and Cité impulsively invited Alice to come to their home for a visit.

"I wish you could come back with us to Brunswick," she said.

"Oh yes, Bama, do come. We'd have such fun," Louise said.

"I'd really love to, but I need to spend Easter with my mother. It's even more important since we lost my father. He died just before the war, and Mama is still in mourning. Perhaps I could come in late April if that would suit you. I haven't been back to Brunswick since I was a child. One of the few people I remember is your grandfather," she told Louise.

The DuBignon sisters glanced at one another, both wondering what she had heard about their grandfather, whose reputation, they both knew, still remained unsavory. They hadn't seen him for ages, but they had heard the terrible stories about his past and feared that Alice had as well. But she made no mention of that.

"I saw him once when I was just a little girl. It was a long time ago, but it's a rather vivid memory. I was with my parents somewhere near the docks, and I heard my mother say to my father, 'Here comes old Col. DuBignon from Jekyl island.' He was with a group of men, and I remember tugging on my mother's sleeve and asking, 'Which one is he?' for I had heard stories about him before."

Neither sister asked what kind of stories. But Alice went on, describing the scene. "Mother said, 'He's the short man with the long cloak and the silver-headed cane.' I'll never forget seeing him that day. He looked so distinguished and so different from the others. I never thought I'd meet his granddaughters one day."

"Well, now you have," Cité laughed.

"And now I have, and I'm so glad."

Alice was pretty with dark shiny hair, merry eyes, lips the color of rosy camellias, and a lively smile for everyone. Louise, like Cité, was very fond of her and wanted Alice to come for her good company, but she also had another motive, which she shared only with her sister.

"Perhaps she might perk Harry up," she told her sister. "He's been so sad since Mama died, and I know that he also sometimes wakes up with nightmares about the war. Maybe a pretty girl would distract him."

Their oldest brother was twenty-two now, five years older than Alice, but during his earlier years, he, like his sisters, had missed so many chances to be young and carefree. He'd been at war and had few opportunities to meet and court young girls. He knew little about women. His sisters thought him a handsome young man, though as Louise pointed out to her sister with a laugh, "We might be a bit biased."

"I don't think so. But let's let Alice judge for herself," said Cité.

And so Alice Symons—Bama—traveled to Brunswick for a month-long visit in April 1866. Cité and Louise together ushered her into the newly-restored parlor and introduced her to Mary Amelia and John Eugene. Only their older brother was missing.

"Where's Harry?" Louise asked.

"I'm not sure," said Mary Amelia. "He was here earlier, but I don't know where he's disappeared to."

In fact, he had been watching for their arrival from an upstairs window. His sisters had talked about this Alice Symons, this Bama, so much that he wanted a chance to have a look at this paragon of perfection before he met her so he could judge for himself. He was shocked by what he saw. She was certainly pretty. There was no doubt about that, but he had never seen such rosy lips and cheeks. And her eyes were so large and full of life. It just didn't look natural. *And what kind of nickname is Bama anyhow?* he thought.

Finally, after Louise had shown Alice to the guest room and left her to unpack, she went to look for her brother. She found him still crouched on the window seat staring out the window.

"Harry, I want you to come and meet our guest," she said.

"I saw her come down the walk, and, frankly, I was shocked that you asked her here."

"Shocked? Why on earth—"

"She's painted by God! No well-bred young lady would go out in public like that. Wearing rouge on her cheeks and lips!" He was outraged.

Louise laughed. "She's not painted, silly. That's her natural color. Isn't she beautiful?"

"Are you sure?" he asked suspiciously.

"Of course I'm sure. I just wish I had her beautiful skin and coloring. And she's very talented to boot. She's smart, and she plays the piano like a dream. Now you stop acting like a ninny and come downstairs to meet her. Right now she's unpacking her things, but she'll be down in a minute. Don't be such an oaf. Come and act civilized," she scolded.

With a sheepish look, he followed her down the stairs and into the parlor. Only a few moments later, Alice came down as well. As she descended the stairs, Harry couldn't take his eyes off her. She looked lovely in a light blue cotton dress, trimmed with darker blue lace around the neckline and sleeves. Her brown hair fell in long curls to her shoulders, and her eyes were bright with anticipation. She was smiling and looked eager for whatever adventure lay ahead. He thought she was the most beautiful girl he had ever seen.

"Bama, this is our brother Henry Riffault, better known as Harry," Cité said.

"I'm so happy to meet you," the young woman said and held out her hand. He could see now that he was closer that her color was indeed completely natural and vivid compared to his paler sisters. He took her proffered hand and gave a polite bow, but he could think of absolutely nothing to say. *She must think me a complete dolt*, he thought.

Finally, he found his voice, though it sounded awkward and

unnatural to him. "Cité tells me that you are an accomplished pianist. I'd love to hear you play sometime."

"I'd be happy to—" she began.

"Well, not now," said his sister. "We're going for a drive so I can show Bama around Brunswick. She hasn't been here since she was a child. Would you be willing to bring the carriage around and come with us?" she asked her brother.

"Of course, but I'm afraid there isn't much to see," Harry said. "So much of the town was damaged or destroyed during the war. I hardly recognized it when I returned. Even our house isn't what it used to be."

"Not yet, but we're still working on it" said Mary Amelia. "The death of our mother was a blow, but we're trying to put things back together as best we can just as she had built it. We miss her so." As the oldest daughter, she had taken over the role of running the household now and overseeing meals and housekeeping. They didn't have many servants, but Beulah had agreed to remain as their cook. They now paid her a small wage, of course, and they had hired a cleaning woman who came in twice a week.

"I'm so sorry about your mother. There were so many losses because of this dreadful war," Alice said. "You're so kind to invite me here at such a time. You must still be mourning her loss."

"We are. I'm just glad I got home in time to see her before she—" Harry could say no more. He cleared his throat to regain his composure.

"But she would have wanted us to get on with life as soon as possible." It was Mary Amelia who spoke.

"I wish you could have met her," said Harry.

"So do I," Alice said, looking with sympathy into his eyes. "I've heard a lot of good things about her from your sisters." There was a momentary silence.

"But we're recovering, and there are a lot of buildings in the works." Again, it was Mary Amelia trying to lighten the mood.

"If we ever get it all put together again, I think Brunswick will be a better place. It wasn't very large to begin with. But I think it will bustle again," Harry said, his eyes brighter than his sisters had seen them in a long time. "Now I'll go get the horse hitched up and we'll be on our way." They no longer had a regular coachman. Harry and John Eugene took care of the horses now.

There was not enough room in the small, new carriage for all of them. Mary Amelia urged them to go without her. "I have some things I need to take care of. All of you go, and I'll have some free time to get them done."

Harry was touched by how determined she was to hold the family together.

"Tell you what, Johnny. I'll hitch up the horses, and you can drive. That way I can show Alice all the sights, such as they are."

"Well, we're going along too," Cité reminded him.

"I know, but you've been in Savannah for nearly a month, and things have changed even while you were away," Harry teased. "Tell you what, you can point out the sights, and I'll tell her about all the things you leave out."

She laughed. "If there are any."

The next evening before dinner, Harry wandered out to the front porch for a breath of spring air. There, seated in one of the wicker rockers was Alice Symons, reading a book. An oil lamp on the table beside her illuminated her face.

"What are you reading?" he asked.

She laughed. "Actually, it's a children's book called *Alice's Adventures in Wonderland*. My mother gave it to me before I left Savannah."

"Why would she give you a children's book?" he asked.

"She said, 'I want you to know there's another Alice in the world who's just as mischievous as you.' I suppose she must have thought me a naughty little girl." Alice laughed. "You must think me childish to be reading such a book, but actually it's fascinating and quite funny. Rather a sophisticated tale for children, I think."

"You must tell me about it sometime," he said.

"Oh, I think you should read it for yourself. It would sound far too absurd in the telling."

"You could read me a passage instead." He liked the sound of her voice.

"Well," she smiled. "Perhaps just a brief one." She leafed through several pages, until her eyes lit on a particular excerpt. "Now listen carefully."

She began to read in her lively tone.

> "You are old, Father William," the young man said,
> "And your hair has become very white;
> And yet you incessantly stand on your head—
> Do you think, at your age, it is right?"
>
> "In my youth," Father William replied to his son,
> "I feared it might injure the brain;
> But, now that I'm perfectly sure I have none,
> Why, I do it again and again."

He laughed. "Is it all in rhyme like that?"

"No, just parts of it, but it's very clever. All about a little girl who grows and shrinks, caterpillars that talk, smiling Cheshire cats, white rabbits who are always late, and quite entertaining tea parties. It's amusing for adults as well as children, I think."

Harry was delighted to hear her talk and to find a young lady who was not only extraordinarily attractive, but one who also played the piano and could discuss books with such eloquence. Nor was she embarrassed to be caught reading a children's book. She seemed very sure of herself. *A rare young lady indeed*, he thought.

"I must read it. Who is the author?"

"An English writer who signs his books as Lewis Carroll. I do hope he writes another."

One evening the following week, he found himself sitting beside her on the front porch in a relaxed silence, lost in his thoughts and enjoying the fragrance of the replanted gardenias just beyond the porch railing. A chorus of crickets chirped their night music, and fireflies flickered like stars lighting the garden. The only other light came from the floor-to-ceiling windows that opened onto the porch.

Finally Harry turned to Alice, whom he refused to call Bama. "Did you spend the entire war in Savannah?" he asked.

"Most of it," she said, "My mother was reluctant to move, since my father was buried there, but when Sherman's army drew closer, she decided it was wiser to leave. We'd heard awful stories about him and his men. Fortunately, we had a friend with an inland plantation, who invited us to take refuge there, which we did. We stayed for several months, but as soon as the war ended, Mother wanted to go home again." Alice had a far-off look in her eye, full of untold stories she wasn't eager to share.

"I'm so sorry about your father," he said quietly.

"Thank you. You know what it's like."

"I do."

They sat in silence for a few moments. Then she said, "Your sisters told me you served in Clinch's Cavalry."

"That's right."

"I've heard that you saw a lot of action."

"I did. Mostly small battles, except for Atlanta, but I lost many friends. It's good to be home again with the war at an end."

"Do you think the war was worth it—all the devastation and death?"

"I'd hate to think so many gave their lives for something of no value. I know we all miss the old ways, but, despite the sacrifice and suffering we went through, I am glad to see an end to slavery. I also think the South has finally learned that a fighting spirit can be better used in peacetime than in wartime," he said.

"What do you mean?" she asked.

"Well, look at Brunswick now—all the things that are happening amidst the ruin, a new town rising like a phoenix, all the new enterprises people are undertaking, all the determination to survive," he said. "It may take us a while to find our way, but we will, and in the end, we'll be the better for it."

"I like your positive spirit. Most everyone I know sits around and mourns for the old South, for the way things used to be, but you…you view an even brighter future."

"It won't be the same as it was," Harry said, "but I don't think we could go on forever building wealth on the backs of enslaved people. My family never had a lot of slaves—a few house servants, but no plantation with field workers. I'm glad they're free now."

"I thought your family owned an island plantation off the coast."

"That was my grandfather. And we lived there for a while, but now he's signed it over to his surviving sons. Unfortunately, my family got no part of it, since my father died long before the land was divided." His tone was grim.

"I'm so sorry," she said. "Your sisters told me how much you loved the island."

"I do. We all did, and we were all disappointed, of course. It's a very special and beautiful place. We didn't even know it had happened until after the war, and by then it was too late even to be part of the discussion or the decision. The deed was done."

"I've heard all about your father from your sisters. He sounds like a wonderful man," she said, steering the conversation away from the loss of the island.

"He was, but I was so young when he died—only seven. At least you and I were old enough to remember our fathers, but John Eugene doesn't remember him at all. He was only a year old. Papa took good care of us and fortunately had the foresight to make some sound investments in Brunswick. Financially we're probably better off now than my uncles who depend only on raising cotton. But times change, and I guess people have to change with them."

"I supposed it's more difficult to do that when you get older. But we're young. We can adapt more easily," she said.

"That's right, and we will. I'm not afraid of the future, and I don't mourn the past—only the lives that were lost in a fruitless struggle. In the end, I think it's a good thing that our country survives as a single nation, however painful it seems right now."

"A lot of people wouldn't agree, but you've given me a lot to think about," she said.

Over the following weeks they often had such talks and exchanged many ideas. Harry was as impressed with her intelligence as he was with her beauty. He had never met a woman, except for his sisters, who had such a lively mind and quick wit, especially for one so young. She was only seventeen. *In fact*, he thought, *it's she who gives me a lot to think about.*

CHAPTER 20

Brunswick, Georgia, early May 1866

Alice proved to be a popular visitor in Brunswick homes, and news of her talent at the piano spread quickly. At every social event where the hosts owned a piano, she was invited to play. Her favorite composer was Mozart, but she could play popular tunes as well and knew most of them by memory. People were always requesting songs like "Camptown Races" and "O Susanna." Alice played them with charming gusto at nearly every gathering, the young people grouping around the piano to sing or even sometimes dance to the lilting music. She was a most welcome guest but her visit was nearing its end. She was scheduled to be back in Savannah in mid-May.

"Oh, can't you stay longer, Bama? We'll miss you so," Louise urged.

"I've been underfoot in your home far too long." Alice laughed. "I suspect your sisters and brothers will be glad to get rid of me."

"No!"

"Not at all."

"We'd love you to stay on." A chorus of persuasion from Mary Amelia, Louise, Cité, and their brothers.

"You're all so kind, but I don't want to outstay my welcome."

Harry most of all was sad that it was nearly time for her departure. He had become very fond of her during the month she had spent with his family. He loved to hear her soft but lively laughter. He'd come to appreciate the vibrant yet delicate colors of her lips, the clear honesty in her eyes, and the gentle sincerity in her voice, as well as her eagerness to learn and share new ideas. She was for him like a flowing stream of sweet water to a thirsty man. How could he let her leave without some guarantee she would return?

That evening the Schlatter family, their home now fully rebuilt and once more a graceful haven, invited the DuBignon family and their guest along with several other neighborhood families to a festive farewell gala for Alice. After a lovely buffet supper and a great deal of conversation, Frances Schlatter asked Alice to play, and she graciously agreed. After several lively pieces, the tone of the music suddenly changed. She played Debussy's "Clair de Lune" and then her favorite piece by Chopin, his Etude Number 3 in E major. Harry listened, letting the music wash over him, its haunting melody making him even more aware of his sadness at her impending departure. She played it with such tenderness, he thought, as though she were speaking to him alone. He could feel tears welling in his eyes, and he had to fight to hold them back.

Finally, he could stand it no longer. He took a scrap of paper from his pocket, wrote a quick note, and folded it. Then he tapped a little boy sitting on a footstool near him and handed him the note.

"Would you take this to the young lady at the piano?"

The boy nodded, waiting for the final notes of the piece she was playing. Then, while the guests applauded, he stepped quickly up to the piano stool and handed the note to Alice. Harry watched her reaction with trepidation. She read the note. He saw her eyes widen and her lips part in surprise, then slowly reshape into a smile. She looked at him and lowered her head. *Was that a nod?* he wondered. His heart seemed to stop. *Was she saying yes?* He couldn't be sure. She tucked the note into her bodice and turned back to the piano.

He immediately recognized the piece as she began to play Mozart's lively "Minute Waltz." It was the happiest of tunes and the briefest in her repertoire. By the time it ended and she had risen to accolades from the piano bench, he was at her side, holding out to her a cup of champagne punch.

She smiled at him. "Was that a serious message?" she asked.

"Absolutely," he said, longing desperately to kiss those rose-pink lips, though he didn't dare do it here in the Schlatters' parlor with so many people standing around. It would cause a scandal. Instead, he bent over and kissed her fingertips, hoping people would take it as a tribute to her talent. "You can answer my question on the way home," he whispered.

When the party ended, as they walked together back to the family home on Union Street, he asked eagerly. "Did I see you nod? Was that a yes? Will you really marry me?"

"I will indeed," she said firmly. "With great happiness, *if* my mother approves."

"Shall we tell the others tonight?" he asked.

"Let's do. I hope they'll be pleased."

And they were. His sisters all greeted the news with squeals, bounces, and hugs

"I'm so happy," Cité said. "Now you'll be part of our family forever."

"*If* my mother approves," Alice reminded them.

She left on a steamer two days later to return to Savannah, taking the news of her engagement with her. Harry waited with trepidation for her first letter. When she wrote back, he opened the letter nervously. As he read, his worried frown faded and was replaced by an irrepressible grin. He need not have worried, for Alice reported that her mother appeared to be pleased and in full agreement with their plans.

Henry sat down at once to write his first letter to his future mother-in-law. He had wanted to write her sooner to ask permission for Alice's hand, but he was afraid she would say no, since she didn't even know him. He had decided to wait until Alice could break the news to her mother about him and his family.

In his letter he wrote that his own "dear, dear Mother" had often expressed her hopes that he would marry a Catholic girl, and if Alice was to be his bride, he would fulfill his mother's dream as well as his own. "Your daughter is, indeed, a treasure. It grieves me to think that I have no wealth to offer her; but rest assured, dear Madam, that all man can do, will be done to contribute to her happiness." Determined to make a good impression he referred to her once as "dear Mother," and then asked, "May I be allowed the pleasure of calling you by that sacred name?" What mother could resist?

Mrs. Symons was delighted with the match and even expressed the possibility of moving to Brunswick herself after the wedding. Thus, with the approbation of his future mother-in-law and to the delight of his sisters, Harry and Alice were married on Valentine's Day the following year.

Their first child, a son, was born before the end of the year. They named him Henry Francis, Henry for the child's father and Francis, for Alice's father. They could not have been happier.

"We're going to need a new house," Harry announced shortly after his son's birth. Even though he had proclaimed himself to be without wealth, he had discovered since his mother's death that she had left a fairly ample estate. He and Mary Amelia as the oldest son and daughter served jointly as executors and took care of all the legal work that needed to be done. Their mother had left no will, and they were surprised by their inventory of her possessions. They knew their lives had always been comfortable, but neither of them had any idea of how much property she owned. They did know that, shortly before the war began, she had received a sizeable amount of money for an indemnity from the French government as compensation for her mother's family's losses in the slave uprising of St. Domingue where her mother had lived. And she had invested it well. As it turned out, she owned not only the remains of their home on Union Street, but also seven additional unimproved lots in Brunswick and almost two thousand acres of land, which the Union forces had now evacuated.

Harry told his brother and sisters that "once the economy finally settles down from the war years," their inheritance would be generous. Harry marveled at his parents' foresight, for land was the one thing that wasn't a loss, as Confederate currency and bonds had been.

"Now, my love," he told Alice, "we can afford to build a new home." Once the estate was settled, construction began on one of his mother's lots on Union Street, on the other side of Gloucester and several blocks south from where most of Harry's siblings lived. Once the house was finished, Harry and Alice stood back to admire it. It had a fashionable mansard roof, a front porch with six columns that faced the street and wrapped around the side, six bedrooms and almost five thousand square feet to accommodate the growing family they hoped to have. They moved in shortly after Henry Francis's first birthday.

"I think we'll be very happy here, my dear," Harry said to Alice their first full day in their new house. "And I hope to see our daughters married here someday."

"We don't have any daughters," she reminded him.

"But we will." The shadow of a passing cloud fell across the room, but it failed to diminish the brightness of their hopes.

Alice was delighted as she watched her son toddle around the spacious parlor and dining room. Keeping up with him was not always easy, but she was a happy and willing young mother. A splendid pianoforte stood in the parlor, a surprise gift from her husband the day they moved in. Little Henry Francis, like his father, liked to hear his mother play. Sometimes he sat on her lap or beside her and pounded on the keys himself, as she tried to teach him how to make softer sounds. Even his discord was music to his parents' ears.

On October 27 the following year, their daughter was born—a beautiful little girl they named Leila Madeleine. The Madeleine part was one of Alice's names as well. It was Harry who wanted to name her, in part at least, for her mother, as their son had been named in part for himself.

"You have an abundance of names to choose from," he quipped. "Alice Madeline Leocadie Symons DuBignon. Did I miss any?" They both laughed at the options. Nevertheless, despite the thought that went into the child's name, her young brother quickly decided that he would call her "Baa," a nickname so like her mother's. Their father, Harry, refused to use it. "We gave her a perfectly good name—the lovely name of Leila Madeleine—which we chose very carefully. Why would we want to spoil it with a dreadful nickname like that?"

Alice laughed good-naturedly and gave him a kiss. "It was our son's choice, my dear. Leila Madeleine was, I suppose, hard for him to say. There's nothing we can do about it. Nicknames just happen, Harry. Be glad you were spared a horrible one, though even Harry is a nickname of sorts. 'Baa' is what little Henry calls her. I expect it will stick."

The year seemed full of promise. Memories of the war were fading, as the young couple looked toward a brighter future. The South still lived under the shadow of the Reconstruction government, and Harry had been required to sign the loyalty oath to the Union if he wanted to open his own business with any hope of success. With high hopes and the windfall from his mother's estate, he had decided to become a dry goods merchant.

"People finally have the resources to spend again for items other than rebuilding their homes. They want choices and fashionable items. I think a dry good store is just what the town needs," he told Newton, who offered his good wishes.

"In a business like that, we won't have the same kind of worries my uncles have."

Many young people in his generation were turning away from cotton growing and toward other types of enterprises. Like Newton, Harry and his brother Johnny both decided that commerce was the way to go, as Brunswick was beginning to grow in population. Harry had even written to his army buddy and half-uncle William, who now operated a small grocery store in Tallahassee, to encourage him to come back to Brunswick.

"I do hope you'll think about it," he wrote. "I'd like continue our friendship, and I think Brunswick holds many opportunities for the future. It would be great to see you again, and we need grocery stores here as much as they do in Tallahassee, so come and fill our need. I hope your life has gone as planned."

William replied promptly to Harry's letter: "It's great to hear from you. I should have written sooner to let you know that I married my Lottie and that we have a little girl. It would be great to get together again, and I promise to think about what you said. I guess people need grocery stores everywhere."

Harry was not surprised when, less than a year later, he received another letter from William, letting him know that he had indeed decided to return to Brunswick. "Most of my family are there and I agree that the town is likely to prosper—if I can just find a suitable location."

Harry quickly informed him that there was a lot available on the corner of Bay and Mansfield Streets, not far from City Hall. It suited his needs perfectly, so in 1869, William and his young family returned to Brunswick, where William opened his new grocery store, intending to sell not only groceries, but also a variety of imported goods.

Not long after their arrival, William and his family called upon Harry and Alice.

"Finally," Harry said with a grin, "I get to meet the legendary Lottie. Needless to say, I heard a lot about you during the war." She was a lovely woman, he thought, though of course not as lovely as his own Alice. Their daughter, who looked like her mother, was about the same age as Henri Francis. Both men were pleased to renew their friendship.

Alice was, of course, gracious to their guests, but she had heard so much about the family problems that she had no desire to carry on any further affiliation with the couple. Harry's sisters were even more reserved in their reactions to the friendship, which they found peculiar. Unable to discard their lingering bitterness towards William's mother, they blamed her for the painful final years of their beloved grandmother, and they staunchly declined even to meet Harry's army comrade.

"None of it was William's fault," Harry tried to convince them, but they wanted nothing to do with him or his family. He was only a reminder of the illicit relationship that had thrown their family into turmoil and stained the family's reputation.

John Eugene, who had just reached his twenty-first birthday, was the only one who even gave William a chance. Harry was proud of his younger brother for looking toward the future and not so much to the past. People liked him, and he had big ambitions. Unlike his sisters, he welcomed William warmly, and the young men got on well with each other from the beginning. The three of them—Harry, William, and John Eugene—chose to greet the present as a whole new world, unencumbered by the pains of the past, either family problems or the war, and they maintained their friendship without the family's approval.

CHAPTER 21

Brunswick, Georgia, 1872

As years slipped by, Harry could not believe how content he was. He and Alice had been married almost five years already and now had two children. It was hard to believe the time had passed so quickly.

Their son, Henry Francis, was already a very grown-up four-year-old, or so he thought. He reminded Harry of himself at that age. He'd been only a few years older than his son when his father, Joseph, had died in the spring of 1850. He smiled to remember how hard he had tried, despite his tender years, to be the man of the house and look after his younger brother and sisters, however inadequate he knew his efforts must have been. He recognized in his son that same effort to protect his little sister and teach her the things he thought she should know. She adored him, of course, Although she was only two years old, she made a valiant effort, mostly with unsuccessful results, to do everything he did.

It was an early October evening. The family had finished their supper and, as in the days of their courtship, the couple sat on the front porch, this time on their own porch, watching their children playing on the lawn. At the moment, Henry Francis was trying to teach his little sister how to play pat-a-cake.

"Remember when he tried to show her how to catch a lightning bug last summer?" Alice asked.

Harry gave a gentle laugh. "I wonder how many poor creatures met their fate, squashed in Leila's chubby little hand." The little girl had been fascinated by the intermittent glow of the slow-flying insects. They weren't hard to catch, but she held them too tightly in her chubby fist.

"She was heartbroken every time," Alice murmured. "But I suppose they'll try again next year."

A light breeze was blowing, but the air was still pleasant, with no sign of the winter chill that would begin in a couple of months. Nothing made Harry DuBignon happier than being with his young family on quiet evenings like this. He was home again, content, and assured. It was the same feeling of quiet joy he had known as a child, a certainty he knew he could depend on. Nevertheless, an unexpected feeling of melancholy washed over him.

"See that full moon rising, Alice?" he asked, pointing toward the eastern horizon." She nodded. "Did I ever tell you that moonlight like that sometimes makes me sad?"

"Why when it's so beautiful?"

"It makes me remember wonderful moonlit nights before the war when my family went to the seashore at Jekyl just to watch the full moon rise and spill its gold across the waters. I guess that, seeing it now, makes me nostalgic for that old life we used to enjoy there, before we learned about what our grandfather had done in dividing the island."

"It must have been enchanting. But we have a lovely life in Brunswick too."

"Of course we do, and I'm certainly not unhappy, just nostalgic, I guess. The last time I was on the island, that time right after the war, there were still a few signs of that lost splendor of my grandparents' old home—but only a few. Pieces of fine French furniture which must have been mementos from the DuBignon estate back in France. Just imagine...having one's own private island. And it had been so splendid, so filled with enchantment when I was a little boy. I just wish it could be a part of our life together—and our children's."

Alice reached out to take his hand. He turned to her and smiled, lightly squeezing her fingertips, a gentle gesture.

"You're the best part of my life, and I think we can be happy anywhere," she said. Then a surreptitious smile crossed her lips. "Besides, I have something to tell you that might cheer you up, dearest," she said quietly. Her voice was a velvet presence in the semi-darkness.

"That you love me?" he asked in a teasing tone.

"Well...that too, but something else equally important."

He waited, trying to decipher the expression on her face.

"I'm expecting another baby," she said.

"That's wonderful! How could I be sitting here talking about being sad? I couldn't be happier! We're soon going to have all those bedrooms full and running over," he murmured, rising from his wicker chair to take her in his arms. "When is he expected?" he asked.

"He? Maybe it's another girl," she suggested, teasing him. She never had an intuition for that sort of thing. Her mother was usually absolutely accurate in all her predictions, but so far, Alice had not mentioned it to her.

"Well, if it's another girl, I'll look forward to one more wedding in the parlor." He chuckled. "When is this little miracle to be born?"

"Sometime in late April or early May," I think.

"I can hardly wait, and you're right," he said, "it does cheer me up and make me realize what a lucky man I am." He settled back onto the cushions of his chair and smiled, holding his wife's hand as, together, they watched their children enjoying the last of the good season, before the autumn storms set in.

On May 1, with azaleas outside blazing in the sunshine, Alice gave birth to another daughter.

"One more wedding to plan for the parlor," Harry reminded her, as he held the baby in his arms for the first time. "She'll be a beauty—like her mother and her sister."

Alice was weary but content, just glad the birthing ordeal was over. It was worth it all to see the smile on her husband's face as his newborn daughter wrapped her tiny hand around his little finger.

"Shall we let the children come in to meet their sister?" Alice said.

Harry handed his daughter back to her mother, kissed his wife's hand, and gently stroked the baby's hair one more time.

"Should we agree on a name first, so we can introduce her?" he asked.

"I thought we had talked about Edith," she said. "I rather like that. And since she was born today, what about Edith May?"

I think it's a perfect name—unless the children change it to some awful nickname."

Alice laughed. "Maybe we should let them call her May. It's easier to say."

"Splendid idea," he said. "Now, shall I let them come in and meet her?"

"Please do."

The children, Henry Francis and Leila, were both waiting impatiently in the hallway just outside the bedroom. When Harry opened the door just a crack, they peeked in.

"Can we come in now, Papa? We want to see," Henri Francis said.

Harry opened the door wide. The children bounded in and Harry scooped his oldest daughter up to hold her high so she could get a better view of the perfect little creature cradled in her mother's arms. "You have a baby sister," he said.

"I know," said Henry Francis, "Nina told us. Does she have a name?"

"Of course, let me introduce her. Or perhaps her mother would like to do the honors?"

Alice pulled back the soft blanket that partially hid the baby's face. "This, my darlings, is your sister, Edith May. But your father and I have decided that you may call her May."

"Look, Baa," Henry Francis said. "Isn't she pretty?" He reached out to caress the baby's cheek. She stirred at his touch and opened her eyes."

Little Leila, her finger hanging from her lower lip, looked at the baby in awe and nodded.

Harry stood there, surveying his family with pride. *God, I'm a lucky man.*

Only four months later, on September 11, the doorbell rang, and Henry Francis raced eagerly to beat his mother to the door. She was close behind, laughing at his eagerness. The little girls were both napping and she didn't want the doorbell to wake them up.

"Who is it, darling?" she asked, as he opened the door. She knew it wasn't her husband. He was at work, and besides, he would not have rung the bell. The boy stood there, silently looking up at a man with an ashen face and a forlorn expression. Alice recognized him as one of the chief clerks at the store. Several men stood behind him. They were carrying something.

"I'm sorry, Ma'am, but we—" Alice saw immediately what it was. She gasped and slammed the door in shock and denial. But Nina, her housekeeper, who had just reached the foyer, hurried forward to reopen the door.

"Bring him inside," she said. It was clear that her mistress was in no condition to make coherent decisions at the moment.

Alice, leaning on Nina's sturdy arm now, could barely breathe. "Oh God Oh God O God," she kept saying over and over, as tears began to pour down her face. Henry Francis, confused about what was happening, backed away to let the men come inside.

"Put him there, on the settee," Nina instructed.

Alice could see pain on her husband's face and cold sweat collected on his forehead. He appeared to be unconscious, but he was breathing. At least he was breathing.

"Tell me what happened," she managed to say.

"We were all in a meeting at the store," the man said. "He stood up from the table to make a point, and then he just grabbed his chest and collapsed. I guess he had some kind of attack, but he's still alive, Ma'am. We got him here as quick as we could."

By now, Alice had begun to recover from her shock and found the strength to do what had to be done. "Go fetch Dr. Hazlehurst. Hurry."

"We've already sent for him, Ma'am," one of the men said.

"Then why isn't he here?" her voice was frantic and impatient. "Nina, bring us some cool damp rags. Hurry now!"

Nina dashed away toward the kitchen with Henry Francis at her heels. They soon returned with the moistened cloths. Alice sat beside her husband to bathe his face and rub his hands.

"Wake up, Harry, darling. Please open your eyes." Her voice sounded desperate.

His eyelids slowly lifted, and she could hear him murmur, "I'm sorry, Alice. I'm so much trouble."

"You're no trouble, my darling. Just stay with me. Talk to me until Dr. Hazlehurst gets here. Don't leave me, Harry. I love you. I need you. Stay with me."

His voice was weak, but he was whispering something. She bent down to hear him, tears streaming down her face, desperately trying to hold on, to be strong for him.

"I love you." His words were but a whisper, but they were unmistakable. He was only twenty-nine, seven years younger than his father had been at his death. This couldn't be happening. "I love you too," she said, her lips brushing his ear. A tear fell on his cheek.

In her heart, she was pleading, *Please, God. Please. Don't take him.*

The men who had brought him home still stood awkwardly in the wide doorway that separated the parlor from the hallway. "Is there anything we can do, Ma'am?"

"What's keeping Dr. Hazlehurst? Where is he?" her voice was frantic. "If you can't find him, find another doctor." One of the men rushed out the door in response to her plea.

"Please, he needs help. Nina," she said, "perhaps a touch of whiskey—there in the cabinet. Hurry." The woman rushed to the glass-doored cabinet, took out a bottle of brandy and brought it to her mistress.

"A glass. There are some cordial glasses on the shelves." One of the men held the bottle while Nina hurried back to find a glass. Her hands were shaking and it was all she could do to keep from dropping it. She handed it to the man holding the bottle and he poured a small amount of brandy into the glass and gave it to Alice. She raised her husband's head and put it to his lips for just a sip. Most of it spilled down his chin and fell onto his white starched shirt. Then he coughed. A good sign, she thought. But it was only a single cough, and Alice could feel herself beginning to despair. *Please. God, please, God.* It seemed the only prayer she could utter. *Please, God.*

Robert Hazlehurst rushed into the house without ringing the bell or knocking. He was out of breath and had evidently either run or ridden his horse rapidly from his office.

"Oh, thank God you're here, Uncle Robert. Please, please save him," Alice pleaded.

"I'll do what I can, my dear." Robert, frowning, quickly knelt beside his nephew, who appeared to be unconscious. He took out his stethoscope and began to listen to his heart. He frowned, not liking what he heard. He took out a small vial and dripped some liquid drops into Harry's mouth

"What is that?" Alice asked.

"Digitalis. It's for the heart. It appears he's had a severe heart attack."

"But he's so young—not even thirty yet."

"There's no timetable for this sort of thing. It can happen to anyone. I think you've done all you can," he said to the men, still standing awkwardly in the parlor.

"Would you want us to carry him up to his bedroom?" the clerk asked.

"He's so weak I don't think it would be a good idea to move him just now," Robert said. "Nina, could you get a blanket and a pillow for him." She rushed off to obey.

As soon as the men left, Robert bent over again to listen to Harry's heart. The beat was weaker than before and he feared the worst. He had seen too much of this sort of thing during the war—young men on the verge of death. There was a time he wasn't sure he could stand any more death and dying, any more grieving widows and fatherless children. Yet here was his own nephew who had served in the war, fought in terrible battles, a young man just starting his life who had come home hale and hearty. And now, without warning, this.

Nina hurried back into the room with a blanket and pillow and helped Alice cover the still body. Robert put his stethoscope once more to Harry's heart. There was no sound, no heartbeat. He was gone. Robert cursed the limitations of medicine, for now he could only turn to his nephew's wife and say quietly, "I'm sorry, Alice. It was too late. There was nothing I could do."

Her eyes were wide with horror and tears. No, this couldn't be happening. Her youngest children wouldn't even remember him. They would never know the love he held for them all. And she would never again lie in his arms, the one place she always felt safe.

She stood there, numb, unable to think what to do next. What was expected of her? How could she survive? Her future had vanished. She fell to her knees and took Henry Francis in her arms and continued to weep.

The following days, as relatives flooded her house with food, condolences, and sympathetic embraces, were like a dream. There was no time to be alone, no time to grieve. Alice felt as though all life had left her as well. She didn't know what to do, where to turn, or even why she was still here. She did what was required without awareness. The funeral mass was held in the tiny chapel dedicated to Saint Francis Xavier, built the year just after their marriage on land donated by a family friend, Urbanus Dart, who was not himself a Catholic. She knew it was the place her husband would want the services held.

Later, she could remember only vaguely how she and the other family members had followed the coffin to Oak Grove Cemetery where a gaping grave awaited the committal of her husband's body, where he would lie near his mother for all eternity. It was all like a bad dream she hoped would vanish before a brighter dawn. But there was no brighter dawn.

When it was over, Alice stood alone in the foyer of her once-wonderful home, its emptiness now like that of her heart. Only when she thought of the three children for whom she was now solely responsible, could she steel herself against her loss. Now they were her only reason for living. *He was so young. We had so many hopes and plans and dreams.* How would she ever cope? Could she even stay here? The memories were so strong, but the world had become a strange and lonely place.

Alice was not the only one whose world had turned upside down with Harry's death. John Eugene was also bereft. He had lost his mother and now his brother. So had his sisters, he knew, but for him it was different. Suddenly, everyone was turning to him, as the only surviving male in the family, to take his brother's place. They had counted on Harry for guidance and help, but now he was gone. Even though Mary Amelia was the oldest among them and far more experienced it the ways of the world, it was he they would now regard as the final authority, the one who should have the wisdom and make the decisions, even though he was only twenty-three. He did not consider himself worthy or ready for this role. It didn't seem fair, he thought, but he had no choice. It was his fate and his duty. Although he would try his best, he regarded the future with trepidation as he felt the heavy burden settling on his young shoulders.

CHAPTER 22

Jekyl Island, October 1872

John Couper and Henry made one of their rare trips together into Brunswick for their nephew's funeral. They sympathized with Alice and the other family members, but they were glad after the service to escape all the gloom and return to their homes on Jekyl, where they were both still trying to rebuild the lives they had lived before the war. Henry was increasingly anxious about the future and the decreasing options for him to restore the DuBignon family wealth. He thought it was easier for John, who was content just to be back on the island. He had his other family, and he didn't care about the indulgences of the past as Henry did. And for a while, that had been true. John *was* happy just to be back, but it wouldn't last.

On a mid-afternoon only two months after Harry's funeral, John and his son Joseph, who was still living at home, were just returning from the beach, where they had had caught eighteen crabs.

"Sylvia," John called as they left their wet sandy shoes and buckets on the porch and came in the front door. "Joe and I are back. We're gonna have a great supper tonight!"

There was no answer.

"Sylvia, where are you?" He looked in the kitchen and the room with the fireplace where they shared their meals and enjoyed each other's company. She wasn't there. "Sylvia!"

Finally, he heard a weak reply. "I'm in here, John. In the bedroom."

He found her lying down. It was unlike her to take a rest in the middle of the day, for with all the children and household duties, she was a busy woman and never indulged in afternoon naps, now that she was free to take them.

"Were you asleep?" he asked as he wrinkled his brow.

"I reckon I must've dozed off for a spell."

"Is something wrong? Are you all right?

"I'll be fine. Just a back pain and a kind of queasy feeling."

She was never sick, and he was worried. "What can I do to help?"

"I had Caroline look after the young 'uns, and I went to see the conjure man dis mornin' while you was out crabbin'?

"What did he do?"

"He said some words over me and give me some miniweed tea to drink. But it don't seem to have done no good."

While she rested, John and the children sat at the table, picking crab meat out of the shells and cutting up the vegetables needed for the dish they hoped she would be able to make. It was women's work, and John wasn't used to helping. Even so, he enjoyed the time with his children, laughing with his daughters as they tried to teach him how to pick the crab from the shells most efficiently. Eventually, Sylvia's pain subsided sufficiently for her to get up and cook a good supper of crab fried rice, green beans, and biscuits for the family.

John, watching her move, could tell she was still in pain. He and Sylvia had lived together for two decades now and they knew each other well. It had been more than thirty years since Robert, their eldest, was born. He was gone now, living in Brunswick with his wife, Charlotte, and his own family. But John and Sylvia still had five children at home—from Joe, the oldest at fourteen, to Cornelia, who was only eight. Sylvia hadn't been with child since Cornelia's birth. She was still young—only in her early forties, but John thought she must already be going through the change. Nevertheless, he still took comfort in her arms at night. He hated the idea that she was feeling sick, for he counted on her to meet so many of his needs. He would be helpless without her, he thought.

In the weeks that followed, she began to lose weight and look more like that skinny little girl who had caught his eye so long ago. She didn't eat much and said she wasn't hungry. Wrinkles began to etch themselves around her eyes and she wore a frown of perpetual discomfort. Now the pain was in her lower belly as well, and the back pain was growing worse.

"Sylvia," John said one night as they were getting ready for bed. "I'm worried about you. Let's go into Brunswick so you can see a doctor."

"Ain't no doctor gone see me," she said. "They all white. Ain't no Negro doctor in Brunswick."

"I can get Dr. Hazlehurst to see you. He's my brother-in-law."

"Ain't no use, John. We both know I got a sickness that ain't gonna be cured. I'll go to town with you, but I ain't gonna see no doctor. I wants to see a lawyer."

"Whatever for?"

"If I die, I wants to make sure you're gonna look after the children till they're grown."

"Of course I will, Sylvia. Besides, you aren't going to die. You can't. We all need you. Me most of all," John said, dismissing the idea, though deep inside he could feel the darkness of possibility stretching out before him.

"I wants a legal paper where you promise to do it." Her voice was as firm as he had ever heard it.

"Is that really necessary, Sylvia?" he asked. "You know you can trust me."

"If I die, I wants to die in peace. That would give me peace." Perhaps she felt she couldn't count on him, he thought. Was that possible, after all their life and the home they'd made together?

He protested several more times, but she was determined and unyielding.

"I don't ask for nothin' else—just a promise on paper." He could see she was not going to change her mind. "I got to make sure my children is cared for."

Finally John gave in. "If it's that important to you, I'll do it." He was shaken and surprised that she thought she needed a legal document to compel him to care for his own children. He was their father after all. Did she think that he was like his own father, that he would betray the people he loved, the people he thought loved him? Did she not trust him after all these years?

But what she said was true. She almost never asked for anything, and he could grant her this with the stroke of a pen. Besides, she was a free woman now and could leave him at any time. He knew that and made more effort now to please her. He couldn't get along without her anymore, but he still felt uncertain about her feelings for him. This would be a small thing, and it might make her feel better. It would show her he cared. At least he hoped so.

On November 8, John hired a few oarsmen from among the freedmen living on the island to row him and Sylvia into Brunswick, leaving the younger children in the care of Joe and Caroline. It was a bright morning with only a slight chill in the air. The fall day was sunny, bringing a golden glow to the amber marsh grasses that had been so green back in the summer. There was a melancholy beauty about the change, and John wished he could hold onto the colors of the marsh somehow, capture this amber morning and keep it forever. He refused to think about why they were going into Brunswick, why they were going to the courthouse to meet a lawyer who would draw up the indenture he had agreed to sign. Instead, he focused on the gentle splashes of water stirred by the oars, the snowy egrets wading here and there, and the small fish that leapt briefly above the water, leaving only small radiating circles as they plopped back in.

"Look at that big alligator, Sylvia," he said, pointing to the creature sunning itself on the edge of a small treeless hummock, a slight rise in the land to make a tiny marsh island. She looked toward the lazy alligator and smiled. John gazed at her, her bronzed skin shining in the sun, only a shade darker than the marsh grass. He thought it beautiful, like warm coffee with a heavy serving of cream. She had been a part of his life for so long, and it made him sad to see the worry that had carved itself into her face. He did not want to do what she had asked of him. It sounded so...impersonal, but if it made her happy, he would do it.

When they reached the Brunswick dock, he held out his hand to help her out of the boat. The few fishermen in their shrimp boats or on the dock stared at him and frowned. *Why was he helping a colored woman?* They glared their disapproval. John barely noticed, but Sylvia, intimidated by their threatening stares dropped back like a servant to walk behind John as they made their way to the courthouse. He didn't seem to notice.

The lawyer looked startled when they entered the ordinary's office, where they had arranged to meet and discuss the agreement, but he made no comment as John explained the nature of the document they wanted drawn up. After clarifying certain details like the names of all the minor children, he informed them that the document would be ready the following day.

"Can't you do it today?" John asked. "We've come all the way from Jekyl Island."

He frowned, thought for a minute, then said, "Come back in a few hours and I'll see what I can do."

When they returned to the office in mid-afternoon, the document was ready. John read it aloud to Sylvia to make sure she understood and that it included everything she wanted. When she nodded, the lawyer signed her name on the document and asked her to make her mark where he had left a small space between the two parts of her name—Sylvia DuBignon. The second section of the document constituted John's agreement in which he promised "to faithfully carry out all of its provisions." Sylvia smiled with satisfaction as he penned his name. There was now a legal paper that guaranteed he would do what she had asked.

They did not speak as they left the office and made their way to the dock, each lost in their own thoughts. Sylvia once again trailed behind, but as soon as they were in the boat, he turned to her.

"That wasn't really necessary, you know," he said.

"Maybe not. But now I can die in peace," she said, her face more serene than he had seen it in the past.

"Please don't talk that way. You can't die."

"We all die sometime, John, to go be with the Lord. It ain't the end of the world. It just be my turn comin' up, I reckon."

She lived on for almost a year, constantly losing weight, until she finally fell asleep one night in the cabin and never woke up again. Her bony face bore the same serenity it had the afternoon they signed the indenture. John thought he saw even the trace of a smile, like the smile of one emerging from a lingering darkness into the longed-for light of freedom. He and the children wept by her bedside. For the first time, he truly understood both the numbness and the grief that Harry's widow had felt at her husband's funeral. Unlike Sylvia, who was sure she was going to be with God, John saw death as the end.

None of the white DuBignons attended her burial. Not even Henry. But the freed people who had returned to the island after the war were all there, singing or humming their mournful hymns of comfort, as they trudged slowly behind the coffin toward the old slave cemetery at the south end of the island. Two mules pulled the wagon to the slow pace of their singing. "Precious Lord, take my hand. Lead me on, help me stand…" Their voices blended like an orchestra with various instruments chiming in at certain moments, and their hymns resonated in the late September woodlands.

The freed people had come to accept John's presence among them, insofar as possible, even though he never came to Sunday meetings with Sylvia and they didn't know him well. But his white skin would always set him apart as a mark of privilege, whether he took advantage of it or not. He felt a heaviness in his heart as he listened to their singing, wishing he could join in. "Precious Lord, take my hand... Lead me home."

John had wanted to bury Sylvia in his family's cemetery at the north end, land that now belonged to his brother Henry, but his children had objected. She would be lonely there, they insisted, alone among all those white folks with none of her own people anywhere about. He had given in, lacking the will to debate the matter. He wanted what she would have wanted. During slavery times, burials had taken place at night, but now, all that had changed. They were conducted whenever the family felt it was right. It was a cloudy afternoon. John held the hands of his two youngest daughters, and, with the rest of his children following, they led the processional. He listened as the people he had once enslaved were now singing softly about the balm in Gilead. *Was it for Sylvia they sang? Or for him?* No doubt his sin-sick soul needed healing far more than hers had. But he doubted they would sing for him.

Once the funeral service had ended, John stood by watching, until the grave was filled and transformed into a mound of earth with a wooden cross tamped into the soil. Then, he stepped forward to lay on the grave the ivory comb he had given her after Joseph was born. It had been her prized possession, and he had been told by his children that such objects left at the gravesite would help the spirit rest and find its way home. One by one, her children placed their own special tokens beside his—a hand-carved box, a seashell, a small basket, a necklace of wooden beads—before they turned to find their way back to the now-empty house they had once called home.

CHAPTER 23

Brunswick, Georgia, late 1872

Throughout the South, people with business interests were beginning to turn to northern investors for capital. Newton had become well known in Brunswick since his marriage into the DuBignon family and was a trusted businessman in the town. Others often consulted him concerning prospective investors from the North. When they needed a representative, especially in New York, they often turned to him. Newton spoke frequently about the possibilities that these connections could accomplish, both for himself and for Brunswick. He was excited by the opportunities the growing economy represented. Thus, not long after Harry's death he had decided to move his young family—his wife Josephine, his eight-year-old son Joseph, and his four-year-old daughter Félicité—to New York.

Although John Eugene could not disagree with the wisdom of his actions, he hated to see them depart. He had counted on Newton for support and advice now that Harry was gone, but he was surprised that his brother-in-law had stayed in Brunswick as long as he had. His sister Josephine had been reluctant to leave her family, but as time went on she became more amenable to the possibility. Newton had encouraged her, suggesting that such a change might even help heal her grief over her brother's death. John Eugene hated to see them go. He would miss Newton almost as much as he missed Harry, and he knew he would have to cultivate other friends and business partners in the future.

John Eugene turned to his new friend, William Turner DuBignon. The two men were both at a loss after Harry's death, and they found a certain consolation in each other. John Eugene knew how much his brother had trusted William, and he was beginning to understand why. Like Harry, William was always willing to listen to whatever schemes or dreams the young man had, and he always kept it to himself. He was reluctant to give advice, unless he was sure, but even talking it out helped John Eugene articulate and clarify his goals.

William sometimes confided his own ideas to John Eugene, but for reasons he never disclosed, he decided abruptly three years after Harry's death to change his name from DuBignon to Turner, which was already his middle name. William's brother Leonidas did the same. John Eugene wondered about William's reasons, which he suspected had something to do with his grandfather or his uncle Henry, who was the executor of their father's will. He knew that there was tension between William's half-sister, Mary, and her stepson Henry. John Eugene did not ask him, deciding that, if William wanted him to know the reasons, he would tell him. But he felt sure it had nothing to do with him. He speculated on the various possibilities, wondering if it was because John's mulatto son, Robert, had fathered a little boy that same year and named him William DuBignon. But John Eugene doubted that his friend even knew about that birth. He himself had learned of it only by happenstance. More likely, he thought, it had to do with anger over his uncle Henry's perceived mismanagement of their father's estate. Mary had taken her stepson to court over some of the issues. It was even possible, he conjectured, that William and Leonidas just wanted to shed the cloud of illegitimacy that hung over them. John Eugene never knew the reason for sure and he never asked. In polite society one didn't openly pry into the affairs of others, and he thought it best to let the reason lie buried in William's heart. That way it need not affect their relationship. It might even be an advantage. Now that they had different surnames, perhaps it would stop people from asking so many embarrassing questions.

Nevertheless, although their common grief over Harry's death and John Eugene's need for someone to talk with about his ideas and ambitions bound them together for a while, it would not last. The demands of the everyday world began to tug at them both, and they met less and less often. The unasked question about the name change festered in a quiet darkness below the surface. Little by little the two men began to drift apart and eventually went their separate ways.

Reconstruction, which had kept southerners under the thumb of Union officials, came to an end in 1877. The war had been over for more than a decade, and the South had recovered from the worst devastation. With Reconstruction over, Union authorities, along with many of the hated carpetbaggers, returned to their homes in the North. There were still lingering resentments and questions about the role of blacks in the new economy, but many of the whites in power felt it was time to forge ahead building a new South. However humiliating they had found Reconstruction, its end permitted them to put the past behind them at last and face the future with determination and renewed spirit. Now, they were more hopeful than ever since the war. The next few years, John Eugene thought, would be a boom time for Brunswick.

Jekyl Island, December 1877

John Eugene's aging uncles, however, did not share that optimism. They were both still floundering in an unfamiliar world. John, lost without Sylvia, hardly bothered anymore about trying to work his portion of the old plantation. A pall had fallen over his household. He provided for his children as best he could, just as he had pledged to do, but one by one, as they grew older, they began to move away and start their own lives.

His brother Henry could never understand why John Couper still carried on so, after all these years, about the death of a colored woman. There were plenty of others around. If that was all he had to worry about, then he was lucky. *It's easier for him*, Henry thought. *He doesn't care about the old days or give a whit for the grace of our former life.* Henry himself could never live like his brother—in a run-down shack in the middle of the woods with a mulatto family who were not welcome in "polite" society and not even in his own family. It didn't seem to matter to John, for he had no desire to be part of that world. He evidently preferred that old cabin in the woods. By now, it seemed that his children looked after him more than the other way around. He was seventy years old and beginning to grow frail.

It's a lot harder for me, Henry thought. Everything he had counted on and hoped for was gone. Everything he had tried to do had failed. He had never believed that the North would win the war and thought that, once the fighting was over and his land was restored, his slaves would come back and he would prosper. He thought he would be able to look forward to an even better future now that he and his brothers owned the island and were no longer at the beck and call of their father. But none of that had happened. His former slaves were free men and women now. He had no work force without paying them, and he had no money with which to pay. Things had gone from bad to worse, and he could see no way forward.

His life was in a muddle. He owed money to multiple people and had no way to repay it. *I'm too old to start over*, Henry thought. He often rode his old horse around the plantation, fuming over the fallow fields, most of them empty of the once-familiar cotton plants. *It's the fault of those lazy darkies*, he thought. *You just can't count on them like you could in the old days when they knew their place. Now that the Yankees are gone, maybe we can whip 'em back into shape.*

Nothing had gone right for him in the past decade. He had been appointed executor of his father's will at his death in 1866, right after the war, when things were especially hard. *I did the best I could*, he thought, *but there was no satisfying those cursed Austs. Those bastards, William and Leonidas, were upset that they had received only $50 in the will and no share of the island—as if they deserved it.* He had left more to Mary and her children, but he thought she too was ungrateful. He spat on the ground, remembering how his father's second wife had even taken him to court, accusing him of mismanagement of the estate. He was furious but had finalized the details as best he could and then resigned as executor. Now, he'd heard, Sarah's sons had dropped the name DuBignon as their surname. *Good*, he thought. *Whatever gave them the right to use it in the first place?*

He was in a foul mood. The harvest, such as it was, was never adequate anymore; cotton prices were low, and he constantly lost more than he earned. He'd had no choice but to borrow money from various sources to maintain his lifestyle, pay a few workers, and keep the big house in reasonably good condition. There had been rumors on the mainland that the Yankees had burned it during the war, but that wasn't so, thank goodness. They didn't bother it at all. They had camped mostly at the far north end, closest to St. Simons Sound, where their ships were anchored. And they didn't stay for long. He had that to be thankful for. The house was still fairly well furnished, with touches here and there of the fine French furniture that once belonged to his grandparents. It had helped with potential lenders. Once inside the house, they could look around and surmise for themselves how wealthy and solvent he still was. More than one of them had made their decisions based on what they saw and assumed that he was rich enough to pay them back with no problem. The scheme had worked so far, but now his creditors were beginning to demand repayment.

Over the years, in order to stay afloat, Henry had borrowed more and more money from anyone who might be willing to lend him something. He no longer had any pride in such matters. He was even compelled to hock his father's gold watch and a diamond pin that had belonged to his grandmother. But he was running out of options. He could no longer maintain the balance of borrowing from one creditor to repay another, and he was up to his neck in an impossible situation. What could he do? What could he do to save his land?

One of those who lent him money had finally sued him for nonpayment of debt—a woman from Savannah named Mary Heisler. The judge had ruled in her favor in the amount of $4,275, which included the amount of the loan plus interest. She in turn, for reasons he did not know, had assigned her claim over to a man named Martin Tufts, a railroad freight agent in Savannah. The following July, Tufts, assuming he could now lay claim to Henry's land and livestock since the man had nothing else to offer, had arrived on the island in his yacht, the *Sunshine*, to look over the plantation, realizing it was all Henry had that could possibly meet the amount imposed by the judge.

The *Brunswick News* had noted the visit and described it as a pleasure trip, but it was certainly no pleasure for Henry DuBignon. Their meeting was tense. Henry had no intention of turning over his land or anything else he owned to Tufts, nor did he show this man he considered an interloper any kind of hospitality. Tufts, assuming the courts would sort it all out, for the time being did not press the matter. It looked hopeless to Henry. Now his land was scheduled to be sold on the first Tuesday of February 1878 by the sheriff of Glynn County. Losing his land would be the final blow. There had to be some way to save it. As far as Henry was concerned, the man just wanted to steal his property.

What could he do? What recourse did he have? Then, one morning as he was riding through the barren fields, it came to him. He would seek a homestead exemption. He thought about it for days—something that, if he could get it, could shield his home and land from his creditors. Yes, that was it. He could apply for a homestead exemption and then declare bankruptcy.

But there was one major obstacle. He needed dependents to file for such an exemption, and he had no one. He needed a wife, but who would marry him now? Or a child. Then it struck him. Perhaps he could adopt a child! It was the only way. He immediately thought of his great-nephew—Harry's ten-year-old son, Henry Francis. *His father's dead now, and I could adopt him and become the child's surrogate father. That way I could claim a family dependent and apply for a homestead exemption.* Yes, that was it! Then he could file for bankruptcy and no one could take his land. He wasn't sure it would work, but perhaps it would, and then he would be immune to some ungodly seizure. Surely he could find a local judge who would be willing to take his side in the matter.

There was yet one more complication. He would have to get the agreement of Harry's widow, Alice, for the adoption. She was a woman alone now, and she probably worried for her son and what he might inherit in life. Henry didn't know what provisions his nephew had made for his family, but surely his widow would welcome another inheritance for her son. Yes indeed. He was quite pleased with himself that he had thought of such a splendid idea, and he had no time to waste.

Henry tidied himself up, put on his best suit, and went into Brunswick the very next day to put the proposition to Alice. She herself answered the door.

"Uncle Henry, what a nice surprise." She was genuinely surprised to see him, for she had laid eyes on him only once since her husband died. He had attended the service and expressed his condolences, but nothing since. Nonetheless, she greeted him warmly.

Her house was well appointed, though not luxurious, which he thought was a good sign. She might welcome his proposal.

"May I offer you some tea?" Alice offered gracefully.

"That would be very nice. Thank you," he said, though he would have preferred a good swig of whiskey. He needed courage to broach with Alice the idea of adopting her son.

She rang for the tea, and while they waited he made a few polite inquiries about her family. She seemed friendly enough, and his hopes rose. He was glad when the tea arrived. It helped fill the awkward moments before he found the nerve to launch into the real reason he had come. He complimented the tea, and the sweets that came with it. Then, finally, he set down his teacup and leaned toward her.

"Alice, I've been thinking about the future and what will happen to my land once I'm gone. As you know, I have no children of my own, and I was thinking that if I could adopt a son—preferably a member of my own family, he could become my heir." He paused to give her time to consider his words. "I was thinking about Henry Francis. Now that his father is gone, I would like to become a father to him. In short, I was hoping you would allow me to adopt your son and make him my heir."

She listened quietly to his proposition, but, taking no time to think about it, her first reaction was totally negative.

"Let you adopt my son? I'm sorry, Uncle Henry, but it's out of the question. I love my son, and I want him here with me."

"But Alice, my dear, it need change nothing in your life or

his," he said. "He could continue to live here with you. The only difference is that I would make him my heir, and I will provide for the child. It seems to me the perfect solution—for both myself and the boy. It need not affect your life in any way. What harm could it do?"

"You could make him your heir without adopting him," she said.

"But the will could always be contested. If he were my legal son, no one could contest that."

She frowned in hesitation. "I don't know. It seems so... odd." She knew nothing of his financial problems, and he saw no advantage in divulging them. He was after all still living on his land in the big house and seemed to most of the outside world to be doing fine. She had never had occasion to go to the island and could only imagine the grandeur of a big plantation house. But she knew how her husband Harry had loved Jekyl, and here was an opportunity to bring part of it, at least, as an inheritance, to their son. Still, she was skeptical.

"But why did you choose my son?" she asked.

"I would like to keep the land in the family. My brother Charles has sons, but they will be well provided for with their maternal grandfather's plantation and wealth. My sisters have sons, but they don't carry the name DuBignon. And since Henry Francis was unfortunate enough to lose his father at such a young age, I would like to help provide for him."

"What about my daughters?"

"Girls marry, change their names, and have husbands to take care of them. It's different for a boy, who will carry on the family name."

"I don't know, Uncle Henry. I'll have to think it over."

"Can't you just decide now? Then we can get the process done while I still live. I am no longer a young man, you know."

"No. I'll need to discuss it with someone I trust." Although she was tempted, she was adamant, and he left, feeling a bit dejected and unsure of what lay ahead.

He waited a week before he returned, this time with a sympathetic deputy sheriff, a friend whom he introduced as W.B. Coker. He had thought that the presence of an authority figure, a man of the law, even in an unofficial capacity, might put more pressure on Alice to agree. Time was short, and his creditors were closing in. Henry was growing desperate.

"I trust you have decided to consent to the adoption, Alice," he said. "And we have brought a statement we would like you to sign."

Alice took the document and read it over carefully. "I can't sign this statement," she said, handing it back to him.

"Why not?"

"Because it's not true. It says that you have contributed to my son's support. You have contributed nothing, as you know."

"Oh, Alice, this is more a letter of my intent. I plan to clothe, educate, and do for him just as though he were my own son. When I'm gone, I will leave all my possessions to Henry Francis."

"Go ahead and sign, Mrs. DuBignon," Coker urged. "It will be good for your boy's future."

"I don't know—" she said.

"Alice, we're family. You know I'm a man of my word.

"But Uncle Henry, he's *my* son. I'm just not sure." She had talked with her brother and a close family friend about the matter.

They could see no harm in it, if Henry was true to his word, and it promised to benefit the boy economically, but she still hesitated.

"Land will only grow in value," Mr. Coker assured her.

Finally, after a great deal more persuasion Alice gave in, not so much because land values might increase, but because it would fulfill a lifelong dream of her late husband—owning a part of Jekyl. If her son could inherit it, perhaps it would be worth it. Still, it was a major step to allow one's only son to be adopted by someone else—even if he would never leave home. But, she thought, perhaps Henry was right, that it would be in the boy's best interest. And finally, she signed the document.

Henry, offering nothing except promises in return, applied immediately to the court to adopt the boy legally, presenting the statement she had signed. With the written permission of the boy's mother in evidence, the adoption was quickly granted. It changed nothing in the life of the child or the man. Henry Francis remained in his mother's home, and few people in the community, including the boy himself, even knew it had been done—that he was now the adopted son and future heir of his great-uncle Henry.

Henry congratulated himself. He had done it. Now he could apply for a homestead exemption. If that were granted, he could file for bankruptcy. He would lose everything, but he would be able to keep the land. He felt sure that, if these actions succeeded, he would outsmart his creditors.

When John Eugene had first learned of his uncle's problems and the judgment in favor of Mary Heisler, he went to Savannah, only to discover that she had already transferred the rights of the claim to Martin Tufts. *Perhaps*, John Eugene thought hopefully, *I can work out a deal with Tufts—for a price of course.* He had his doubts that a railroad man from Savannah would take much interest in an island in Glynn County.

After much time and discussion, Tufts finally agreed to his offer, and John Eugene hurried home, jubilant to share the news with Fannie. Soon, he thought, he would at last own a part of Jekyl Island. But, as yet, he knew nothing of the subsequent adoption of Henry Francis or his uncle's application for a homestead exemption.

Martin Tufts was the first to learn of Henry's efforts. He was furious. Fearing that the money John Eugene had offered might slip through his fingers, he filed a caveat in the Glynn County court, protesting that Henry's petition for a homestead exemption was based on a fraud. He argued that the man had no family, that the adoption was a sham, and that a homestead exemption was unjustified. The boy did not live with him. He did not support the child and took no interest in him. His only purpose for the so-called adoption, Tufts contended, was to obtain an undeserved homestead exemption and cheat his creditors.

The court agreed to look into the matter and presented an interrogatory to Alice. By now, learning of Uncle Henry's situation and realizing that she may have been duped, she submitted a statement to the court, alleging Henry's "misleading conversation and advice" and stating that "Mr. DuBignon has never given or contributed anything to Henry's support in any way and has never had any control or authority over him." In fact, she claimed, "He has never even asked after him when he would meet me." On her lawyer's advice, she declined to speculate on Henry's reason for adopting her son.

Despite Alice's testimony, the judge went by the letter of the law and granted the homestead exemption. Almost immediately, Henry made his next move and declared bankruptcy. Should that succeed, on the basis of the homestead exemption, he would have the right to keep his land.

But the final judgment would have little effect on Henry's life, for even before the litigation came to an end, he would be compelled to leave his home on Jekyl Island.

It had all begun on a Thursday morning at the end of February 1878. Despite his proclaimed poverty, Henry still kept a housekeeper who cooked and cleaned as well as a man to take care of all else. They were man and wife, Patsy and Ned, who did the work because they could find no other means of support as an aging couple. Although he paid them only a pittance, at least they had a place to live in the old cook's cabin, and they could grow their own garden. Even so, Henry saw them as a drain on his diminished funds, but he couldn't live without some servants, he thought. He wouldn't know how.

On the Thursday morning in question, Henry got out his shotgun and ammunition, saddled and mounted his horse, and set out to hunt some game. It was cool in the early morning as he trotted along the plantation road toward his favorite hunting area. It was nearly March and signs of spring were awakening on the island. Fragrant and familiar hints of honeysuckle were beginning to perfume the air, and camellias still bloomed. Wild sweet William created patches of color along the roadways, and yellow jessamine climbed the trees. These horseback rides through his own land just as spring was about to burst into full flower gave him a sense of anticipation that made him feel almost young again—as though he were still a boy, riding the same roads and trails he had ridden as a child. Only his aching joints reminded him it was no longer true.

All morning, despite his efforts, he managed to shoot only a small wild turkey and a pigeon. *Better than nothing*, he thought. It was the old couple's day off, and he had to clean the birds himself and hang them in the smokehouse until Patsy was ready to cook them. He added some good hardwood and hickory chips to the firebox, and by the time it was finished, he felt a bit weary.

He went back inside and ate the light meal Patsy had left for him. Then, feeling content with himself, he poured a snifter of brandy and settled for a time in front of the parlor fire to relax. It had been a strenuous morning, and he had to confess, he wasn't as fit as he once was. Little by little, the brandy warmed his insides as the fire warmed his outer body. Finding himself growing drowsy as he stared into the flames, he swallowed the rest of the brandy in a single swig and rose, thinking that a short nap would refresh him.

A little after three o'clock, he woke up, suddenly alert. He could smell smoke. Jumping from his bed and not even stopping to put on his boots, he raced to the top of the stairwell that led to the foyer. He could see no flames, only leaping shadows on the wall and smoke pouring out of the front parlor. For a second, he wondered whether he had bothered to replace the fire screen when he lit the kindling and put a log on the grate.

He rushed down the stairs, intent on putting out the fire. To his horror, it had already spread to various parts of the room. One of the rose-colored sofas was ablaze, and flames were leaping up his mother's draperies.

There was no water in the house, no time to draw it from the well, and no one to help. He thought of the kitchen, separated from the main house by a dogtrot. Perhaps Patsy had left a bucket of water standing near the stove, which she often did in case of a kitchen fire. The blaze was spreading quickly now, and he wasn't sure he could get back in time. But he had to do something. The house, built from island timber cut more than fifty years ago, would burn quickly. For lack of any other choice, he rushed to the kitchen to look for a pail of water. Sure enough, Patsy, who was always careful, had left a full bucket sitting by the stove. He grabbed it and rushed back to the parlor, leaving a wet trail of splashes behind him.

The small amount of water in the bucket did little to quench the flames. The fire was moving rapidly now and had spread to the front hallway. Everything between him and the front door was burning. It was too late to go upstairs and try to salvage anything, for now the staircase itself was on fire. He couldn't believe how quickly it had spread. He hesitated for only a moment, grabbing any random object that was close by and that seemed to be of any value, his pocket watch he had left on a hall table, a silver pitcher, a candelabra—whatever he could seize before he ran through the dog trot again and out the back door as the flames chased him.

He stood outside, helpless and miserable, and watched the house burn.

Soon John's son Joseph came running down the road to help. The children had seen large clouds of black smoke rising and knew that something big was burning. But it was too late. Nothing could save it now. The boy could only stand beside his uncle, who never acknowledged him as such, and watch the stately old house burn to the ground. By this time, Henry's brother John, who no longer moved as fast as his son, had joined them. The roof blazed bright against the calm blue sky, and Henry felt sure they could see the smoke as far away as Brunswick.

"You'd be welcome to stay with us," John said when the big house lay only a smouldering ruin. They had little extra room in their cabin, but no matter how small it was, there was always room for family. It was something John had learned from Sylvia, a spirit of welcome she had brought with her from the black community. There was always room for someone in need.

"You gonna rebuild, Mister Henry? I reckon we can help," John's son Joseph said.

Henry stood in dejected silence for a moment, gazing at the smoking ashes and knowing he had no money to reconstruct the fine house that once stood grandly there, though in recent years it had begun to fall into disrepair, despite his efforts.

"I think not, Joe," Henry replied. "I can't afford to rebuild. It looks like I'm done here." This was the final blow. His knew that his life on Jekyl was over. He had lost his home, the only thing of value he had except his land.

"What will you do?" his brother asked.

"I don't know. Maybe I'll go live with Eliza if she'll have me. She has that house she built on Union Street, and she might welcome the company."

It was all gone now. Everything. All that was left of the finery, the memory of wealth the family had enjoyed in better days—gone—the wealth he had once hoped to restore. All their elegant furnishings, fine china, silver trays, and— His mind could hardly take it all in. All he had tried to preserve of home as it was before the war was now reduced to piles of ashes.

When the ashes had sufficiently cooled, John and Henry, wearing too-large shoes that belonged to his brother, picked through the ruin to see if there was anything at all they could salvage. They found some charred cutlery, an iron cook pot, and a few silver coins that must have been in one of Henry's pockets, but nothing of real value. It was too late by then to get to the mainland. Henry reluctantly spent the night at John's cabin, staying for the first time under the same roof as colored folks—except for servants, of course, which to him hardly counted. John's oldest daughter, Caroline, made a fine dinner, and they gave him the best bed in the house, while some of the children made do on pallets. *Well, beggars can't be choosers,* he thought, but he lay awake much of the night, reminding himself that he could never adapt to such primitive living.

The next morning, as soon as the sun was high enough, he had Joseph and some of his friends row him into Brunswick, carrying the few items he had saved and preparing to break the bad news to his sister Eliza, who he hoped would invite him to stay.

Eliza opened the door herself, astounded to see her bedraggled brother standing there, wearing disreputable shoes that didn't fit, clothes that looked as though they had been slept in, and clutching a lumpy croker sack.

"Henry, what on earth? You look terrible," she said.

"Can I come it?" he asked. His voice was plaintive.

"Of course," she said, opening the door wider. "Let's go into the sitting room." It was a small sunporch off the parlor, where she often read in the afternoons. "Tell me what's happened."

"It's all gone, Eliza—the house, the furniture, everything. It all burned to the ground yesterday. There was nothing we could save, except these." He held out the sack. It contained the candelabra and the silver pitcher. He had the watch in his pocket. "They're yours. It's all I can offer. All I have left," he told her.

"Oh, Henry, I'm so sorry." She looked at him in dismay. "And now," she said with resignation, "I suppose you'll want to move in with me?"

"I have nowhere else to go. Will you take me in?"

"Well, of course. You're my brother. You shouldn't have been out there all by yourself anyhow. I guess we can just dodder around here together. I'm sorry you lost everything, but I guess we'll manage."

"I don't know how to live in town," he told her.

"Well, I mostly keep to myself, except for Sunday mass. And you'll go with me, of course."

Henry wrinkled his brow at the thought. "Is that my penance?"

She smiled at his discomfort. "Yes, I guess it is."

"Oh, well. My life is almost over anyhow," he said with resignation "I might as well try to make my peace with God." He could see that his days as a free man were over and his dreams of being lord of his own grand manor had come to an end.

CHAPTER 24

Brunswick, Georgia, 1878

While 1878 was a disastrous year for Henry, his nephew John Eugene DuBignon was enjoying one of the best times he had ever known. So much had happened in the last two years that had brought him happiness he never dreamed of. He had finally married the love of his life—Fannie Schlatter—on September 28, 1876, and she'd given birth to a baby girl on their wedding anniversary one year later. By this time John Eugene had established himself as a well-respected businessman in Brunswick. He was prospering as the town slowly transformed itself after the war, with a growing population and many new businesses springing up.

In his eyes, his marriage to Fannie was a miracle—a gift from God, as was their daughter, whom they had named for John Eugene's sister Josephine. The child was beautiful like her mother, and he doted on her. He had never been happier. But as he remembered all too well, it had almost not happened.

Fannie was the daughter of their old family friend and neighbor, Charles Schlatter. She and John Eugene had known each other most of their lives. They were good friends as they grew up—both attractive, close to the same age, and fond of one another. A marriage between the two of them seemed inevitable someday, and their families approved of the match.

But things had changed dramatically not long before Fannie's seventeenth birthday. She had fallen in love with a handsome and sophisticated Englishman named Eardley Graham Westmorland, a British vice-consul who had arrived in Brunswick during the war. When peace came, he stayed on as a representative of an English mercantile firm. He was ten years older than Fannie and far more knowledgeable in the ways of the world. John Eugene, at only eighteen, was not yet prepared to support a family and knew he did not stand a chance against the more mature, refined, and dashing vice-consul, who had won her heart.

As it turned out, Westmorland had another rival as well—a Virginian named Egbert J. Martin who had recently moved to Brunswick. He had served honorably during the war and had the distinction of being the nephew of a well-known Confederal general, the late Edward "Allegheny" Johnson. At first, Martin and Westmorland were friends—until Martin also met and was smitten by Fannie Schlatter. But he was too late, as he would learn bitterly. Westmorland and Fannie were already secretly engaged, though her parents were dead set against the marriage. They thought she was too young and feared he would sweep her off to England and they'd never see their daughter again. They were also concerned, given his age and experience, that he might be too worldly for their daughter and was seeking to seduce her. They forbade her to see him, but Fannie was headstrong and intensely in love with Eardley Westmorland, and she would do anything to be with him. Thus, the young lovers began to meet in secret and make plans to elope.

However, on July 4, the eve of the planned elopement, Fannie's mother intercepted a message from Westmorland, intended for Fannie's eyes only. She grew red-faced with fury as she read the passionate contents of the note and learned of her daughter's defiance. She summoned Fannie to the parlor and closed the doors with a thud.

"Your father and I have forbidden you to see that Englishman. You have obviously defied our wishes." Her voice was stern. Fannie did not flinch.

"And I will continue to defy them," she said, raising her chin. "I love him. I want to be his wife, and I will be with him one way or another." Her voice was bold and rebellious.

"And just what do you mean by that?" her mother asked.

"Make of it what you will, Mother, but I am going to marry him tomorrow with or without your permission. And if you interfere, then I will run away and live with him as his wife anyhow."

"How can you say such a thing? You would be ruined." Her mother was aghast.

"I don't care," she said. "At least I would be happy. I would prefer to have your blessing, but if you and Father try to prevent the marriage, you'll never see me again."

Early the next morning, as she was packing her bags behind the locked door of her room, her father knocked and asked her to come to the parlor once more. She followed him down the stairs into the room where her mother was waiting. He said nothing but sat sad-faced and silent throughout the painful conversation, allowing his wife to do all the talking.

"Last night your father and I discussed the terrible things you said to me yesterday. We have come to the decision that we can't let you ruin your life and reputation. We can't lock you away in a convent, as much as we might want to. But neither of us approves of this marriage. Let's be very clear about that," Frances Schlatter said, standing as tall as she could. Her back was rigid, and her jaw was set.

"Here's what we have decided," she went on. "You will marry today here in this house. That way at least your reputation won't be ruined. We will obtain the marriage license and send for a minister. We have already instructed Mr. Westmorland to be here at 9:30 this morning. The two of you will accompany your father to get the license, and the ceremony will take place at 11:00. That way we can make sure it is all legal and that you don't drag our good name through the mud any more than you already have. But you will *not* have our blessing."

Fannie looked at her father. She could see the anguish on his face. He loved his daughter and wanted nothing to mar her happiness, but his wife was adamant, and he did not interfere.

"Why do you hate him so?" Fannie asked her parents.

"It's not that we hate him," her mother said. "But you've just turned seventeen. You're too young to be married. We know nothing about his family except what he has told us, and I think he would say anything to have you. Furthermore, he is too old for you. He's ten years your senior, and he has clearly tried to seduce you, if he hasn't already succeeded," her mother said bitterly.

"We simply don't trust him, but you leave us no alternative. You have threatened that, if we don't allow you to marry, you will ruin your own reputation so that no decent man would ever want you after that. We will make sure this marriage takes place and that the ceremony is legal and performed by a minister. Then you and Mr. Westmorland will leave this house, and he will never be welcomed here again." Her mother's face was stern. "Just keep in mind that you are making your own bed and you will lie in it. Don't ever come to us for help."

Fannie looked at her father again. He was staring at the floor, a miserable expression on his face, but still he said nothing. His wife had convinced him the night before that these actions were, in the long run, in their daughter's best interest.

When the girl saw no support coming from her father, she turned to her mother once again. Her voice was hard. "Fine. If those are your terms, I accept."

The wedding took place in the parlor of the Schlatter home at eleven o'clock. There were no flowers, no candles, no attendants—only Fannie and Eardley, the minister, and a pair of grim-faced parents to witness their vows.

Once the ceremony was over, Frances turned a still-angry face toward her daughter and her new son-in-law. "Now, get your things and be gone. Neither of you is any longer welcome in this house."

"Father," Fannie stepped forward to embrace her father. He did not return her embrace, but she heard his whispered words, "I love you." Her vision blurred with tears she managed to blink back.

Eardley picked up the small valise she had packed, and they left the house together. He had no home of his own and had given up his rented apartment with their intention to wed and leave Brunswick that very evening on the steamer *Sylvan Shore* headed for Savannah. The only place he had to take his bride to await their departure was his office on Gloucester Street. Despite the unpleasant circumstances, the couple were delighted to be married and to start their life together.

As they walked to his office, Eardley said to everyone they met, "I want you to meet my wife, Fannie Westmorland." He beamed at his own words and Fannie gave a blushing smile. Word of the marriage spread rapidly, and several of Eardley's friends stopped by the office to wish them well. To their surprise, one of those who came by was Egbert Martin, who asked to speak to Fannie. Being a trusting man, Westmorland allowed him to enter the office, where Fannie was waiting. She was apprehensive as he entered, but he seemed calm enough and spoke to her in conciliatory tones.

"I want to congratulate you, Fannie. And I wish you and Eardley well," he said stiffly. She relaxed then and thanked him for coming by. What she would never know and what no one ever revealed was what happened later at the Schlatter home, where Martin went as soon as he left Eardley's office.

About four o'clock in the afternoon, Martin showed up again at the office. Eardley was sitting on the doorstep talking with a friend. He nodded to Martin, thinking he was just passing by. But suddenly Martin's face hardened. He pulled out a pistol and fired, hitting Eardley in the chest. Fannie heard the blast and ran to the front door of the office, opening it just in time to see Martin fire again, this time hitting Eardley in the groin. Fannie stared in horror at her dying husband, then at his assailant.

"You monster," she said, collapsing in tears to take Eardley's body in her arms. Martin did not run away but waited calmly to be arrested. He was taken to Savannah for his own safety to be jailed as he awaited trial for murder.

Fannie was distraught and could not be comforted. Friends took her to her parents' home. She did not want to go there, but there was nowhere else for her to go. *How could anyone do such a thing?* townspeople wondered. This beautiful woman, a girl still, shattered on the happiest day of her life. The whole of Brunswick was shocked by the senseless killing. How could such a thing happen on the main street of their town?

John Eugene learned these details later. He had grieved over the love affair but had not known of the planned wedding. Like everyone else, he was shocked to hear of both the marriage and the murder. All he wanted to do was go to Fannie, put his arms around her, and console her in her grief—his childhood friend, the girl he loved, the woman he had given up hope of ever marrying someday. He did, in fact, call at her parents' home, as soon as he heard. It was her mother who answered the door.

"She won't see you, Johnny. She refuses to see or talk to anyone. She blames me for it all. She's refusing to eat. She's just locked herself her room, and she's been crying endlessly. I can hear her through the door. I just don't know what to do." She was wringing her hands, as though in despair. But he couldn't read the expression on her face. Anguish? Grief? Remorse? Guilt?

For weeks Fannie refused to see him or anyone else. She dressed in black and became a virtual recluse. The only time she emerged from her father's house was the Saturday after the shooting, the day of her husband's funeral at St. Mark's Episcopal Chapel in Brunswick. John Eugene and most of the town attended the service. Some were friends of Fannie or Eardley. Others, he suspected, were there merely out of curiosity. Her parents were present at the funeral and tried to comfort her, but she shunned them and insisted on sitting alone. John Eugene watched her obvious misery during the service. He wanted to take her in his arms and hold her. But all he could do was sit through the funeral, unable to take his eyes off the weeping young widow.

When the service ended, mourners followed the hearse to Oak Grove Cemetery, where Eardley's body would be buried. One of Fannie's good friends walked by her side, her arms around the girl to steady her and keep her from stumbling as the procession made its way along the unpaved street.

The town was outraged, and public opinion ran rampant against the killer. It appeared to be an open-and-shut case. There had been eye witnesses to what happened who proclaimed that the shooting was unprovoked. Egbert Martin's trial was set for September, but for various reasons it was delayed. Friends of the killer insisted that there were "extenuating circumstances" that would come out in the trial, and everyone knew that Martin had powerful connections throughout the South. One local newspaper described him as "a Virginian, of a good family, and a relative of Gen. Edward Johnson." It would be a highly controversial case. When the Superior Court finally convened in mid-November, they found it impossible to seat a jury. Everyone, it seemed, had already made up their minds. The trial was postponed, and bail for Martin was set at $20,000. As one Northern newspaper predicted, "Of course, that will be the last of it, and Martin will go unpunished." And he did. Things had not changed so much under Reconstruction. It seemed that a white man of means with good connections in Georgia could still do pretty much whatever he wanted

Fannie continued reluctantly to live at her parents' home for she had nowhere else to go, but she never forgave her mother. For many months she closeted herself in her room, refusing to come out, even to eat at the table with her parents. She didn't want to see anyone, and her grief seemed endless. She spent many long hours sitting alone beside Eardley's grave, where a fine marble monument, which her father paid for, was her only comfort. Only on rare occasions did she appear in public wearing her widow's weeds. It would take years for her to regain any semblance of her former gaiety.

John Eugene waited patiently. He had never loved anyone else, and he waited—using the time to try to make himself worthy of her, doing all he could to enhance his standing as a good citizen and businessman. He would wait forever, he told himself, if it was necessary.

As soon as Fannie was willing to take social calls, John Eugene began to visit her again, not at first as a suitor, but just as a friend. He tried to tell her light-hearted stories, which she greeted with only a sad smile. Then one day, he heard her laugh out loud. He sympathized with her quixotic moods and tried to keep her entertained by telling her what it had been like to spend his boyhood on Jekyl Island, how he had loved its quiet beauty and wildlife and how it had helped to heal his family's grief after his father died. He made it sound almost magical.

"It would be wonderful to live someplace like that," she said, "in the middle of nature and away from Brunswick and all those prying people." Despite her words, there was still bitterness in her voice.

"I'll take you there someday," he promised.

By her twenty-second birthday, John Eugene, now twenty-four and a partner in a successful dry goods store called DuBignon and Beck, finally declared himself a suitor. He had waited a long time—almost six years—but he knew he would never love anyone else. When he finally found the nerve to propose, to his surprise, she reacted with a charming, even grateful, smile, but she refused to marry him.

"I won't give my mother the satisfaction." she told him. Fannie had never forgiven her mother whom she blamed for all her misery, and she would not allow her the happiness of seeing her only daughter wed an "appropriate" young man.

Fannie waited until after her mother's death on June 2, 1876, before she finally agreed to marry him. John Eugene had waited three more years for that answer. It had been a long wait, nine years in all, *but it was worth it*, he thought. At last everything in his life was falling into place.

Their September wedding was glorious, and he felt that the whole town rejoiced with him. At last she was his. Everything seemed perfect. It had been the beginning of a whole new life. It had given him increased confidence and optimism toward the future. People had responded in kind, beginning to recognize him as a town leader. The year they were married he was chosen as an alderman, and not long after his daughter's birth, he was elected as a member of the city council. With Fannie at his side he felt he could accomplish anything.

As his prestige in the city grew, so did his pride in his family's noble ancestry, and he began to make small efforts to remind townspeople of these origins. He began to write his name as his great-grandfather had written it when he left France to come to America, separating the French *particule* "du" from the name Bignon; signing documents as "J. E. du Bignon," he felt he was restoring his rightful legacy. It was his grandparents who had changed the spelling to "DuBignon" to make it sound and look more American. But he thought it important to remind people of his family's highborn French origins.

His interest in Jekyl Island was a part of these efforts. The du Bignon family had owned it ever since they fled France during the French Revolution. It was their heritage, their home for almost a century. The Jekyl Island plantation had replaced the fine manor his grandfather had boasted about back in France. How many families in Brunswick could make such claims? His only regret was that his branch of the family had, thanks to his grandfather, been cut off from any ownership there whatsoever. That slight still rankled. But, as fate would have it, he found a way to make another dream come true.

It had been only eight months after his marriage to Fannie, not long before his daughter's birth that, as he was drinking his morning coffee in the parlor and reading the local newspaper, his eyes fell on the announcement of a sheriff's sale to be held on the first Tuesday in July.

"Good heavens!" he said to himself. "Fannie!" he called out. "Fannie!"

She rushed into the parlor at his excited tone. "What on earth?" she asked, distressed at his sudden agitation.

"You'll never guess. My chance has come!'

Already six months pregnant, she settled heavily in the nearest chair by the fireplace. "What chance? What are you talking about?"

He could hardly contain his excitement. "Do you remember my Uncle Charles—the one who lived on that big plantation near Milledgeville? Do you remember I told you that he had died two years ago?"

"Yes," she said, still puzzled by his reaction. "What about him?"

"His land at Jekyl Island is going up for auction on the first Tuesday in July. He never took any interest in it, and it looks like his widow is going to sell it to settle one of his debts. I'm going to that auction," he told her.

"Of course you are," she said with a knowing smile.

He talked of nothing else for the next week. Even over dinner, where Fannie had made a special effort to have the table elegantly set with their Haviland-Limoges china and Baccarat crystal, he could talk of nothing else. She had not seen him so excited since she had told him she was expecting a baby. John Eugene sat there, glowing as he gazed around the table, adorned with red roses from his wife's garden.

"You, my dear, are a treasure," he said to his wife. "You continue to bring me not only happiness, but luck as well. With you at my side, I can't fail. And now I have an opportunity to accomplish a lifelong dream."

"And what is that, my dear?" she asked with a smile. She knew perfectly well what he was going to say, but she also knew that he wanted to say it all over again.

"To own at least a part of Jekyl Island, which, as you know, is a part my family's legacy. My branch of the family was left out when my grandfather divided the island." He grinned broadly. "I intend to rectify that."

She had heard the story many times before. It had become almost an obsession with him.

"I hope it all works out," she said as she took a sip of wine.

"It will," he said, his voice ringing with certainty.

On the morning of the auction, John Eugene was anxiously waiting on the courthouse steps. As it turned out, he was not the only bidder, but he proved to be the most determined. At first he stood quietly, watching the bids. As the bidding slowed, he stepped forward and shouted his own higher offer. To his surprise, no one bid against him.

He felt relief and exhilaration when the auctioneer banged down his gavel and announced, "Sold to Mr. du Bignon for $4500." Whether it was a good buy from a financial perspective, he wasn't sure and he didn't care. It was worth every penny to him. He now owned one-third of Jekyl Island. It was a great start. Now, he knew his life was blessed beyond the wildest imagination of the boy he had once been.

CHAPTER 25

Brunswick, Georgia, September 26, 1877

It was on the first anniversary of John Eugene's marriage to Fannie that their daughter, Josephine, was born. She was his third miracle in only a year, and he thought it a sign that she had been born on such an auspicious date.

"She is our gift from God—a blessing on our marriage," he told his wife, who gave him an exhausted smile as she lay against the pillow with the newborn in her arms.

"I never thought I could be happy again," she said softly, "but you've proven me wrong. I love you." Her eyes were soft, and she gave a gentle kiss first to the forehead of little Josephine. Then she stretched toward her husband, who leaned forward to accept her kiss, like an angel's wing brushing his lips. It was the most tender kiss they had ever shared.

John Eugene blinked away tears of joy. It was the first time she had ever made such a declaration of happiness to him.

"You, our marriage, and our daughter have blessed my life," he said. It was as though his entire existence had been transformed.

"Even more than acquiring part of Jekyl Island?" she teased.

"Even more than that," he said, squeezing her hand.

From that moment on, he made it his goal to give his wife and daughter all they could ever want, and when he was not at home doting on his family, to involve himself more in the important affairs of the town. Suddenly, he seemed to see opportunities everywhere—in banking, railroads, shipping, and maybe even a canal that would link Brunswick to the Altamaha River. Those things would prosper, he was sure, and he was determined to be part of it all. Already he felt he had become a truly influential man in town. His marriage to Fannie and the birth of his daughter had spurred his ambitions beyond anything he could have imagined as a sad and disappointed young man of eighteen. With his wife at his side, everything seemed right in the world.

But Fannie was right. John Eugene had not forgotten his dreams of Jekyl Island. The very next day after he bought his uncle Charles's portion at auction, he had written to his sister Josephine and his brother-in-law Newton Finney, who were now living in New York, to tell them his exciting news. Newton had prospered in the northern city and had many times shared the good news of his success with John Eugene. His letters frequently began with the same or similar words. "We are all fine here. Things have been going exceptionally well for my business. Our future is, from all indications, on the rise." Shortly after their arrival in New York City, Newton had formed a partnership with a man named Oliver Kane King. Over time, the partners had tried out diverse roles, with varying success, calling themselves at various times merchants of railroad supplies, bankers, and brokers. Their offices were on Broadway and at a 21 Nassau address, and by now they were thriving.

John Eugene was impressed and determined to do equally well in Brunswick. He wrote to his brother-in-law and sister to inform them of his own recent accomplishment.

> *I've just bought Uncle Charles's one-third of Jekyl Island at auction. You know he died a while back, and Aunt Ann wanted to sell it to settle a debt. Uncle Henry is still fighting to keep his land on Jekyl, and I'm keeping an eye on that situation as well. I don't want any part of the island falling into the hands of strangers. It's been family land for a long time, and I'm going to try to keep it that way. Wish me luck.*

Newton responded almost immediately to his brother-in-law's letter.

> *Good for you and best of luck. I think it will be a good investment, for I predict the island will grow considerably in value in the near future. Did you by any chance read the article in Harper's last November? It was all about the Georgia sea islands and their "picturesqueness and tender beauty," as the writer described them. Mark my words, there's going to be more than one rich northerner who will be interested in that area. I expect you could make a fortune on it. If I can help in any way, just let me know.*

John Eugene was a bit surprised by the reaction of Newton, whose first thought had been to turn a profit by putting his part of the island up for sale, but then, he had never lived on Jekyl. As for himself, he had not thought about *selling* the island—only about acquiring it and making it whole again, as he thought his noble ancestors would have wanted.

Then, not long afterwards, Fannie came across another article in *Lippincott's Magazine* extolling the "Edenlike retreat" of next-door Cumberland Island, describing in poetic terms the abundance of birds and butterflies, the "graceful pennons of Spanish moss" that waved in every wind and changed in every light.

"Is Jekyl as nice as that?" she asked.

"Every bit as nice—I recall it as a place of peace and beauty, a place with so much history, and best of all, it was my family's first home in America."

"I know you're proud to own a part of it now, and I hope it all stays in your family and you and your uncles will keep it that way." Her encouragement provided him with another reason to pursue his now-expanded dream—to reunite the entire island under his ownership.

It didn't take long for Newton's prediction to come true. The very next year after the *Lippincott's* article appeared, Thomas Carnegie, the brother of the more famous Andrew, bought 4,000 acres of Cumberland Island just south of Jekyl and set out to rebuild the old mansion of Dungeness that once stood there. The first one, which had belonged to a Revolutionary War general, Nathanael Greene, had once been a fine plantation house, but the new owners intended for this new Dungeness to be even grander, a showplace where the Carnegie family could invite their wealthy and influential friends. This rich New Yorker had paid $35,000 for only a part of Cumberland. *A mere trifle to a wealthy man like him, I suppose,* John Eugene thought. But it was a fortune to him. Both he and Newton took notice.

He still had no intention of selling his part of Jekyl Island, despite encouragement from his brother-in-law. He hadn't bought it to make money. Rather, it was a family legacy. Nonetheless, the idea had planted itself in his mind and nagged at him, despite his will to cast it aside. Should he ever decide to sell it, it would have to be for a very good reason and to someone worthy, someone who would not divide the land yet again. Jekyl contained between eight and nine thousand acres, considerably more land than the Carnegies had bought on Cumberland. If it were sold as a whole, it would surely be worth a great deal more. But the idea of reselling it for a profit was distasteful for him. Above all, he wanted to be able to share it with his wife and daughter, to let them experience it as he had when he was a boy, to let them feel the freedom and oneness with nature that he and Harry had enjoyed. *No*, he thought, *I could never sell it off to strangers who might not value it as my family did.*

Finney, on the other hand, whose mind seemed always fixed on getting wealthier, could see only the island's potential profitability. He wrote again to John Eugene, pushing that goal to the forefront:

I belong to the Union Club now, thanks to my business partner, Oliver Kane King, who's the club's treasurer. He says it's the oldest and most exclusive men's club in New York. People call it the Mother of Clubs, and it's quite an honor to be a member. Members include not only those of the old Dutch families of New York that people call the Knickerbockers, but also, and perhaps more prevalent, are men who have helped to develop the commercial side of America—industrialists, bankers, railroad tycoons— people who can afford anything they want. You wouldn't believe the people I get to hobnob with—Vanderbilts, Rockefellers, even J.P. Morgan. If I recall correctly, that portion of Jekyl you just bought is right across the Sound from Cumberland. I'll bet one of them would pay a pretty penny for it. Something to think about.

But John Eugene was determined to save the island from strangers who might divide it up in various ways, maybe even build things like sawmills or factories of some sort. The risk of that was increasing daily, given the financial failures of his two uncles, and he was keeping a close eye on the situation to make sure it didn't fall into the wrong hands.

One evening after dinner, he brought the matter up to Fannie. They were sitting before the fireplace where he was enjoying an after-dinner cordial and she was working on a sampler for their daughter's room, squinting in the lamplight to make sure her stitches were straight. Josephine had long been in bed, and they always took this private time just to be together and say to each other whatever was in their hearts.

"I hear that my old uncles at Jekyl, John and Henry, are both having a hard time of it financially. I'm told that there are threats against their land to settle their debts," John Eugene said thoughtfully.

"I feel sorry for them. Is there anything we can do to help?" she asked.

He wasn't surprised by her reaction. She was always sympathetic with those in distress, but he thought people made their own luck and their own misery. Truth be told, he still felt some resentment at his uncles for manipulating his grandfather into deeding the land only to them—with no thought for anyone else.

"They've brought it on themselves," he said. "Ever since the war, they've done nothing constructive to help their situation. They just tried to carry on as though nothing had changed. It's absurd."

"I suppose it's the only life they know," she said. "Maybe they were just too old to start over."

"That may be true, my dear, but they seem to have made no effort at all. They just relied on my grandfather to provide for them. They persuaded him to give them the island. Then, when he died, he willed everything that was left to his new family. I don't know what my uncles expected, but they seem to have made no real effort to adjust to the new way the South is."

"You mustn't be so hard on them, John. Neither of them has had much experience in the business world. All they knew was the old plantation life. It seems that the only time they tried to make money in another way was by allowing that slave ship to land on the island, and that didn't work out very well."

John Eugene nodded. Both he and Fannie had been too young to understand what was happening at the time. But the memory of that episode had long lingered in the area, and they had heard talk of it many times.

"In any case," she went on, "I don't think you should take this as an opportunity to acquire their land, if that's what you have in mind. It would be unkind."

"But if they lose the land, it could be gone forever. Would you object to my trying to acquire it from a new owner if the opportunity came along?"

"Well...no. That's a different matter. I think that would be justified to keep the land in the family. I'm sure that even your uncles would want that, provided you still let them live there if they wish. It's all they know, John. It would be cruel to make them move away at their age and try to adjust to a whole new world."

Her words, as always, reminded him that, to her, compassion mattered more than money. It was one of the things he loved about her. It was a virtue he knew he did not always live up to, but, in this case, he knew she was right. They *were* family after all.

John Eugene was proud of his wife and her intelligence. Each of them had their own role to play, but theirs was an equal partnership, which was more than most of his married friends could say. She was an amazing woman, who read constantly and wrote poetry that had been published by prominent magazines like *Lippincott's* and *Harper's*. She was admired by the community as much as he was—probably more, he thought. He had heard one person describe the "ineffable beauty of her character" and "the charm of her delightful grace and splendid intellect." It was a perfect description of his beloved Fannie. He never hesitated to ask her advice on important matters and she was usually right. He thought for a moment about her words. They were so much a part of her character.

He smiled. "That's a good thought, my dear. And I promise not to make any moves as long as my uncles still own their part of Jekyl, but if they lose it, well, that's a different matter."

She laid down her sampler and looked at him earnestly. "And promise me that you won't evict them from the land even if you do acquire it," she said. "Others might do that, but we couldn't look the rest of the family in the eye if you did."

"I promise," he said, raising his right hand as though he were in a courtroom. "Whatever happens, they will have a lifetime right to remain there if I am ever the owner."

She stood up and went to him, leaning down to kiss him lightly on the lips. "Thank you, John. You're a good man."

But John Eugene was anxious, for he knew that both his uncles had debts they could not pay. He was well familiar with the court case against Henry and was well positioned should his uncle lose, thanks to his arrangement with Martin Tufts to buy the land. But it was all still uncertain at this point.

He had also learned that Henry's portion was not the only part of the island that was under threat. John Eugene was not surprised to learn that his other uncle, John Couper DuBignon, was also in financial trouble. Unlike his brother, John had never longed for a lavish lifestyle. All he cared about was providing for himself and his children. But even with his frugality, he had almost no income and was doing nothing substantial to earn money. The only planting he did now was a garden to feed his family. He had lost all his spirit after Sylvia's death, but the children needed clothes, and there were things they couldn't grow on the island. The debts of his accounts had mounted over the years, and there was no way he could repay them. His creditors were a local Brunswick merchant, Gustavus Friedlander, and his attorney, William Anderson. Finally, they too began demanding payment for his debt. He had chosen not to fight it in court, for he knew that he owed the money and would repay it if he could. He certainly didn't want to face the humiliation of another public legal case. His appearance in the Savannah courtroom during his trial after the *Wanderer* debacle was still raw. All that uncertainty. All those people staring at him. All that gossip. He was determined to avoid it. But, like Henry, the only thing he owned of any value sufficient to cover his debt, as his creditors pointed out, was his part of Jekyl Island. It seemed he had no choice.

Thus, at the insistence of Friedlander and Anderson, he traveled to Brunswick for a day to meet with them and try to settle the matter. He went alone to Friedlander's office.

"We can no longer provide you with any credit, Mr. DuBignon, and I'm afraid the time has come that we must insist on payment." Friedlander's voice was friendly, but firm. Anderson nodded in affirmation.

"You know full well that I have no money with which to pay the debt I owe you," John admitted in his most dignified manner. "You have been most generous in extending the credit as long as you have, but there's nothing I can do." Then they raised the possibility of the feared solution.

"You own land, Mr. DuBignon. Land has value," Anderson pointed out. "Gustav and I have discussed it, and we have decided that we might be willing to accept the deed to your land on Jekyl Island in lieu of payment?"

"That land has been in my family for three generations. I just don't see how I can part with it. Where would I go?"

Friedlander was quiet for a moment before he spoke. "What if you didn't have to leave at all? You could stay there if you like, but we would own the land. It's security for your debt. We'd be happy to sell it back to you if the time should come when you're able to make sufficient payment."

John sat in silence, contemplating their offer. Then Anderson spoke again. "How many acres do you have, and what is your land worth?"

"I don't know exactly. I think it's about 3,000 acres. I don't know what it's worth now. You'd have to have it appraised. I want to be sure I understand what you say. If I agree, the land will be yours, but are you saying that I could still live there with my children? I could stay in my home?"

"Until your death, but you couldn't leave it to your children in your will. Frankly, Mr. DuBignon, it's a good offer and one you can't afford to turn down." Letting the man and his family live there was no inconvenience for them. From the looks of him he wouldn't live too much longer anyhow. And so the matter was settled.

When John Eugene learned of the situation, he decided to waste no time. The land no longer belonged to his Uncle John, and Fannie had agreed that, once it was in the legal possession of someone else, she had no objection to his trying to buy it. It was the perfect chance—one he could not forego.

Only a day after he first heard of the settlement, he made an appointment with Friedlander. On the agreed-upon afternoon, he put on his frock coat, his black silk string tie, and his new Homburg. He wanted to look stylish, reasonably well off, and certainly serious about the transaction he intended to propose.

When he reached the office of the dry goods store of G. Friedlander and Company, he doffed his hat and waited until Mr. Friedlander was free. The office door soon opened, and a tall, heavy-set man stood there.

"Do come in," he said to John Eugene. "It's very nice to see you." The man spoke with a German accent. John Eugene knew he had come to America as an immigrant to escape Jewish persecution in Germany. Like so many others of his faith, he had gone into the dry goods business and had prospered. John Eugene had encountered him only briefly once before, but this was the first time he'd dealt with the man or had the opportunity to assess him closely. He seemed for the most part a genial fellow, though like most merchants, he had a shrewd look in his eye. When Friedlander had first arrived from the old world, he settled for a time in New York City before arriving in Georgia to sell Yankee notions. And he had prospered. He had expanded his business and now had a large store that included all kinds of merchandise ranging from coats and hats to groceries, and even liquor. He had done well in Brunswick.

The two men exchanged pleasantries for a minute or two before Friedlander asked, "What brings you to my office on such a nice day?"

"A proposition, which I hope will benefit us both," John Eugene replied.

Friedlander's curiosity was piqued. "And what might that be?"

"I have learned that you and Bill Anderson have recently accepted my Uncle John DuBignon's land on Jekyl Island as payment for his debts."

"Yes, that's true. But we've told him he could stay there for the rest of his life."

"That's quite generous of you," John Eugene said. "And what will you do with the land?"

"I don't know. I suppose we'll eventually sell it."

"What will become of him if you sell the land to someone else?"

"Well," Friedlander said, "I suppose that if someone else buys it, they may require him to vacate, particularly given his ... unusual family circumstances."

"I do understand. But it would break his heart to have to leave the island," John Eugene said, hoping to appeal to Friedlander's better nature. "He has always told me that he was born there and that he intends to die there." He was sure the German immigrant knew what it was like to be compelled to leave one's life-long home.

"Yes, I agree," he said sympathetically. "It would be a shame, I suppose, especially at his age."

"I'm here to discuss an offer that will compensate you for his debt and also allow Uncle John to remain there."

"And what might that be?" Friedlander asked, suddenly very interested.

"I would be willing to pay the price of his debt, or most of it anyhow, in exchange for the land. And, as the new owner, I would allow Uncle John to stay on Jekyl with his...family."

"Do you even know how much the debt is?"

"Somewhere in the range of four thousand dollars, I'm told."

"And would you be willing to pay that much?" Friedlander asked.

"Yes," I would, "if it would help my uncle."

"Hmmm," Friedlander said thoughtfully. "That's a magnanimous gesture, but before making any decision in the matter, I will, of course, have to talk with Mr. Anderson."

"Of course. How much time do you need?" John Eugene asked.

"Shall we say a week from today? I should have an answer by then."

"A week from today will be fine. I'll call again at that time. Is three o'clock satisfactory?"

"It is indeed," Friedlander said warmly, and the two men shook hands.

Friedlander walked John Eugene to the door and ushered him out of his office, with another cordial handshake. "Good to talk with you," he said.

"You too," John Eugene replied and, with a smile on his face from rising hopes, he made his way outside. He had intended for his proposal not to sound in any way mercenary, but rather altruistic. He was doing this to help his old uncle rather than just to acquire the land for himself. And he had no trouble convincing himself that it was true. Above all, he thought, Fannie would approve.

One week later, John Eugene arrived at the precise hour they had agreed upon. This time both Friedlander and Anderson were waiting in the office. They greeted him warmly.

"Gustav and I have talked about the matter," Anderson said, "and we have agreed that your proposition could be a good solution to a potentially difficult situation, *if* you are willing to pay a sufficient amount."

"And what would that be?" John Eugene asked, trying to hide his enthusiasm.

Again Anderson spoke, "Four thousand five hundred would cover the debt." John Eugene would have paid that amount rather than let the land escape him, but he had learned from his brother-in-law Newton Finney that it was always best to bargain a bit. He also knew that these were experienced businessmen quite accustomed to haggling over the price. "That seems a bit steep. Would you accept $3500?"

Anderson's face held no expression as he said, "The debt was a good deal more than that, but $4500 would cover it."

"And then some, from what I hear," John Eugene recounted. He took a pen and a small writing pad from his pocket and began to jot down figures, finally raising his head and replying,

"Current obligations would not allow me to pay that much." He hoped the two men were as eager to unload the land and settle the matter as he thought.

They looked at each other, and some kind of signal passed between them. This time it was Friedlander who spoke. He turned to John Eugene and said gravely, "We couldn't take a penny less than $4,000."

John Eugene hesitated for a moment, as though he were thinking it over and doing mental calculations. Finally he said, "I think I could manage that, but no more." In fact, despite his sober appearance, he was delighted with the price, though he hid it as best he could. He knew it didn't quite cover the full amount of his uncle's debt, but it would relieve the two lenders of any property tax responsibilities and having a useless piece of real estate on their hands. And at least, it would give them some capital to invest. The men shook hands to close the deal, and John Eugene went home to take the happy news back to his wife. "We now own two-thirds of Jekyl Island," he told her jubilantly, "and I didn't break my promise." She smiled her appreciation.

CHAPTER 26

Brunswick, Georgia, 1883

Time passed, and John Eugene fretted that the matter of Uncle Henry's land had still not been decided. It was his last important hurdle to owning the island. Even though his uncle had been compelled to leave Jekyl after the family house burned, he still clung tenaciously to the land. It was his last claim to his family's wealth.

Even if John Eugene could acquire his uncle's part of Jekyl, he reminded himself that there would still be the small portion of Aunt Eliza's thirty acres. He would put that off until last. He feared it might violate his wife's caveat about not buying directly from his uncles. Fannie had, of course, not mentioned his aunt, but he suspected she had simply forgotten about Aunt Eliza's small acreage. He saw no advantage to his aunt's clinging to the land. She never went there, and it seemed to him only a tax burden, but she had no financial problems like those of her brothers. She was frugal, never spent beyond her means, and carefully guarded what little she had managed to acquire. She was cautious in business matters, and he knew she could be obstinate and inflexible. *She may be attached to the land for nostalgic reasons,* he thought uneasily, *and she can be stubborn.* To be honest, he was a bit afraid of his aunt, and he wanted to delay approaching her as long as possible.

He would first wait to see what the court decided in the case of Uncle Henry. He agreed with Tufts that his uncle's claim for a homestead exemption was a sham, but he was nonetheless amazed at how cleverly and quietly he had gone about it. John Eugene had to admit that his uncle was a shrewd man.

Another year went by before the matter of Henry's Jekyl land was finally decided. The decision was in his favor, but he would not celebrate his victory for long. One morning in January 1885, there was a knock on John Eugene's front door. When he opened it, he was surprised to see a dark-skinned middle-aged man standing there. He recognized the visitor as Aunt Eliza's yard man. Negroes rarely came to the front door, so John Eugene assumed it must be important.

"Mornin', Fred," he said. "What brings you here? Is somethin' wrong?"

"Miss Eliza sent me over here to tell you that Mister Henry done passed away just 'fore daylight." His voice was appropriately sorrowful.

With what he hoped was a similar sorrow in his own voice, John Eugene said, "I'm so sorry to hear that, Fred. Tell Aunt Eliza I'll be over directly to help her see to things." He gave the man a dime for his trouble and closed the door, ashamed of his momentary feelings of renewed hope.

After the funeral, which was attended only by family members, there was the matter of settling Henry's estate, such as it was. He had left no will and appointed no executor. Alice wasted no time in petitioning the court for the guardianship of her own son, Henry Francis, which she was granted, but only after paying a substantial bond. Then, on behalf of the boy, she quickly persuaded her brother, Wilfred Francis Symons, to apply for the executorship of Henry's estate. She was determined that Uncle Henry would keep his promise, whether he'd intended to or not.

The court agreed that the sole heir was Henry Francis DuBignon, the deceased man's "adopted son." In his role as executor, Symons had the estate, primarily the land, appraised. It was estimated to be worth $5,000. John Eugene waited impatiently to see what Symons and the boy's mother would decide to do with it.

Alice wanted to keep it. "It was a dream of my husband to own a part of that island. That's the only reason I allowed that ridiculous adoption in the first place," she said.

"But, Alice, what on earth is Henry Francis going to do with it?" her brother asked. "He's more a scholar than a farmer. The land is too valuable to just sit there, and it could pay for a fine education for the boy. I know you loved your husband and want to preserve his dream, but your son is more important now, don't you think? I would advise you to sell the land."

Alice allowed herself to be persuaded. They both assumed that the Jekyl property would sell at auction for at least as much as Charles's had all those years ago and perhaps more. She remembered what the deputy had said when Henry came to persuade her to give her permission for him to adopt her son. "The land will grow in value." Maybe her brother was right. She should sell it.

John Eugene had made no attempt to approach either Alice or Wilfred to try to influence them one way or the other. Nor did he offer to buy the land outright. Given his promise to Fannie, he knew she would frown on him for trying to convince the representative of a seventeen-year-old boy to sell it to him. She would think him an utter cad for trying in some underhanded way to wrest land from a child. Besides, the boy was Harry's only son, and John Eugene had loved his brother and wanted to stay on good terms with his family. He would wait for the auction.

The court approved the sale to be held the following June. John Eugene breathed a sigh of relief and thanked God for this new opportunity. Even Fannie was pleased. He was determined to buy the land whatever the cost. This might be his only opportunity.

There were fewer bidders waiting for the sale at the courthouse steps than John Eugene had expected. The bidding was brisk at first but began to slow quickly. It had opened, surprisingly, at only two hundred dollars, the bid offered by a young, bearded man with an eager look on his face.

"Two fifty," shouted a swarthy-looking man with heavy jowls, who appeared to have been drinking. It was an absurdly low price, John Eugene thought.

"Three hundred," the younger man called out.

They kept raising each other until the bid had reached $800. At that point, the swarthy man dropped out to the younger man's delight. Up to that point, John Eugene had merely watched, observing the demeanor of the bidders and calculating the best moment to jump in. The hopeful young man clearly wanted the land. But during the early bidding John Eugene had studied his manner of dress and decided that he was probably unable go much higher with his offer. He decided to test the waters.

"One thousand dollars," he said loudly, jumping the bid to a new level of competition. He hoped his voice was calm but determined enough to discourage the other bidder. The young man paled visibly at his offer. Everyone, including the auctioneer was looking in his direction, awaiting a counteroffer. The young man hesitated, took out a pad and pencil to jot something down. He was clearly wavering, but a jump of $200 in the bidding suggested resolve on his rival bidder's part, as it was intended to do.

John Eugene was trying to appear composed and nonchalant. He would go much higher, if he had to, but, in truth, his available funds were depleted. He had already been compelled to borrow money, and he did not want to take on much more debt. He held his breath as he waited for a response.

The young man looked perplexed and disheartened as he gazed at his opponent and pondered whether there was any point in continuing. John Eugene had tried to distinguish himself from other bidders by wearing his very best clothes. He was even carrying a silver-headed cane like the one he'd heard his grandfather always brandished to make himself look wealthy and important. It was intended to intimidate the other bidders. Whether it was working or not, he couldn't be sure. So, he waited.

Finally, the young man reluctantly shook his head. The auctioneer hesitated for a few moments to see if he would change his mind or to give any other bidders an opportunity to make an offer, but there was only silence in the small crowd. Finally, he banged down his gavel and announced in a loud voice, "Sold to John Eugene du Bignon for one thousand dollars."

John Eugene breathed a sigh of relief and stepped forward to settle the matter. It was definitely a bargain. He suspected that his sister-in-law Alice would be disappointed at the price, but he felt no guilt. In fact, he was elated. His bargain with Tufts had been for a much higher amount. This time, given the public nature of the auction, he felt sure that his ownership could not be questioned. *Alice and the boy will always be welcome on the island,* he thought, soothing his conscience. *And Harry would be pleased to see it all coming together again.*

Now, there was only one small piece of land to acquire before he accomplished his goal—the thirty acres that belonged to his Aunt Eliza. It was the one he dreaded most.

It was a warm afternoon, and a gentle breeze was blowing through the open windows of the sitting room. Fannie was seated at her writing desk with a pen in her hand, gazing thoughtfully out the window at a robin perched on a limb of the live oak tree.

"Hello, love. I hate to interrupt, but do you have a minute?" John Eugene asked.

He had decided to talk with his wife before he approached his aunt. He knew he could always trust her advice, especially when it came to dealing with women.

"I always have time for you, John," she said with a smile, brushing back a curl that had come loose as she worked. She laid down her pen. "What's on your mind?"

"Remember when we talked about the possibility of acquiring

Jekyl Island, and you told me I shouldn't take advantage of my uncles' misfortunes and try to buy their land directly from them? I'm sure you thought it would make me appear calculating and greedy."

She nodded. "I do think it would have been in poor taste. But we both agreed that, should someone else take over the island, it would be acceptable to try to save the family land and buy it back, which you did. I thought you were very patient and that you handled it quite nicely."

"Patience is my specialty," he said with a laugh. "Remember how long I waited for you?"

She smiled and blew him a kiss. "I do indeed."

"Well, I want to ask your advice again. As you know, I own most of the island now, but to have it all, I still need to acquire Aunt Eliza's thirty acres. I think her situation is different from my uncles'. She isn't destitute like her brothers were. And she isn't dependent on the land. She never plants crops there or uses it in any way. But I *need* that one small piece of land to make it all complete."

He paused and took a deep breath, watching his wife's reaction as she considered his words. Before she could speak, he went on, "She has the right to say no, of course. But I'm so close to my goal now that I can taste it. Do you think it would be all right if I approached *her* directly about selling it?"

Fannie, always thoughtful about the feelings of others, considered it for a long moment before she replied. "Well, perhaps. But you shouldn't put any pressure on her. She's elderly now, and she has the right to leave her land to whomever she chooses."

"That's true, and she can certainly be ornery."

Fannie laughed softly and raised her eyebrows. "Now John, you know it's a family trait. So can you."

"Well...maybe." He laughed. "But she has no children of her own and probably hasn't even been to the island in ten or fifteen years. Maybe more. I don't know why she'd want to hang on to it."

"Maybe because it belonged to her parents?"

"Maybe, or maybe she just never thinks about it one way or another. But even if that were the case, she's sharp-witted, and she won't agree unless I can make her see merit in the offer."

"Then make the offer in a tactful way. And if she says no, accept her answer gracefully without any argument or additional effort to persuade her," she said firmly.

"That sounds fair enough." He gave her a quick kiss. "You're always so wise, my dear wife," he said, and he meant it. "I never want to do anything that would displease you. You know that." But more than that, he was glad he had asked her opinion, for he felt reassured that she didn't think it in bad taste to discuss the matter with his aunt.

It was just before teatime when he called on his aunt Eliza. She was already sitting in the parlor.

"Do come in," she said. She gestured to her maid Miriam to fetch another cup. "It's always nice to have a visit from my nephew. And how are your lovely wife and adorable daughter?" She looked as she always did, a well-groomed spinster with rigid, upright posture, wearing a black dress with a white lace collar, her silver hair gathered in a neat bun behind her head.

"Fannie and Josephine are both doing well, Aunt Eliza, and we would love to have you come for a visit whenever you can."

"Well, Johnny, you know I haven't been doing well recently, and I don't get out much. To tell the truth, I miss Henry. He was more company than I expected."

"I'm sure he was. We are all so sorry about his death, Aunt Eliza. But it was a lovely funeral." He knew that she had planned it and made sure that all the family attended.

"I have reserved the burial plot next to his at Oak Grove for myself," she said.

"Oh, it's much too soon to think about such things. You have many years left, I'm sure."

"Well, I doubt it. I'm eighty-five now, Johnny. I've already lived a long time—longer than any of my brothers. John Couper is still with us, of course, but I'm two years older than he, so I've still lived longer," she said with a satisfied smile.

"You'll probably outlive all of us, Aunt Eliza," he said.

"I rather doubt that. Besides, it's sad to be left here all alone. I had grown rather accustomed to having Henry around." She paused for a moment, as she poured him a cup of tea. "And to what do I owe this delightful visit from my nephew?" she asked. "Is it strictly a social call or do you have something else on your mind?" Her eyesight wasn't good anymore. Nonetheless she looked at him sharply, with her faded, but piercing eyes, as though she already suspected why he had come.

For the first time in all these negotiations, he felt flustered. "Well, both, I suppose."

"And just what is on your mind?" she asked.

He could see that there was no tactful way to work around to the real reason for his visit. Perhaps, he thought, the best thing is to get right to the point. "Well," he said in a nervous voice, "I've come to discuss Jekyl Island."

"I suspected as much," she said without emotion. "I've heard from various people that you have recently acquired all my brothers' shares of the island and I suppose you are now here to talk about buying mine."

"You are a discerning woman, Aunt Eliza," he said. "I've always admired you for that."

"Don't try to flatter me, Johnny," she said with impatience. "Just get to the point."

"I've always wanted to own a part of the island, Aunt Eliza, but you know that when my grandfather divided it, only his *living* sons received a share—and you, of course."

"And I've always suspected that, as Joseph's sons, you and Harry, God rest his soul, felt some resentment about that, though you never said anything."

"Not so much resentment as disappointment, and perhaps a bit of hurt that my father's family had been overlooked. You know that my family lived at Jekyl for a number of years—both before my father entered the legislature and after his death, when it became a place of healing for us all. It meant a lot to us." He paused and then went on. "Both my father and my mother were born there, as were my brother and sisters. My father and both my grandmothers are buried there. We felt it was our home, and we all loved it growing up, and yet we were left out. It hurt." It was the most candidly he had ever spoken to his Aunt Eliza or anyone except Fannie about his feelings on the matter.

"You were barely a boy when you lived on the island."

"Old enough to remember how Harry and I used to play together on the shore and explore the woods. I longed to grow up there like my father did. I've always missed it," he said.

"You've certainly succeeded better in Brunswick than you would ever have done there as a planter. The example of Henry and John Couper should make that clear."

"That's probably true, but it's not so much about financial success as about preserving our family heritage. It was your grandfather's land—the land for which he sacrificed everything he had in France. When the portions of all my uncles were in danger of falling into the hands of strangers, I was horrified. I just couldn't let that happen if I could prevent it. If it did, some part of our family's heritage on the Georgia coast would have been lost."

She nodded thoughtfully and took a sip of tea. "I suppose that's true," she said.

"I've made it my goal to preserve it intact, as it was in my great-grandfather's day, so that no one will ever forget the noble French family that settled there. I feel that I owe that to the family. And I know Harry would have agreed with me. He also loved the island."

"A *noble* endeavor, I'm sure." Her voice sounded a bit skeptical, then it softened. "Since I anticipated your visit, I have already thought about it. The island is special to me as well, and I also grew up there. but I haven't been there for a long time now," Eliza said.

"I know that, my dear aunt. And since you don't work the land, I suspect your portion is something of a tax liability."

She put down her teacup and looked him squarely in the eyes. "And you? What would *you* do with the island?"

"Well, I've always wanted to take Fannie and Josephine there—to see where I grew up. And I hope to build a house where we could stay for extended visits. After that," he said, "I'm not sure. Maybe raise some livestock. Mainly, I'd like to be able to go there whenever I want to. You and the other family members would always be welcome, of course. I just want to see it have a future worthy of our lineage."

"And just what is your offer?" she asked.

"Well," he hesitated, "I bought Uncle Henry's three thousand acres for a thousand dollars at auction. I figure that suggests that the value of the land is about $3.35 an acre."

"You paid a good deal more for the others."

"That's true, but it was not at auction, but to help settle my uncle's debts. I think an auction gives one more insight into the true value of the land."

"So, what would you offer for my land?" she asked.

"I think a hundred dollars would be a fair market price."

"A hundred dollars. Well, it's not much."

"True," he said, "and I would be willing to pay more. But you don't really need the money or the help as they did."

"It would, I suppose, be good to see the lands reunited. I'll consider it, but I'd like to discuss it with my attorney before I decide."

"Take your time, Aunt Eliza. And do what you think is right," he said, remembering his wife's advice.

When they had finished their tea and their discussion had reached its logical conclusion, he said his farewells, and she showed him out. Standing at the door, she said, "I'll have an answer for you by Monday."

Well, at least she said didn't say no, he thought with relief. His hopes were high as he made his way home.

When John Eugene walked in the front door, Fannie was waiting for him in the foyer. "Well, what did she say?"

"She said she'd think about it and let me know by Monday.

I'm hopeful, but by no means certain that Jekyl Island will soon be restored intact, just as my great-grandfather bought it. If and when that's the case, I plan to build us a house there so that we can spend comfortable periods of time—just you, me, and Josephine. And the servants, of course."

"Don't count your chickens too soon, John. She hasn't said yes yet."

CHAPTER 27

The following Monday, John Eugene went once again to call on his aunt. He was nervous about the visit. Although he knew it was only a small part of the island, it was important to him, for without it he could never fulfill the totality of his longed-for dream of reuniting the lands.

His aunt's long-time housekeeper, Miriam, who had once been a slave at the Couper plantation on St. Simons, opened the door and ushered him into the parlor, where he waited nervously for his Aunt Eliza to arrive. He sat stiffly on the settee, with nothing to do but study his surroundings. There was the old mantle clock his aunt had brought from the big house on Jekyl. The carpet on the floor was one that had come from his grandmother's dining room, and the kerosene lantern on the end table, he suspected, was also from the big house, for she had gas lighting everywhere else. But most of the furniture and fixtures she had acquired after she moved into Brunswick—the blue velvet settee, the mahogany tea table and wing-back chairs beside the fireplace. Only one of them had a matching footstool, where he had seen his aunt prop her feet to keep her ankles from swelling. It was a comfortable house that looked a bit old-fashioned and prim like its owner.

Ten minutes or more passed, and John Eugene was beginning to worry. Finally, he heard his aunt's uncertain footsteps on the stairs.

"Please forgive me for keeping you so long, Johnny," she said merrily, as she made her entrance leaning on her walking cane, "but I don't move as quickly as I once did."

"I'm happy to see you anytime, late or early, Aunt Eliza. I should perhaps have given you a more precise time of my arrival. I hope I haven't inconvenienced you."

"Oh, not at all. I assume you've come for my answer to your offer," she said.

"That, of course, but more so to see my favorite aunt."

"Nonsense," she said. "Would you care for some tea before I give you my answer?"

"That is entirely up to you, Aunt Eliza."

"Well then," she said and rang the little silver bell on the tea table to summon her housekeeper.

"Miriam, bring us a pot of tea and some of those molasses cookies you made this morning."

The woman nodded, curtsied slightly, and hurried off to the kitchen to prepare the tea.

While they waited, Eliza made small talk about the weather, other family members, and a church social she had attended. John Eugene tried to show interest in what she was saying, but he was restless to know her decision.

Finally the tea and cookies arrived. Eliza took her time pouring, offering him sugar and cream and commenting on Miriam's cookies. "These are her specialties, you know, but she also makes the most tasty currant cookies."

He tried not to seem anxious, but he knew she was teasing him intentionally with her delay. Finally, when they had finished the cups of tea, she brought up the question.

"I have thought about your offer, and while it is not overly generous to be sure, I have decided to accept it. My solicitor thought I should ask for more, but I thought *why, what's the point?* I will die soon anyhow, and it will save me a painful decision as to whom I should leave it in my will. I'll have my lawyer draw up the papers this week. Would you like another cookie?"

He would have eaten all her cookies, drunk all her tea, and kissed her feet, if it made her happy. It was a dream come true. "You are too kind, Aunt Eliza," he said, taking another cookie, even though he didn't much care for the taste of molasses. But today everything was delicious.

He wrote to Newton at once to relay the good news.

I've done it, Newton. I have acquired the entire island of Jekyl. Fannie and I are going to build a house there, nothing fancy, but a good house where we can either live or just have short visits with little Josephine. She's six years old now, pretty as her mother, and she has never set foot on the island, I'm ashamed to say. I'm sure she will enjoy all the things one can do there. To me it was the dream world of my childhood. Ask your Josephine just how wonderful it was growing up there. You are of course welcome there any time, or with us here in Brunswick for that matter. I hope you'll visit soon.

John Eugene's memories of Jekyl dated from some of the earliest years in his life, yet they left an enduring impact in his mind. He couldn't be absolutely sure which ones were real and which were painted with a fanciful brush based on stories that had been told to him. They represented in his mind the reality and wonders of his early youth, not just an amalgam of small past moments of joy coupled with gilded recollections and idealized anticipation. He recalled his family's life on the island as simple, where home and nature were conjoined, where one lived both indoors and outdoors under the live oaks, and where he found simple entertainment, like watching dolphins leaping in the salty river waters near his house or hummingbirds hovering over the bluebonnets and beebalm his mother had planted alongside the front porch. It was a tromp through the woods or along the beaches with his big brother Harry. It was Cherokee roses announcing the spring and hazy memories of finding turtle nests and beautiful seashells, which his mother had told him were gifts from the ocean. If possible, he wanted to recapture, even for a while, that simple but carefree life he thought he recalled there, and he wanted to share it with his wife and his daughter.

In his excitement he had already selected a plan and begun the building of the new house. It would not be a showplace, but a modest home with a wide porch, a dog trot to the kitchen, and tall windows one could open to let in the breezes, like the ones he remembered from his childhood. It would be a place where ease and comfort were more important than style, a place where he and his family could relax from all the hubbub of their lives in downtown Brunswick.

Despite his determination to keep it unpretentious, the Brunswick newspaper nonetheless reported it, sight unseen, "an elegant home." John Eugene thought perhaps it was difficult for the journalist to imagine him and Fannie building anything less. But he had made sure the design was restrained—nothing so elegant as the home he planned to build in Brunswick someday. Besides, after borrowing so much to invest in the land, money was growing scarce.

When the house was finished, he brought his family out to see it. Little Josephine loved the boat ride through the marshes. Venturing through the marsh creeks was not something her family had ever done together. She sat beside her father, who pointed out a snowy white egret hunting for supper in the murky waters and a great blue heron on a stately march across a grassy hummock. She caught sight of a large alligator sunning himself on a muddy bank and huddled closer to her father at the sight.

"Do you think he'll eat me?" she asked. She had seen alligators before, but never up so close.

"I think he's already had his dinner and is taking a nap," John Eugene answered with a soft laugh.

She relaxed then and hummed to herself for a while as they moved swiftly through the waters. "Are we almost there?"

"Almost," her father said.

As they drew nearer to the island, he pointed to the new house, which loomed large in the empty landscape. It was the only structure interrupting the natural beauty of the land with its sprawling live oak trees and Spanish moss waving gracefully in the island breeze. Brick chimneys rose above the housetop like rigid fingers pointing toward heaven. Three gables, their shutters open and welcoming, pierced the roof. Once they docked on the riverbank, they left the boatmen to secure the craft and the three of them walked toward their new home. As they approached, Fannie said, "I like the shady porch that wraps around the front and side of the house."

Once inside, an excited Josephine ran here and there, laughing, her voice echoing through the empty rooms, "Here's the parlor, Mama!" or "This can be my bedroom. Come look out the window!" Her excitement seemed to dim as she said with dismay, "But, Papa, there's no furniture."

"I thought I'd let you and your mother choose the furnishings," John Eugene said, glancing at Fannie for confirmation.

She nodded absently and half-smiled, distracted as she examined the house's details, the fireplace mantles, the flowered wallpaper in the dining room, and the staircase newel posts.

John Eugene was concerned by her silence. "I know it's rather plain, but I thought the real attraction here was the island itself. I wanted it to be a place to relax, where we didn't need to worry about the demands of business and society."

"I think it will do very nicely," she said, and he could see that she was already arranging furniture in her mind. "I doubt we'll be spending a great deal of time here, but I like it."

A fleeting sense of disappointment passed over him. He had hoped they'd be able to spend summers here at least. "You don't think it's *too* modest, I hope," he said.

"Of course not. Hmmm, maybe wicker chairs for the front porch or several wooden rockers," she murmured, more to herself than to him. He could see her mentally at work, making decisions about her selections, contemplating draperies for the various rooms, and considering color choices. She seemed happy enough, he thought.

As it turned out, Fannie was right. They didn't spend as much time there as John Eugene had hoped. Their visits were usually only fragments of time. Josephine was in school now, and they could come only on weekends or rare school holidays, though he still had hopes for the summer. In the meantime, he didn't want the island to lie idle, considering what he had spent to buy it. He decided to invest in some good Devon stock, known for its fine beef. He had no intention of planting cotton as his predecessors had done. It was too risky, too labor intensive, and subject to insect plagues, storms, and drought. But livestock was a different matter.

During one of their brief visits, John Eugene and Fannie were sitting on the front porch of their new Jekyl house, relaxing in the late afternoon breeze and waiting for the multi-hued sunset to spread its special aura over the marshes. Suddenly, a lone doe wandered out of the forest and stopped in front of the cottage. She paused and fixed her eyes on John Eugene. *Lucy,* he thought, remembering the little fawn he and his brother had found alone in the woods that day so long ago. For a moment, he was four years old again, and this was Lucy, all grown up and standing before him. *But it can't be,* he thought. *Deer don't live that long.* Then, a buck and a fawn stepped out of the brush, cautiously following her into the open area. As John Eugene watched, lost in his thoughts, they loped into the forest once again. *I hope she found the mate Mama said she'd find. Perhaps this doe is her daughter.*

Then, as his thoughts circled back to the present, John Eugene took a deep breath and turned to Fannie. He hesitated for a moment, then finally asked the question he had wanted to ask for a long time. "How do you like being on the island?"

"I like it fine, dear," she replied with a vague smile. "But it does get a bit lonely here on occasion, and Josephine has no one to play with. I don't think I'd want to live here all the time." Sometimes, he knew, she appreciated the solitude, which permitted her to contemplate, read, and compose her poetry. The leisure and absence of human distractions provided a good setting for such a solitary task, but her poems did not comprise her entire life, as she made clear.

"I must confess that, when we stay here for longer periods, I miss my friends and some of the social events we enjoy in Brunswick."

John Eugene had to admit, at least to himself, that, except for these serendipitous moments when memory carried him back to his childhood, even he didn't find Jekyl as exciting as it was when he was a boy. Then, it was full of adventure and constant new discoveries, but now, at his more mature age, he no longer wandered the woods, like he had as a boy, looking for deer antlers and arrowheads or scanning the beach for sharks' teeth. Instead he took his family on more staid carriage rides along the old plantation roads. The sunsets were still like daily miracles, and he loved strolling on the beach with his daughter and taking occasional solitary horseback rides. But it was no longer the remembered home of his childhood. Like his wife, he found he missed the hustle and bustle that had begun to characterize the growing town of Brunswick, where he was well known and highly respected. He now had so many responsibilities there that even his brief absences could become a problem. Together, he and Fannie were a part of everything of significance that went on in the town. He served on the board of directors for the Brunswick Savings and Trust Company. He was president of the Brunswick Club and presiding board member of the Brunswick and Florida Inland Steamboat Company as well as of the local newspaper, the *Times-Advertiser*, and he had to confess that it all pleased him very much.

Given his success, few people in Brunswick even remembered his grandfather's peccadillos. He felt certain that he had helped restore the family name, which he continued to spell "du Bignon," to encourage the prestige it once had when his noble ancestors first arrived in Georgia and were said to be one of the richest families in Glynn County. A man could ask for nothing more.

His latest success in acquiring the whole of Jekyl Island had convinced him that he could achieve whatever he set out to do. If time stopped there, he would feel proud of all he had accomplished. Nonetheless, he had not bought the island just to raise cattle. That was only a stopgap measure to justify the purchase, and it made him nervous. He kept remembering Newton's last letter, which encouraged him to sell. *"Now that you own the entire island, I'll bet you could sell it at a handsome profit, probably as much as a hundred thousand dollars—maybe more."* That was a fortune, and John Eugene was tempted. *Perhaps it might be interesting to test the waters*, he thought. But should he sell it—after all his talk about buying back the island for the du Bignon family? He certainly wasn't willing to sell it to just anyone. It had to be someone special—someone who would help the island regain its former prestige. After considering it for a while, he finally wrote to Newton.

> *I'm willing to have some of your wealthy friends down for a hunting party to get their reactions. I can host them in my new house on the island. But I'm still not sure whether I'm interested in selling.*

Newton sprang into action, and in the spring of 1885 a group of wealthy hunters, mostly members of New York's Union Club, arrived on Jekyl as guests of John Eugene du Bignon. The hunting trip was not a raving success, for the hunters managed to bring down only one deer among them. They left the island unimpressed. John Eugene was disappointed at their reaction, but Finney did not give up.

A month later he sent a second set of distinguished visitors to Jekyl. One of these was a wealthy thirty-five-year-old merchant named John Claflin, an attractive man of short stature and son of a prosperous dry goods merchant. He was accompanied by an affable cousin named E. E. Eames. Both men worked for the family firm, H. B. Claflin & Company, which, Finney had informed him, was valued at something in the neighborhood of $9 million. Following his father's death, the younger Claflin would inherit it and become president of the company.

This time, the visit went well. The weather was ideal, wildflowers were at their peak, and the visitors commented more than once on what a nice break it was from the cold weather of New York. Their hunts were successful, as deer and wild turkeys seemed more plentiful. During their visit, Fannie decided that she and Josephine would remain in Brunswick and leave the men to their hunt. Thus, unencumbered by any female presence save a housekeeper and a cook, they shared stories, cigars, and brandy late into the nights. John Eugene found Claflin to be an eloquent storyteller. Each evening after the hunt, the young man would recount fascinating tales of his travels throughout the United States and abroad, especially of his exploits in South America, where only a few years earlier he had trekked through unexplored jungles with only a native guide. Even compared to his earlier adventures, Claflin said, he found Jekyl much to his liking, with enough wilderness and game to suit his adventurous tastes.

"But here," he said, "I can also enjoy the comfort of a good bed and a warm evening meal, not to mention the brandy." John Eugene enjoyed those evenings as well, and he had to admit that he found Jekyl far more interesting with other businessmen there.

"Would you consider selling the island?" Claflin asked. "If so, I might be interested."

"I'd consider it for a sufficient price and with certain conditions."

"What conditions did you have in mind?" Claflin wanted to know.

"Well, if I decided to sell, I would want to make sure that the island remains intact as my grandfather and great-grandfather owned it. I want to be certain that portions would not be sold off to investors, who might bring who-knows-what to Jekyl. It means a lot to me to keep it whole, for I put a lot of effort into acquiring it in its entirety for that purpose."

"And what price would you be asking?"

"I haven't given it much thought, but probably somewhere between a hundred and a hundred and fifty thousand."

"A reasonable price, no doubt, but a great deal to invest in a place I might only use once or twice a year. Let me think about it."

"Well, I'm not yet sure that I'm even willing to sell." The hour was late and the men had begun to talk after several glasses of brandy. John Eugene's tongue had been loosened a bit more than usual, and he found himself telling Claflin, "To be frank, I still owe some of the debt I acquired in purchasing the island and making it whole again. I only hope I can hold on."

Claflin, who had also imbibed rather freely, remarked, "Oh, but you mustn't let it be lost to debt. Let me lend you the money with the island as security. That way," he said, "if you don't pay it back, I'll get a bargain."

Both men laughed. But John Eugene did not forget the impulsive offer, and the next day, when their minds were clearer, John Eugene brought the matter up again.

"Were you serious last night when you offered me a loan to cover my purchase of Jekyl?"

Claflin hesitated for only a moment. "How much do you need?"

"A little less than eleven thousand dollars should take care of it." It was a small amount for a man as prosperous as Claflin, he thought.

"Well, as I suggested, it would be a bargain if you default," Claflin said again.

"I won't," John Eugene said with an assured smile. The two men shook hands. They would sign an agreement the following June.

John Eugene wrote his brother-in-law once again to tell him all that had transpired. And Claflin returned to New York's Union Club extolling the virtues of Jekyl Island and telling members how tempted he had been to buy the island outright. Finney wrote back to John Eugene.

> There now appears to be a good deal of interest in Jekyl Island here, although no one seems willing to invest what I think the island is worth. But I have another idea. Perhaps we could form some sort of group, a consortium of some type, to purchase the island. We could ask a higher price, and I think many people would be willing to buy into a part of it. Perhaps we could form a gentlemen's club of some sort at Jekyl, something based on the model of the Union Club. Would you be interested? We, you and I, I mean, could even become members and, thus, we could still

use the island as your family always did.

John Eugene thought it an intriguing idea—especially the part about their being a member of the group and still having access not only to the island, but also to all those successful and wealthy men. It could be very useful to him. *Such an arrangement would meet all my goals*, he thought. *The island would remain intact as a single entity owned by the many. And Newton and I could be a part of it.* The idea excited him, and he shared it with Fannie over dinner one evening.

"I'd like your opinion of Newton's idea—a Jekyl Island Club with only wealthy and exclusive members. And Newton and I would be members. We would make that a condition of the sale."

Fannie thought for a moment, then smiled. There was even a sense of relief in her voice. "I think it's a lovely idea, Johnny, if we can still go there as a family. I have no doubt that it would be more lively and less lonely if others were there as well. But where would people stay? There would have to be some kind of hotel or clubhouse on the island."

John Eugene thought about her comments for a moment. He knew that ladies were not permitted in the exclusive men's clubs like the Union Club and the Knickerbocker Club in New York. But this could be different. Perhaps they could make it a family vacation spot more like Newport. It could still be a hunting club, but it could include other activities as well, which might have more appeal to the ladies. Members might even want to build homes there—though it would have to be a lease-only agreement in terms of the land. He was determined not to see the island divided again. If they made it exclusive enough, he suspected, many would want to join. The idea appealed to him more and more, and he suggested it to Newton, who wrote back:

What a splendid thought! I think that many in New York, especially the society ladies, would find that most appealing. They might even encourage their husbands to join if they could also be part of it. Let me talk it over with some of the Union Club members and get their reactions. I also agree with Fannie that we would need a good clubhouse. I know an architect here in New York who might be interested in such a project. How much would you require for the club to buy the island?

John Eugene relied promptly.

You once suggested that you thought we could get more than a hundred thousand for it. Do you still think that's a possibility? If so, I'd like to ask a little more to allow for bargaining room. And I'd like to make a condition of the sale that both you and I would be among the founding members.

It all moved quickly after that. Newton discussed the matter with some of his associates in the Union Club, and found that even J. P. Morgan, the richest man in America, expressed an interest, along with many others of great wealth. They were eager to commit, especially when Finney suggested that they limit membership, at least initially, to only fifty, each of whom would receive two shares for the price of $1200. With that limitation, not every wealthy man in New York—not even all members of the so-called Four Hundred—would be able to obtain a membership. Such a fee was prohibitive for most Americans, but for people like J.P. Morgan, William K. Vanderbilt, Pierre Lorillard, and even Joseph Pulitzer, it was a relatively small investment, and they would get a lot for their money—the prestige of membership and a wonderful vacation spot away from both the busy life of New York and its frequently disagreeable weather. It would be a relaxing and beautiful setting to discuss business matters with other successful men.

Word of the new club leaked to Chicago and other parts of the north. Marshall Field heard about it and wanted to join along with various other members of the Chicago Club, which was similar to the Union Club in many ways. The membership list, when it was finalized, read like a Who's Who of northern industrial wealth. The only member from the South would be John Eugene du Bignon himself, the least rich of them all, but a man of great ambitions.

By this time, Newton was sure that the club would be a success. Thus, when John Eugene named a starting price of $125,000 for the island, to his surprise, there was no counter-offer. The prospective members agreed. Each of them would invest far less than Carnegie had paid for his Cumberland Island property and, at the same time, gain access to more land and hunting grounds as well as the social benefits the new club would provide.

Fannie was pleased that they had adopted her suggestions and that John Eugene had made his own membership as well as Newton's a condition of the sale. But she had one other concern nagging at her. She raised it to her husband only a month before the scheduled signing.

"What about your Uncle John, my dear? You told everyone that you purchased his part of the land so that he would never have to leave. You know his circumstances would never allow him to be a part of such an exclusive club. What will you do?" she asked with a troubled frown. "You must find a way to keep that promise."

John Eugene was perplexed. He had almost forgotten that promise, but, as always, Fannie prodded him to do what he knew was right. He wrote to Newton again:

I must add one more stipulation to the sale. I promised that

Uncle John and his family could live on the island for the rest of his life. It was the only way I could get the owners to sell it, for they had made him that same promise. He's an old man now and lives quietly in a remote part of the island, and I doubt he'd ever cross paths with club members. I'm sure the latter won't be pleased, but perhaps you can convince them that it's the charitable thing to do. Otherwise, I just can't sell it. Fannie would never forgive me. You know how soft-hearted she is. And, in this case, I agree.

It was indeed a wrinkle in the plan, and it took a good deal of persuasion on Newton's part, but those who would most likely be the club's executive committee finally acceded to the demand, rather than give up the opportunity. Even then, they wanted the assurance that John's family would remain as invisible as possible and would in no way interfere with club operations. Once he died, his uncle's family, those few left on Jekyl, if there were any, would no longer be allowed to live on the island. John Eugene concurred. His promise was to his uncle alone. Thus, they finally signed the agreement on April 15, 1886. Club ownership would include not only the land, but everything on it, including du Bignon's fine Devon stock, and any other animals, wild or domestic, that inhabited the island, as well as John Eugene's cottage.

The club's reputation was touted almost at once. *The New York Times* predicted that the Jekyl Island Club would be the "swell" club, a "winter Newport" that attracted the *crème de la crème* of New York society. It even publicized that ladies were welcome there, though they could not become members. John Eugene was elated. Not only was $125,000 a veritable fortune in his eyes, he would be rubbing elbows with the richest men in America, for he and Fannie would belong.

Fannie was delighted with the news that the buyers had agreed to make it a family club, not just an exclusive men's club. She was certainly not averse to spending time in the company of America's elite families. And Josephine would, no doubt, have their children to play with. Along with John Eugene, they would be able to enjoy not only the beauty of the island, which her husband still raved about, but also an exciting social life.

Club officers made sure that John Eugene, as the only local member, was willing to handle a fair amount of responsibility in overseeing and reporting on the construction of the clubhouse and providing any local labor that was required.

"I only wish Harry had lived to be a part of all this," he confided to Newton on the day they signed the agreement. "I wish there was some way I might honor his memory in this endeavor." Newton listened sympathetically.

"Perhaps there is," he said.

"How? What do you have in mind?"

"Do you remember that fellow who served in the army with Harry? Your brother was especially fond of him. Perhaps we can find some way for him to be a part of all this, to let him fill in for Harry and keep his memory alive."

"William Turner?" he asked. John Eugene remembered that the two young men had been almost like brothers during the war years. Harry had vigorously defended him to other members of the family, who were less willing to accept him. "But he could never afford to be part of all this, and you know he would never be accepted."

"I don't mean as a member, but perhaps he could serve in some capacity. For example, we'll need an assistant superintendent, a local man who can look after things when the regular superintendent is not there. You know they'll pick an experienced northerner for superintendent and in all probability, they won't be willing to pay him year round—only during the club season. But they could find a local man much cheaper for year-round oversight."

"Would he have to live on the island?"

"Well, I expect so, if he's going to oversee it properly," Newton said.

John Eugene's mind was racing ahead. William knew the island well, having also lived there as a boy, and he was attuned to business in the Brunswick community. "He sounds like a good possibility, perhaps even an ideal one. But how could we make it happen?"

"Don't they look to you for recommendations involving local labor."

"Yes, but won't they see it as a form of nepotism?" John Eugene asked.

"You don't have to mention that he's connected in any way with the family. Now that he's changed his name to Turner, there's no apparent connection. Besides, I think they could use a man with a thorough knowledge of the island."

And so it was done. The executive committee accepted the recommendation without question. And when John Eugene made the offer to William, he jumped at the opportunity. He too recalled his boyhood on the island with fondness. In this position he would be able to live there again. He also liked the idea of getting to know some of those New York millionaires. It could be useful.

When everything was more or less in place, the clubhouse

completed, the landscaping done, and the rest of the staff in place, the club opened for its first season in 1888. On January 21, the club president, Henry Howland, who had just become a justice in the U.S. Supreme Court, was the first person to sign the club register. Other members present from the executive committee signed. The signature of John Eugene, his name written in bold letters and in his usual aristocratic style, "J.E. du Bignon," was number seven. He was pleased to see his name there among some of the nation's wealthiest and most influential men.

When he returned home, he told Fannie about the first day. "It was exciting and elegant. The clubhouse is by no means full, but reservations are pouring in. Even the Vanderbilts are coming. If you want to, you can meet Alva Vanderbilt, the reigning queen of New York society, I'm told. She's coming down with her husband."

"I wouldn't know what to say to her," Fannie said quietly.

"They're no different from us, I've discovered. Just richer. A lot richer," he said with a laugh.

"I would feel she was judging everything I do, if she even noticed me."

"You'll do just fine, my love. And I'll be proud to have you on my arm."

The club season lasted from January until mid-April, with more than two hundred members and guests arriving in their yachts or private railroad cars and bringing with them their retinue of maids and valets. Everything was not perfect. The club encountered difficulties that first season in hiring the best kitchen staff, and Alva Vanderbilt and others complained about this or that. There was insufficient hot water; the gas lighting was inadequate; the stables were too small. Nonetheless, when the season ended, members of the executive committee deemed it a huge success.

CHAPTER 28

Jekyl Island, Georgia 1889

John Couper DuBignon found himself living on an island that was well populated in the winter months, something he was unaccustomed to, but it was still a quiet place the rest of the time. He had grown old in recent years, his hair and beard were white, and his health was beginning to fail. It occurred to him that he might be the oldest surviving DuBignon of his generation. His sister Eliza had died three years earlier. His children had grown up and started families on the mainland. But he still lived alone in the run-down cottage he once built for Sylvia. It was where he wanted to be. He hardly noticed the club members when they were on the island, except for the sounds of their shooting that echoed through the woods, and they ignored his presence. He could hear them, but he never saw them, which suited him just fine.

His sons and daughters visited occasionally during the off-season, but never when club members were on the island. Then, they weren't allowed. Each time they came they could see that their father was growing increasingly feeble.

"He needs somebody to live with him and help him," Robert told his family after one of their visits.

"Why don't he just come live with us," his wife Charlotte asked.

"I tried to get him to do that, but he's a right stubborn ol' cuss, and he ain't never gonna leave Jekyl Island."

"Now, Robert," his wife had said, "you ought'n talk like that about yo' daddy, even if it be true."

"He always says, 'I was born here and I'm gonna die here.' No two ways about it. That's his plan and he's stickin' to it."

"Maybe one of our boys could go stay with him for a spell," Charlotte suggested.

"Now that's a good idea. Which one of you boys is willin' to go?"

They all looked down at the floor. Then Robert said, "What about you, Willy? Yo' schoolin' be 'bout done, and yo' big brother already got a job. How 'bout you go?"

"Aw, Pa," he objected. But it didn't matter. If that's what his father wanted, he had no choice. And so, he soon found himself living with his grandfather on Jekyl Island. He didn't mind nearly as much as he thought he would. It was where his pa had grown up, and he had heard about it all his life.

Jekyl Island, December 31, 1890

John Couper hobbled out of the cabin, with the aid of a cane and his grandson William. He wanted to sit on the narrow front porch and watch the setting sun, as he had always done at the end of the day. It was blocked from clear view by trees that stood between the cabin and the marsh waters, but it didn't seem to matter to the old man. He couldn't see too well anyhow. It was just something he had always done. The rest of the time, he sat in what he called his "comfy chair," gazing at nothing in particular, lost in whatever memories he could recall.

"You've been good to me, Willy," John Couper said to the tall, gangling sixteen-year-old, who had helped him up and was guiding him toward his cane-bottomed chair on the porch.

"I like livin' out here with you, Grandpa," the boy answered. "I had a hankerin' to come, so I could learn about the island where you and my pa both grew up."

"Pshaw. I know your pa and your ma sent you out here to look after me. And you've done a right good job. But your work is nearly done. We both know I don't have long for this world, Willy. I'm just an old remnant of a dead society—good for nothin' anymore. But when I die, I want you to make sure they bury me here—in the old family cemetery. It's where I belong."

"I'll try, Grandpa, but it don't belong to yo' family no more. It belong to that fancy club now," William answered.

"How can my family's cemetery belong to a bunch of strangers?"

"I don't rightly know," William answered. "But it do."

He had been on the island looking after his grandfather for more than a year. Now that he was here, he'd found that he rather liked it most of the time, except from January to about mid-April, when all those rich club members came down from the North to get away from the freezing weather. During those months, William had to keep pretty much to the cabin, which his grandfather never left, and the small plot of land that contained their garden, the milk cow, and the chicken yard. The rest of the year, however, unless his grandfather needed him, the boy felt free to go anywhere he chose, except for the clubhouse grounds and the places where club members were building houses.

William knew his grandfather was not well, and he had gotten worse in recent months. He could no longer get about on his own, and he forgot things. Sometimes he couldn't even remember his grandson's name. Other days, like today, his mind seemed sharp enough. But still he slept much of the time, struggling to rise at mealtimes and to watch the sunset. That was something he never seemed to forget. Only lately had he started to complain about a pain in his chest that came and went, sometimes several times a day. William held his arm as he sat heavily onto the cane-bottomed chair.

Once his grandfather was settled, William said, "If it's okay with you, Grandpa, I'm gone go to see if I can catch us some fish fo' supper." It was the end of December, and a handful of club members were already on the island. But there were so few of them that he could still move about the island more freely than he did during the regular club season, which didn't begin until after the new year.

John Couper nodded. "You go on, Willy. I'm just gonna sit here and wait for night to come."

While his grandfather sat on the front porch gazing westward toward where he knew the invisible sun hung low in the sky, William left him there and made his way with his fishing pole to the nearby river, which ran between the island and the marsh. He wasn't gone long—half an hour at most. When he returned, he found his grandfather slumped in his chair, his head hanging forward. William thought he had fallen asleep.

"Grandpa, wake up. I got us some good fish."

But when he tried to awaken him and get him back to bed, he realized that the old man wasn't breathing. He was dead.

William was unsure about what to do. He reckoned he could bury his grandfather himself somewhere on the little plot of land they occupied. But the old man had said he wanted to be buried in the island's family cemetery. It was the last day of the year, and William knew that club members would be arriving soon. A few of them were already here. He didn't dare dig a grave in the little cemetery without permission. What should he do?

He struggled to carry his grandfather's body inside to lay him on his bed. He didn't want to leave him outside where some critter might find him. Then, when he was stretched out in his usual place, William laid his hands across his chest the way he had seen it done in coffins. The old man could have been just sleeping for all anyone could tell. Once he had adjusted the body in a dignified way, he set out to look for the assistant superintendent, William Turner. Although the superintendent himself was on the island, a man named Ernest Grob, William had never met him, and he knew that his grandfather and William Turner were half-brothers. He seemed to the boy the best choice. Maybe he would be willing and able to help.

Before he got to the clubhouse, he passed by several cottages. Behind one of them, a black man was leading a horse toward the stables. It was Charlie Hill, the coachman for the family of Stewart Maurice, who often spent Christmas on the island. William had known Mr. Charlie in Brunswick, before he was hired at Jekyl.

"What you doin' around here, son?" the man called out. "You

know you ain't supposed to be anywhere near the club. You gone get in trouble."

William rushed over to him. "Mr. Charlie," he said, his voice almost frantic. "Mr. Charlie, My grandpa—he's dead! He wanted to be buried in the cemetery at the north end."

"I'm sorry to hear that, but you know that ain't gone happen, Willy."

"But I promised I'd try. Do you know where I could find Mr. Turner?"

"You ought to let his nephew, Mr. John Eugene du Bignon, know first," Charlie suggested.

"But I made my grandpa a promise to do somethin' that will need me to talk to Mr. Turner."

"Okay, Willy. But you stay here by the stable. Don't go anywhere near the clubhouse. I'll go see if I can find him."

William waited for what seemed like hours before Charlie returned with William Turner at his side.

"Charlie here tells me your grandpa has died. I'm real sorry. I'll send somebody to let Mr. du Bignon know, and he can come for the body and take you home to your family," Turner said.

"But Mr. Turner, like I told Mr. Charlie, he said he wanted to be buried in the cemetery here on the island," William explained.

"Now you know that's impossible, boy. The club would never allow that."

"But it's his family cemetery. His ma is buried there and his brother."

"I'm sorry, Willy, but club members will never permit it. I'll send someone to inform Mr. du Bignon, and he can deal with it."

John Eugene came out the next morning, and when Willy told him what his grandfather had requested, he said, "Well, I doubt they'll permit that."

"Can't we at least ask? I promised him I'd try."

John Eugene looked at the boy—almost a young man, strong and with the handsomeness of youth. He wanted to help the boy, though he himself had promised his uncle only that he could stay on the island for the rest of his life—nothing more. But a promise was an obligation, and the boy had made a promise. It would do no harm in asking.

He went to Mr. Grob, the club superintendent, who was sympathetic but told him he had no authority to grant such a request and that it take could a week or more to contact Mr. Howland, the club president, and hear back.

"By then, if you leave him on the island, that body will be attracting buzzards—even inside the house. And you know as well as I do that Mr. Howland will say no. The best thing to do is take him back to Brunswick for burial, and for the boy's sake, you better take him back today." After the brief meeting, John Eugene returned to his uncle's cottage where William was waiting.

"Well, we tried, Willy, but Mr. Grob said no. That's all you promised him—to try. Now let's get him back to town, where he can be buried." The boy nodded but looked disappointed.

John Eugene arranged for his uncle John to be interred in the family plot at Oak Grove Cemetery next to Eliza and Henry Jr. He even paid for the funeral at Fannie's insistence. That was all he was willing to do. If his sisters were agreeable to paying for a tombstone, that would be fine, but he felt he had done his part. However, none of his sisters wanted anything to do with John Couper's funeral, after what they considered the shameful life he'd led.

"He embarrassed our family—almost as much as our father did. He can be buried there, but with no marker. None of us want to put one up. It would just remind people of what I hope they will forget," Mary Amelia said.

The yawning mouth of John Couper's empty grave waited beside the granite stones that marked the burial sites of his brother and sister. It was a quiet afternoon, as the small procession approached the spot. Only the priest, Fannie, and John Eugene followed the coffin, carried from the funeral wagon by six hefty men. No one stood with the priest at the graveside except John Eugene, who considered this his absolute final duty to Uncle John, and his wife Fannie.

Across the road the old man's son Robert with his wife and children, brothers and sisters, gathered under the deep shade of a large live oak tree, watching as the priest said the final words, and the coffin-carriers lowered the pine box that bore the body of their father and grandfather into his grave. Unobserved by those at the graveside, tears stained the dark cheeks of several of those who stood on the other side of the road. One of the women began to hum a soft and doleful melody, and others, one by one, joined in. They stood with their heads bowed, the men with their hats in their hands. They watched as the pine box that bore the body of John Couper DuBignon was lowered into the grave. They could see the priest mumbling his prayers, as John Eugene and Fannie bowed their heads. None of those at the graveside showed any emotion as they went through the perfunctory ritual. Then it was over. As the three of them walked away, the men who had carried the coffin began to fill the grave from the mound of dirt piled to the side.

The dead man's children and grandchildren watched silently as the men chunked shovelfuls of dirt onto the coffin, and they could hear the thumps of the heavy soil against the pine box. They had learned that the white DuBignon family refused to pay for a tombstone to match the large granite slabs that marked the graves of Henry and Eliza. Robert knew that his own family could not afford one. There were no objects of remembrance placed on the tomb. White people didn't do that. Only a small wooden cross marked the place where their father's body lay. In the rain and the thick, humid heat of summer months, it quickly rotted away, and an autumn storm blew down its final vestige. Nothing marked the place where John Couper DuBigon lay.

One evening at dusk, Robert, with his brothers and sons, all toting heavy croker sacks on their backs, slipped unnoticed into the cemetery. The shadows of evening crept over the graveyard, and no one else was in sight. They all knelt beside the grave that contained the body of the man they had known as their father or grandfather. Each man in turn opened his croker sack, removed the bricks that were inside, and began to lay them end to end to outline the place where he lay. He might lie forgotten by his nieces and nephews, but the sons of John Couper were determined he would not be forgotten by everyone.

CHAPTER 29

Jekyl Island, March 1891

It was late afternoon, and John Eugene stood with his wife on the front porch of the Jekyl Island clubhouse, proudly surveying his domain. At least he still thought of it that way. The clubhouse itself was graced with wide porches, balconies, a splendid tower, and a porte-cochère, where one could step out of a coach without getting wet in case of rain. It was a splendid structure, he thought, a landmark designed by a well-known New York architect named Charles Alexander. One reporter had even claimed that, from a distance, it looked like an "English castle." John Eugene liked that description. It made him smile.

He was imagining for the moment that it was his own castle, his alone, one even grander than the manor house his great-grandfather had left behind in France so many years ago. The club grounds were well-manicured, in striking contrast to the majority of the island, which remained untouched. He was delighted that the club landscaper, William Shaler Cleveland, had agreed with him that the island should be kept insofar as possible in its natural state, just as he remembered it from his boyhood. It was a large part of the club's charm, and it was what made Jekyl so special to him. He could still ride among the huge live oak trees that shaded the roadways and smell the fragrant jessamine vines that bloomed in late February, announcing the coming of spring. He could still listen to the wind that rustled the leaves and caused the Spanish moss to wave like flags in the breeze. He could still see the resurrection ferns spring to life after every rain. He could even walk the beaches with his wife and daughter as they collected seashells cast ashore by a recent storm. Best of all, as the only local club member. he could visit any time of year, whenever he wanted, enjoying the mysteries and changing hues of the marshlands and tidal creeks that led from Brunswick to Jekyl.

He could see the club's steam yacht, the *Howland*, tied up at the dock and silhouetted against the western sky. Everything looked so peaceful. He felt the same serenity within, as he watched the splendor of the setting sun mark the end of a long and satisfying day. *One of Jekyl's many spectacular sunsets just for our benefit*, John Eugene thought, remembering how often he had stood like this on the leeward side of the island and gazed in awe at the setting sun's magnificent display.

Fannie had spent much of the afternoon strolling, enjoying tea, and chatting with Charlotte Maurice, who was interested in learning all she could about the history of Jekyl, for she and her husband, Stewart, were planning to write a little book about the island. She enjoyed talking with Fannie and learning about the earlier generations of the du Bignon family. Just as the ladies had spent their afternoon together, so John Eugene had joined the men in one of the parlors to listen as they discussed their lively views of the new president, Benjamin Harrison, and the impact on business of the recently-passed Sherman Anti-Trust Act.

Now, all the millionaires and their families had gone in to change for dinner as they did each evening, with the help of their maids and valets, donning their elegant gowns and tuxedos in preparation for their grand entrance into the clubhouse dining room to greet their equally elegant peers. Staff members were all inside, finishing their daily chores or preparing for the lengthy and sumptuous dinner to come.

The club and the grounds were both quiet and no one was in sight, giving both John Eugene and Fannie the illusion that they were all alone on their own island, as they used to be. As a courtesy, Mr. Grob had invited them to spend the night in what was once their home on Jekyl, but which was now the superintendent's cottage. In order to give them privacy, he was having their meals delivered from the dining room, while he spent the night with the boat captain's family.

With no one there to observe, John Eugene put his arm around his wife and kissed her softly on the lips. This was the club's fourth season, and things seemed to be running smoothly. The superintendent and his staff were well liked by club members, a couple of whom had already built cottages on the island and were making plans to come with their families and friends to spend at least part of the winter at Jekyl. There was no sign of the difficulties they had experienced that first season in hiring staff members, who had already made other commitments. Now, New York establishments like Delmonico's were providing them with well-trained chefs, while their waiters, maids, and other white staff members, many of them young immigrants, were interviewed and hired in New York, brought to Brunswick each season by Mallory steamer, and then transported to the island on the *Howland*.

Ah, yes, John Eugene thought, *it's all going splendidly.* And he and Fannie were a part of it. As the only local club member, he had accepted much of the responsibility in the construction of the clubhouse, overseeing the landscaping, and hiring local workers—most of whom were black. He recalled those few bumps they'd had during the opening season, and Alva Vanderbilt had not returned, but overall things were going very well now.

Fannie looked up at her husband with an affectionate smile. "How does it feel to have finally accomplished your dream?" she asked.

"It feels wonderful," he said, "but it feels even better to have you at my side. You've been with me every step of the way, and I'm grateful for your support and encouragement. I don't think I could have done it, at least not the right way, without your help and suggestions."

"Nonsense. It was your idea, and somehow you have managed to create all this grandeur and make a small fortune at the same time." She laughed softly. "I know it's inappropriate of me to speak of financial matters, but what you have done is amazing. There were times when it seemed impossible to accomplish all this and still keep your promises to Aunt Eliza and Uncle John. But you did it. Somehow it all came together. You are responsible for this wonderful place, and we are part of it. I'm so proud of you," she said, putting her arm through his.

"We did it together, my darling. I only hope my great-grandfather would be proud. I think he would appreciate that so many club members are among the industrial elite, men who, like him, may not have been born rich, but by dint of hard work, have come to be like royalty in America. Remember when the *New York Times* called it the 'richest and most exclusive club in the world.' We've made the island famous and worthy of our family's heritage. And so much of it is still exactly as I remember it from my childhood. We have the beauty of the island to enjoy, but we also have the social life we lacked when we were here alone. I can only thank God that what was so special about the island before remains untouched. And it's still ours."

"I love you," Fannie whispered. Then they fell silent as, side by side, they watched the sun dip below the horizon, leaving behind a trail of glory, with shifting shades of orange and rose, slowly transforming into transient hues of blue and violet. The sky was awash with colors that danced slowly across the river and through the marsh grasses swaying in the breeze. The island was once again, as it was in the days of his father, a spot of grandeur and unequaled beauty, a place where the wealthy club members tried to ignore its past transgressions of slavery. It seemed destined for a glorious future.

"Do you like coming to the island more now?" John Eugene asked.

"Infinitely more. Of course I liked it before, but it's even better now. There is always something interesting to do and someone interesting to talk with. Yes, I must confess I rather enjoy the social life, but the natural beauty is still here. It's become the best of all worlds."

He smiled with satisfaction, took Fannie's hand into his own, and squeezed it, feeling his heart expand with joy. He remembered the words his brother Harry had so often spoken: "How can I be so lucky?" John Eugene knew exactly what he meant. His life was at its peak, as he stood there beside his beloved wife, basking in the echoes of the past and the promises of the future in this brand-new world he had helped to create. Life could get no better than this.

AUTHOR'S AFTERWORD

Many readers prefer stories with a happy ending, For that reason, I have chosen to end the book here. Thus, if you are a reader who only wants a happy ending, close the book now and put it away. If, however, you are like me and want to know the rest of the story, read on.

John Eugene du Bignon and Newton Finney maintained their relationship with the Jekyl Island Club for almost a decade, enjoying its benefits and hobnobbing with the wealthy club members. Newton's Manhattan office at 52 Broadway served as the Jekyl Island Club's New York office until the mid-1890s, when a new club leadership emerged. It was dominated by a man named Henry Hyde, whose son labeled him the "Czar of Jekyl Island." He was the wealthy and powerful owner of the Equitable Life Assurance Corporation in New York. Although he was never its president, he made up his mind to bring more businesslike and efficient leadership to the Jekyl Island Club.

It was Hyde who proclaimed in 1895 that Finney's club office in New York had become a mere "sinecure," costing members unnecessary funds. Under his influence, the New York office was moved from 52 Broadway to 512 Washington Street, the business address of another club member named Frederic Baker. John Eugene, possibly miffed at the changes and the loss of influence he and Finney originally had in club operations, dropped his membership the following year. Finney, whose wife Josephine had died in 1889, also ceased to be a member in 1897, thus marking the end of all association between Jekyl Island and the du Bignon family.

This book is based on a true story, and the family vicissitudes are all real. I have no specific evidence for the friendship between William Turner and Henry Riffault DuBignon, other than the fact that they did serve throughout the Civil War in the same unit. Had there been animosity between them, it seems logical to assume that one of them would have requested a transfer. The fact that neither did suggests to me that the two young men got along well enough. The hiring of William Turner as the club's assistant superintendent, would seem to strengthen that probability. Someone in the family knew him sufficiently well to trust him in this important role, and the most logical person would have been his military comrade, who may at his death have passed that trust on to his younger brother.

William Turner did not hold the position of assistant superintendent for very long. In 1892, his name disappears from club records and is replaced by that of a new assistant superintendent, Julius Falk. Turner was only forty-eight years old when Falk replaced him. I assumed at first that he had either quit the job or was fired, but I later discovered that he died on December 21, 1891, in a shooting that some believed to be a self-inflicted, accidental wound while others suspected it was murder. Driving a wagon on a country road on the mainland, he was shot dead by his own gun, fell from the wagon, and was dragged for more than a mile. A concerned black man followed the trail of blood, found him on the road, and notified the authorities. Turner had been known to quarrel recently with certain parties, unnamed in the records, which led to speculation that he had been intentionally killed. But no one was ever accused, and no case was ever brought against another person.

The episode of the *Wanderer* is well known, and the Jekyll Island Authority has now developed a Wanderer Memory Trail on the island's south end that features the stories and photographs of some of the captives who were so brutally ripped from their west-African homelands and brought to Georgia against their will. Many of their descendants still live in the area. Others are scattered throughout the country.

I would like to clarify one detail concerning Sylvia DuBignon, the common-law wife of John Couper DuBignon. Some who claim to be descendants of this relationship contend that her name should be spelled "Sylva," as it is in at least one census record. However, the only legal document I have found that contains her name, the indenture that John Couper signed accepting responsibility for their children until they had reached their majority, spells it "Sylvia." Since census records of the time often contain misspelled names, and since Sylvia was a far more common name and appears in the only legal document we have, I have chosen to use this spelling. All else that we learn about her from this document is that she clearly cared about the welfare of her children and that she could not write, signing her name with an X. I only wish we knew more of her story. I have assumed that she was preparing for death as the document was drawn up. Given the concern for her children the indenture suggests makes it unlikely, in my view, that she planned in any other way to abandon her family. A copy of the indenture the couple signed is still on record in the Glynn County courthouse.

Sylvia is the featured character in this book about whom we know the least. We can ascertain her approximate age from census records, as well as the names and approximate birth dates of her children with John Couper. But the way in which the two of them became a couple, as well as the date of her death, are shrouded in the silences of history. I have speculated on what was an all-too-common situation in relations between enslaved women, who had no choice, and their masters. Whatever the beginning of their story, she and John Couper lived together for many years and had six surviving children. She did return with him to Jekyll Island after the Civil War, even though she was legally free. Descendants of that common-law marriage, like descendants of the *Wanderer* captives, still live in Brunswick and throughout the country today .

One other matter: I have abbreviated somewhat the trial of Egbert Martin for the sake of narrative brevity. There was a later trial in which he pleaded "temporary insanity," which resulted in a hung jury. Finally, on the basis of a petition signed by eighty-six of his supporters, the case was dismissed.

The varied spellings I have used of the name du Bignon or DuBignon are not arbitrary. I have made an effort to spell it as the character in question would have spelled it at the given time. The spelling varied from person to person, and, after the first generation in America, was for the most part written as "DuBignon," John Eugene, in contrast to others in the family, and in all likelihood to underscore the family's nobility, returned to the original French spelling of du Bignon, sometimes writing it Du Bignon, but always separating the "du," as a sign of nobility. I should also point out that the spelling of Jekyll Island varied as well. It was spelled Jekyl until 1929, when it was officially changed to Jekyll by the Georgia state legislature.

The Jekyll Island Club existed as a legal entity from 1886 until 1947. It had closed in 1942 for the duration of World War II, when many club members lent their money and influence to the war effort. By the end of the war, most club members had lost interest. Although then club president, Bernon Prentice, and a few others gave lip service to trying to reopen, it never happened. In 1947, the state of Georgia, by right of eminent domain, took over the island and reimbursed the club and its few remaining members who still owned houses there, a total of $675,000. Today the island is an undivided state part. People and businesses can only lease the land or the structures. It remains intact, as John Eugene du Bignon left it.

This book brings to an end my trilogy about the du Bignon family. The first book, *Marguerite's Landing*, recounts the adventures of Christophe Poulain du Bignon and his wife Marguerite Lossieux, who left France in 1792 to escape the French Revolution and settled as the first generation of the family on Jekyll Island.

The second, *The Truth Keepers*, continues with the shocking tale of the next generation and focuses primarily on Marguerite and Christophe's youngest and favored son, Henry DuBignon, and his relationships with his French wife, Amelia Nicolau, his mistress, Sarah Aust, and her daughter, Mary, who became his second wife.

The present book relates the tangled stories of the last two generations to have legal ownership of the island. For more than a century, the family's story was intertwined with that of Jekyll, one of the famous Golden Isles of Georgia. It has not always been a pretty story, filled as it is in the early generations with the horrors of slavery, family misfortunes during the War of 1812 and the Civil War, and internecine squabbles. Nevertheless, I have found their saga fascinating. They are certainly one of the most intriguing families I have ever encountered. I can only hope the reader will be as interested in their story as I am.

ACKNOWLEDGMENTS

The historical sources for this book come from many archival collections and repositories in Georgia. These include Glynn County Court records, the Georgia Historical Society in Savannah, the Georgia Archives, and the National Archives and Regional Administration, both located in Morrow, the Coastal Georgia Historical Society on St. Simons, as well as the Jekyll Island Museum and the special collections of the Brunswick-Glynn County Library, all of which have provided invaluable documents concerning the lives, relationships, and legal entanglements of various du Bignon family members. The digital library collection of Georgia Historic Newspapers has been particularly useful in providing details about many incidents in the book. I appreciate the help of the staff in all these establishments and all those who contributed to this book.

I have had help from many individuals as well. Kyle Ward, Southeast Navigation Manager at the National Oceanic and Atmospheric Administration Office of Coast Survey, helped me find the official records of Newton Finney's career. My thanks also to Michael Martin, my son and a marine biologist, who pointed me to the appropriate NOAA resource. I am grateful to John Hunter, Director of Planning and Development in Brunswick, who guided me through historic city maps and land records to locate the site of Josephine du Bignon's home on Gloucester Street in Brunswick. My thanks also go to Cliff Gawron, Director of Landscaping and Planning at Jekyll Island, who provided useful information on the island's native plants. I am, as always, grateful to Amy Hedrick, whose web site is a treasure trove of historical information about families, individuals, and events in Glynn County.

My friend, Susanne Hebden, has assisted me in many ways during my various trips to Jekyll for the writing of this book and various book signings of previous novels. I am grateful for her support and willingness to travel anywhere to help. Suellen Beverly, a longtime friend, and Faye Johnson, both friend and former colleague, read early versions of the manuscript and made useful comments that helped to shape the book. I am especially grateful to my designer, Art Growden, not only for a beautiful cover and interior, but also for his patience in making all the changes I have requested. Most important of all, I'd like to thank Vicki Brennan, my editor, for her many suggestions that led to the final draft of the novel. Without the help of these people and the archival resources, this book would never have been written.

Readers who might be interested in learning more about the Jekyll Island Club are encouraged to consult the nonfiction book I wrote with my late husband, William Barton McCash, *The Jekyll Island Club: Southern Haven for America's Millionaires*, published by the University of Georgia Press in 1989. I have explored the pre-club history of the island in *Jekyll Island's Early Years*, also published by the University of Georgia Press in 2005.

It has been a joy to learn so much about Jekyll and the fascinating people who have lived on the island over so many centuries. I feel fortunate to have had the opportunity for more than three decades to explore its extraordinary history.

QUESTIONS FOR DISCUSSION:

1. The title of the book invites the reader to consider the following questions: To whose memory do you think it refers? To whose home?

2. What do we actually remember? How much of our memory is based on personal recollections and how much on what others have told us? Are our memories influenced by the way we want to remember? Why do people frequently recall the same event in different ways?

3. Are the memories of and aspirations for the island the same for all the characters or do they differ?

4. All the major characters referred to in this historical novel were real people. What aspects of the book seem to you most likely to be based on evidence? And which aspects do you suppose are derived from the author's imagination?

5. The book touches on a variety of love stories. Which one do you find most compelling and why? Which one is the most complex and how? How are they all relevant parts of the primary story line?

6. Is the complex relationship between John Couper and Sylvia one of those love stories? Is there love between them? What evidence can you provide to support your idea?

7. What does the *Wanderer* episode tell us about the characters involved?

8. In writing historical fiction, one must find the story among the varied documents and scattered facts we have about history. Has the author succeeded in your view in finding that story?

9. In what ways does the Civil War impact the lives of the different characters?

10. Which of the characters in this novel do you like best? Why? Which one do you most dislike? Why?

11. Could any of these characters have been omitted? Are they all part of the same story? Or do they each have their own story? Or both?

12. In your view, did John Eugene make a good decision in the end?

ABOUT THE AUTHOR

JUNE HALL McCASH is the author, coauthor, or editor of fifteen books (six historical novels, eight nonfiction works, and one book of poetry) as well as numerous articles. With a Ph.D. from Emory University, she is the recipient of an Outstanding Alumna Award for Distinguished Career from Agnes Scott College, and both a Distinguished Research Award and the Outstanding Career Achievement Award from Middle Tennessee State University. A fellow of the National Endowment for the Humanities and the American Council of Education, she recently completed a nine-year term as a trustee of the Jekyll Island Foundation. Named Georgia Author of the Year for her historical novels in 2011 and 2013, she is also the author of *Jekyll Island's Early Years*, *The Jekyll Island Cottage Colony* and coauthor of *The Jekyll Island Club: Southern Haven for America's Millionaires*.